"A brilliant novel, Alfie! Dense with wordplay, literary learning, Harvard lore of our time (Donald Fleming was something, I agree). I like Larkin more than you do, I think, and Heaney less. I came to Joyce maybe later than others and look at him from a distance. I don't like Nabokov at all. But I thoroughly enjoyed your interweaving of them with your narrative—and I thought the novel-in-progress in the main novel was a terrific idea, beautifully done … But I admire your wit and daring here. This is very different from your earlier books—something else I admire." —*Max Byrd*

"My dear Alfie: I really appreciate your sensitivity in sending me the extracts from the novel that concern Seamus and me. So let me set out by saying I found them moving and marvelous. Your love for Seamus and your deep understanding of him and his work pervades the extracts. They make me feel grateful and proud and they bring back so many memories … Many, many thanks." —*Marie Heaney*

"*Time is the Fire* is a delightful book. It is also swathed in layers of wisdom and deepest insight that reward attentive reading far beyond the clever and charming send-up of James Joyce's *Ulysses* which it may superficially appear to be. *Time is the Fire* captures the literary life of a whole era, in a particular place (Harvard Square) during an era of unusual concentration and achievement. Two central characters, the real-life poets Stratis Haviaras and Seamus Heaney, were indeed at the center of a stage of literary camaraderie, productivity and excitement that has and will have historical importance. Alfred Alcorn was a participant and a rich contributor to this scene, and he captures with wit and graceful charm the way it was, both internally for each individual writer—the way ambition and misgivings wage war and seek balance in each literary psyche—and the bustle and preoccupations of a community of artists who read each other, cheered each other on, and cross-pollinated in ways that future scholars will be studying and researching for generations to come. This book will always be central for it captures the way it felt—it feels—to be smack dab in the full rush of ongoing literary life." —*Bob Scanlan*

"Alfred Alcorn's life of relocation, loss, wide reading, adventure, and mind-stretching curiosity flavors this most moving and personal of his novels. *Time is the Fire*, sitting lightly to plot, gives us a piercing search for human wisdom through literature and philosophy. A staccato book, a literary feast, it is playful, mocking, self-aware, with a vintage Alcorn knife-edge ending." —*Ross Terrill*

"I think the book is a blooming (intended) masterpiece, a pro vita summa; it's wiping out everything I've read in the last couple of months, Joycean not only in theme but also in its infinite inexhaustible imagination and inventiveness, the combination of the transient quotidian and the timeless tragic verities. I'm blown away, thanks for letting me see it early on." —*Morty Schiff*

"That was an adventurous reading and re-reading of *Time is the Fire*, Alfie … I read it through many interruptions, but I enjoyed re-reading it with fewer ones in Athens. Sure I liked the judiciously placed here and there the usual Harvard-Cambridge suspects including myself, but the stakes here are high and you have gone out of your way to surpass both Joyce and yourself. I love it and, yes, it identifies an era and a culture vibrant in all its depth." —*Stratis Haviaras*

"Great 1st book to start year. Sometimes slow going—but by choice—not a negative—it was the pace of savoring. Sometimes I wonder if the literary and artistic references in the Books would make a good Humanities survey course. I am planning to dig into some of it—especially the Poetry—No, I am not going to reread *Ulysses*—you can't make me. A window into an author's mind which is rich in scholarship, imagination, and generosity of spirit." —*Jay Gaffney*

TIME
Is The
FIRE

ALFRED ALCORN

Published by
Pleasure Boat Studio: A Literary Press

Time Is The Fire
by Alfred Alcorn

ISBN 978-0-912887-43-2
Library of Congress Number: TBA

Design by Susan Ramundo
Cover by Laura Tolkow

Pleasure Boat Studio books are available through your favorite bookstore, as well as the following:
SPD (Small Press Distribution) Tel. 800-869-7553, Fax 510-524-0852
Partners/West Tel. 425-227-8486, Fax 425-204-2448
Baker & Taylor Tel. 800-775-1100, Fax 800-775-7480
Ingram Tel. 615-793-5000, Fax 615-287-5429
Amazon.com and **bn.com**

and through
PLEASURE BOAT STUDIO: A LITERARY PRESS
www.pleasureboatstudio.com
201 West 89th Street
New York, NY 10024

Contact **Jack Estes**
Email: pleasboat@nyc.rr.com

For Marie, Catherine, Christopher, and Michael
and in memory of Seamus

Time is the fire in which we burn.
—DELMORE SCHWARTZ

Mr. Leopold Bloom O'Boyle ate with relish and a dab of bright mustard the inner organs of beasts and fowls. That is, he chewed slowly and with pleasure the first of two frankfurters bedded in the warmed piths of lightly greased and grilled white bread rolls served up by Charlie in The Tasty in the heart of Harvard Square. He chewed and swallowed and tasted timelessness, hot dogs being his humble madeleines.

He said, "You know, Charlie, frankfurters ..."

"You mean 'dogs." Charlie, spatula lifted like a baton, back to the counter, did not approve of 'dogs for breakfast.

"Indeed, 'dogs. I mean, when you stop and think about it, 'dogs are little more than reconstituted flesh."

Leopold or Leo or L. B., as he was variously referred to, spoke ostensibly to Charlie and to Marty, one of the irregulars, who was seated on the stool next to his. You could say anything to Marty, who wasn't always lucid, who shuffled in his pockets, and who looked a squat Robert de Niro having a bad face day. Ostensibly. Because L. B. O'Boyle's peripheral vision and range of voice took in a young woman with shapely legs wearing a skirt so short it might have been a stylized loincloth, of a piece with a belted, high-cut jacket and dark pixie hair. She perched on one of the stools against the narrow wall counter, near the cased-in map of the world stuck with pushpins emblematic of missives from Dublin, Nome, Rome, Arusha, Tel Aviv, Udaipur, Dachau, Magadan, Antofagasta, and North Chelmsford, among many others. Which meant, in the confines of the tiny eatery, almost within touching distance. She was sipping an honest cup of bad coffee from one of the establishment's thick mugs and smoking a filtered cigarette she held downwards between fingers tipped with inch-long nails lacquered scarlet red. From her look of attentive distraction she might have been a recent arrival on the scene, possibly a tourist stopping to imbibe some local authenticity as tourists do.

Thought L. B. O'Boyle, who, not so mutely craving to adore, had proffered this sample of badinage as an example of local authenticity. That she appreciated his effort appeared evident from the half smirk on lips rouged to match her talons and from a quick glance of eyes too large and luminous to need the mask of mascara.

"Don't ask and we won't tell," said Charlie, unsmiling behind the counter, flippant with customers and their eggs.

1

"Don't ask what?" asked Marty.

"What they put in the hot dogs."

L. B. O'Boyle chewed and swallowed what they put in hot dogs. "Or, to quote Bismarck, the making of sausages is not a pretty sight." Then, like his namesake, prattling on about the grinding of meat and the making of laws.

"Who's Bismarck?"

Not that Leo, some while now in the married state, knew why he wanted to impress this striking example of young womanhood. A bit of male display brought on by her show of gams? Force of habit to play the authentic Harvard Square character in an authentic Harvard Square milieu? The dawning, inescapable terror of ... Because at this juncture in his life he was not inclined to give chase even if he were to interpret the acknowledging glance as encouragement.

So why today, of all days, this sense of irrevocable loss, of possibilities foreclosed, of unacted desires, when she slid off the stool, snubbed out her cigarette, paid for her coffee, smiled a "*ciao bello*" at Charlie, and paraded her unmercifully beautiful rump out into the warming September morning? *Venus Kallipyge* aside, why did her leaving and the manner of it leave behind an audible silence in that landmark hole in the wall?

A silence into which L. B. O'Boyle, clearing his throat and quoting his friend Alf, intoned, "The beauty of women makes good men suffer."

"How would you know?" Marty, too lucid by half, even laughed like de Niro–downwards, privately.

L. B. heard the rue in his own voice. He chewed more of the reconstituted organ and non-organ meat and pondered: Ari Krasnick would not have let her walk off like that. Ari Krasnick, friend and co-conspirator, would have followed her out the door, would have stopped her on the sidewalk, oblivious to annoyed pedestrians having to skirt them as he entreated her with his Spaniel eyes, importuned her with a fusillade of words, telling her he had to, just had to talk to her, meaning, naturally, another kind of intercourse. Women found his ardor either hilarious or convincing and ended, figuratively, doubled over one way or another.

That was no longer tenable for L. B. O'Boyle, who forebear, who let diffuse to mere regret the lust in his heart. Not out of any invocation of conscious morality as out of a fidelity compounded of marital inertia, a dash of the uxorious, and a recurring enchantment he took for love. Leopold Bloom O'Boyle—yclept thus by a deceased father, a devout Joycean who had gone slightly daft and finally died while attempting to commit *Finnegans Wake* to memory—was married and on the verge of getting more married than he already was. To a Protestant. To a Protestant preacher. To a more than likely pregnant ... They would know for sure today. Which prospect rounded on him spasmodically with strange, exhilarating terror.

"Ellbee, don't be calling me a preacher. I'm a minister. Preachers is what they got in the south." Going full Cracker on him. It was not what he anticipated some several years back when he took up, during a brief infatuation with the notion of White Trash, with Annabel Folsom Chance of the Deep South.

She deceived him. Right from the start. From that first glance in the aural and atmospheric miasma of The Plough and Stars, that species of desolation, to quote the bard Heaney. Gotten up like a cheerleader, she was, breasty in a rolled-top sweater of dubious pink, flared mini-skirt, soft boots, everything but the pompoms. Which went with the coquettish swing of straight blond tresses and a voice that got to him when the organized noise abated.

He had stood one back from the bar stools where Annabel and a female friend sat. There was noncommittal talk of sharing the ashtray. A flit of a smile on shapely lips. Be my guest, her inflections such that he inquired, as perhaps he was meant to: "Where are you from? If you don't mind my asking."

"Montgomery, Alabama." Drawling it out as though it didn't already have enough syllables. "And ya'll ...?"

Y'all ... Jesus. "I'm indigenous."

"That's a big word."

"It just means local."

"Does local mean Irish? I've noticed a lot of Irish around here."

"A regular infestation."

"We don't have any real Irish in the South."

"Indeed?"

"They're all Baptists."

"Except Scarlet O'Hara."

"Yes, that's true, isn't it? My name's Annabel. This here is Dorothea. She's my special friend."

"I'm L. B." Handshakes, neutral smiles.

"Elll … Beeee. And what does Ellbee stand for?"

"Leopold Bloom."

"Then you must be Jewish."

"In a fictional sort of way."

"Yes …" As though she didn't know but pretended to. Or wanted to give that impression.

Dorothea had turned to talk to the bearded gentleman next to her. Nominally fictive Israelite Leopold Bloom O'Boyle pointed at Miss Annabel's nearly empty glass and spoke with mock chivalry, "May I be so bold to offer you a recharge of what you are imbibing?"

Smile showing brilliant teeth, pantomime flutter of eyelids, "Why kind sir, I do declare I would be honored."

The voice and then the eyes. What did he see in those blue depths? Dawning attraction? And we are attracted to what we attract.

A moment later, "Would you mind if I called you?"

"Called me what?" Toying with him.

"On the telephone."

She took out a pen and tore a piece of paper from a spiral notebook. She had sensible hands, which should have alerted him, and a deliberate way of block printing the letters of her first and last names to go with the seven numbers.

"Annabel Chance," he mused aloud, reading her legibility.

"The very one."

She deceived him. Turned out to be Wellesley, Class of '84, and a student at the Harvard Divinity School writing her Doctor of Divinity thesis on Karl Barth's influence on the fiction of John Updike.

For Christ sake.

Leo O'Boyle stopped consuming his second hot dog and put the remainder on the plate. He stared at his nearly empty mug and pondered a refill of the alleged coffee. He pondered as well taking out a small notebook in which to write notes about a novel he felt particularly anxious this morning about not writing. Or, more accurately, about not finishing.

Leo's wandering glance caught and moved away from the small wall clock but not before registering the time: 8:11. He had a watch on his left wrist, but he had yet to use it that morning to tell time.

Outside, through the glass door, upright, blond Jim Block went by holding a large model in his arms. An architectural model. Great guy, Block. Upstairs in the bend of windows among a nest of fellow practitioners. Building the built world. Friend of Alf Brooks-Denny's. Nice family.

Family. The frightening word.

Because Leo, as his mother called him, suffered from, among other things, a persistent case of Philip Larkinism. That is to say, what he took to be the poet's aesthetic of futility appealed to him in the form of an easy, lulling nihilism. Might say the anesthetic of futility. *They fuck you up, your mum and dad* ... and all of that. Though in Leo's case he had done most of the fucking up by himself.

Stately, plump L. B. O'Boyle, the well-known travel writer and the less well-known chronophobe, stood up from his leftovers and glanced at the push-pinned map of the known world. Another wince of disquiet. Petra, his next assignment, had no pin. Supposed to be there two weeks from tomorrow. Copy due no later than ... He paid his bill, said his good-byes, and issued out into the mild September day.

Not really plump. Well fleshed, he would concede. Even full bodied. But not plump, not even stout, certainly not corpulent, a word he associated with crapulent. Well fleshed. And not un-stately. For which he relied on his voice, which was comfortably bass in its testicular resonance and adept at a facetious formality, traces of a year spent knocking around Dublin. The oft-squinting eyes were more shy than sly, hazel green and humorous under heavy lids; the mouth expressive even in repose, becoming fuller and authoritative with articulation. Of late he was given to keeping his chin up, out of its encroaching double. Of course, you couldn't keep your chin up and your nose down at the same time so that he appeared to some, given the voice, as just a bit sniffy. In his sniffier moments, L. B. O'Boyle liked to think he possessed the pseudo-Celtic good looks ascribed to Humbert Humbert by his creator. Not so pseudo in that he had also been likened in physique and physiognomy to *The Dying Gaul*—a rather fleshy dying Gaul— what with the strong nose, shapely mouth, and noble brow, but without the moustache or the knobbed torc. Curly and ginger with a tendency to bush outward if not given a monthly shearing at LaFlamme's, his hair had a pronounced, tapering, upward sweep towards the front, an Elvisian touch he cultivated because the Reverend Annabel Chance, Doctor of Divinity, thought it was cute.

He stood five feet eleven inches on a good day though, what with slackness of age, having turned thirty-six in July, and perhaps of character, he seldom reached more than five feet ten. He wore vaguely pressed chinos, a button-down white Oxford shirt from the Coop, loafers, and a gray brown nearly new wide-wale corduroy jacket from Keezer's, the used clothing purveyor near Central Square.

From his shoulder on sturdy straps depended a bag of a species somewhere between a purse and briefcase. Its reddish brown, un-tooled and slightly abraded leather rendered it fashionably unfashionable. Not for him one of those trim little knapsacks. They appalled him, especially on the back of a smartly dressed woman. Why not go all the way? Get an alpenstock and learn to yodel.

For Christ sake.

His hanging bag contained the unfinished novel that kept tapping him on the shoulder with some persistence on this particular morning. Titled *Ice Object 13*, it constituted in its extant state approximately one hundred and thirteen pages, single-spaced in twelve-point Courier, each page with a two-and-a-half-inch margin to the right on which to make notes. These pages, some close to a finished draft, others little more than narrative scaffolding or verbal doodling, were punched with holes and secured in a three-ring binder along with a growing volume of post-its, foolscap, sheets of A4 from Easons on O'Connell Street, a five-by-eight lined notepad, four-by-six index cards, etc., all scribbled or block-printed with notes and footnotes to notes and all in dire need of organization.

The novel revolved around a mysterious thing uncovered by an avalanche on the upper reaches of the Hubbard Glacier in the state of Alaska. At one level, it was an adventure yarn. On another level it was to be a profound exploration of the nature of time, the Object being not only extraterrestrial but extra-temporal. Or so the author wanted to think. On down days and even on some up days, he thought of this slowly gestating literary effort as *mon bébé mort*.

His other dead baby, snug in a manila folder with pockets, he called *The Caper*. An earlier effort at the novel form, *The Caper* had been slowly shriveling until revived by Ari Krasnick and a couple of his friends as a living implausibility, at which point it began slowly shriveling again. Another wince, an inner bristling. Lunch later today with The Committee. A black hole sucking in time.

Under its buckled flap, the satchel, for that's what it was, also held a brown accordion folder containing a selection from the literary remains of his late and lamented father, Francis Xavier O'Boyle. These included a sheaf labeled *JN*, meaning, he found later, journal notes, jottings meant for inclusion in a bound black journal that remained virtually untouched. And, most interestingly, a notebook titled *Working Class Hero*. He wasn't sure why he carried the files around with him. A kind of balance. *Mon père mort.* Until the week before it had been on the shelf over his writing desk in the spare room. Some fascinating stuff, at least to a son. What he meant to do with it he hadn't decided. Resurrect the man with his own words?

There was also a plain manila folder enfolding an unfinished, indeed, scarcely started, travel piece on the wonders of Petra, the narrow gorge in Jordan culminating with classical facades sculpted into the living sandstone. A few notes on the extinct Nabataeans, the former inhabitants. Did they speak Aramaic? Like Christ?

Liam Walsh, habitué of McDaids and drinking pal during L. B. O'Boyle's Dublin *Wanderjahr* and now doing public relations for a well-capitalized start-up airline based in Saudi Arabia, had commissioned the piece for the carrier's on-board magazine. For which L. B. had received a generous advance along with meal and hotel vouchers and two first-class round-trip tickets from Boston to Amman via New York.

Also: A slender appointments calendar purchased at Slates and seldom used, calendars being a kind of clock. A black, bound journal of his own, also from Slates. A half can of peppermint Altoids. Paper clips. Scraps of paper with notes. Almost clean handkerchief. A pair of Ray-Ban Aviators, classic now. Receipt for two rolls of Kodachrome, the resulting prints ready at Ferranti Dege.

More handily, he carried in the inside pocket of his jacket a three-and-a-half inch by five-and-a-half inch black Moleskine notebook for on-the-fly notes about *Ice Object 13* and the occasional phone number

or address. A back section he devoted to yet another literary entangle-
ment, one well beyond his competence if not his confidence. Friend Alf,
off the cuff, asking, "Hey, Leo, why not do a day in the life of yourself? A
kind of updated Bloomsday. Set it in and around Harvard Square. Hour
by hour. Hyperconsciousness, you know, get in the flow."

"What flow?"

"The stream of consciousness."

Alf going on about Nabokov on the *Circe* episode of *Ulysses*—the
novel dreaming itself.

Novels begin like that. Or in dreams. Waking dreams. His ice object
story began its uncertain life during a flyover of the Hubbard Glacier a
couple of years before. Something in the snow resembling a downed
weather balloon or stylized igloo glinting in the angled sun. The author
thinking, dreaming what if? Before the plane dipped, the light shifted,
and the thing resolved itself into an outcropping of ordinary rock. But
not before the image embedded itself in his mind, gestated, hatched,
grew claws and the stubs of wings. And demanded to be fed.

Especially this morning for some reason or reasons. The thing had
turned loud and ravenous on him, all but chewing the inside of his bag.
He promised to attend ASAP. After a few small errands. Perhaps in
Lamont after dropping by the Poetry Room. Soon, he soothed, soon.

Out the door of The Tasty, he turned right to cross what had been
a spur of Massachusetts Avenue, now a paved part of a redbrick pedestrian plaza where gathered the young and the restless, the lost and
the homeless, the dazed and the clueless. All in the shadow of Dmitri
Hadzi's twenty-foot granitic, semaphoric *Omphalos*. Umbilicus of the
intellectual universe and right there in Harvard Square.

Omphalos.

The fact is, the suggestion to pen a kind of *Ulysses Redux* had also
taken hold, had become an inner itch that scratching only made worse.
Leopold Bloom O'Boyle had the right authorial handle for it. But it
meant a lot of work. He would have to reread *The Odyssey* and take notes.
And then climb Mount Ulysses yet again. He knew the routes, some of
them by heart. He knew the dazzling views, the dizzying heights, the
alluring by-ways, the webs of connections, the endless minutiae, the
thin air. Still it meant digging out the guidebooks and an oxygen mask.
For what? The trials and tribulations of an Odysseus thrice removed, a

take on a take, the danger of inadvertent parody never far off. Another neglected fosterling in his bag of dreams clamoring for attention?

Still ...

To the right of where he stood the subway entrance engorged and disgorged all variety of riders, gliding up out of and gliding down into the underground on the escalator, motionless yet moving. The sight nagged L. B. O'Boyle's inner author with something metaphoric just beyond his reach. Something to do with the nature of time. Or something to do with Dmitri's sculpting and his Joycean dad poking gently baby Leo's naked naval and intoning, "The cords all link back, strandentwining cable of all flesh." Umbilicus. Reverend Doctor Annabel Chance's enticing bellybutton and what now grew beneath.

He noticed a bank of pay phones just beyond the sprawl area. Call Annabel? Wish her the luck she probably wouldn't need. Tell her he loved her. Remind her to ask about the alternatives? The alternative.

Across the busy traffic, just before Massachusetts Avenue turned sharply left, stretched a long commercial block, coigned redbrick, mansarded, as though part of Harvard. Probably owned by Harvard. There stood the street clock in front of the more modern Coop, the time showing as 8:22. He did not avert his gaze. What time is it? Mistaken question, really. It's never the same time as when you looked. Even as you looked. A kind of uncertainty principle. If only by seconds, then minutes, hours, days, years. Better to ask, what time was it? Or what time will it be? Which both presumed there was a time, an actual point of time, called the present. When, of course, there isn't.

Now he was not so sure that the present didn't exist. He glanced again at the street clock and this time checked it against his father's watch. 8:23. They agreed. Which, for reasons he could not fathom, reassured him. Heretofore he had not only avoided looking at public clocks unless absolutely necessary, but he had been unable to wear his late father's elegant Lecoutre Master Mariner for more than a few minutes at a time.

And something else. To his bemusement, the travel writer *cum* novelist *encore manqué* took in the scene with more than his usual acuity. He could imagine that it was all new, that he was seeing it for the first time—as though he were a tourist just off the plane or a perspicacious travel writer, but one from Tokyo or Canberra or Moscow. Or as though someone else was looking through his eyes. Or he was looking through their eyes. Because he was struck by the prevalence of redbrick, the size of the cars, the directed, striding people, the gray steeple of the church on the corner of Church Street pointing into the blue gray sky. And for just that instant, he felt relieved of his fear of time.

Out of Town News in the old repurposed subway entrance stood just beyond the information kiosk. All the newspapers he couldn't read. Inside the smell of newsprint. *Corriere della Sera. Bella sera.* Got that much. *Frankfurter Allgemeine Zeitung.* Hot dog wouldn't work there. *Le Monde* he could handle and *The Irish Times.* No more *Pravda*, no more *Izvestia.* No news in the truth, no truth in the news. The Soviet Union dumped unceremoniously into the trash bin of history. If only Dad had lived to see that.

The Boston Globe for September 8, 1992, featured front-page stories about the Bush-Clinton race, each candidate wrapping himself in the banner of give 'em hell Harry. A page 2 headline read, "Sarajevo food stocks dwindling fast." Another story had a picture of the Sinologist Ross Terrill, a friend of Alf's. It was about a dissident being arrested shortly after visiting Terrill in Beijing. Inside a photo of Mrs. Clinton, Mrs. Hillary Rodham Clinton. Someone to watch.

A fleeting thought: Joyce used the *Evening Telegraph* and other papers published close to June 16, 1904, as sources of record for his masterpiece. Buy the *Globe* and do the same with it? But who was he, Bloom or Dedalus or both? Telemachus looking for his father? Or Odysseus trying to get back to his besieged Penelope in Ithaca? He much doubted that Annabel would be fending off suitors or lying abed waiting for the moral equivalent of Blazes Boylan to come ravish her. That little creep Bernie Lusk didn't quite fill the bill. Boylan at least had a spurious *élan.* Holding a carnation in his lips by the stem. On the other hand, the three o'clock appointment Annabel had at Brigham and Women's reverberated at a level he couldn't plumb.

No. Can't do it. Wouldn't work.

Still, he paid the aproned attendant and folded the daily into his satchel.

He glanced at *Le Monde. Lundi.* Only a day late. Front page story about a record number of murders in Los Angeles County during August. Must seem like the Wild West to the civilized French.

Another thought blooming. Out of Town News. A squat Tower of Babel. Sheldon Cohen presiding. For the newspaper scene? The *Aeolus* episode, perhaps? It was an island, a traffic island. Or had been before becoming a peninsula for pedestrians. No shortage of local windbags. Could play with that. Better than the *Harvard Gazette* Office up in Holyoke Center. Knew folks there. House organ. Not the same. Holyoke. Curious name.

No. Cannot start yet another novel.

• • •

L. B. O'Boyle turned back in the direction of The Tasty, then past the Wursthaus. The worst house, in common parlance, domain of the Cardullos and mother lode of authentic Italo-American German cuisine. Guys hanging around the entrance foyer like stage Mafioso. Also the eponymous Cardullo's across JFK Street. Real deli. Smoked eel. Had that at the University Club on Stephen's Green. JFK was Boylston Street until Councilor Alfred Vellucci read Bob Levy in the *Globe* that the Kennedy School of Government was thinking of changing its name, the better to better its fund-raising. JFK. Our martyred President. Dad turned teary that day in late November, muttering to himself, pacing around their apartment. Luck of the Irish. History the nightmare … *Sic transit gloria mundi*, he kept repeating.

Who was the novelist had a character named Gloria Monday?

Standing under the stack of illuminated signs,

> Wursthaus
> Gutes Essen
> Restaurant
> Delicatessen
> Liquors

Leopold Bloom O'Boyle suffered a nearly debilitating nostalgia for the present he didn't believe in. These things, these people, this instant, were all passing, would keep on passing. And be forever gone. He glanced around at the hurrying faces and marveled that he alone appeared to be suffering this sense of continual, irretrievable loss.

But then he suffered from all kinds of nostalgias, including what might be called vicarious nostalgia for the lost worlds of others—the pristine America of the natives before the Europeans arrived; Nabokov's butterfly-collecting boyhood; the vibrant culture of Europe's Jews before the advent of Hitler; the Brahmin Boston of Henry James and John Singer Sargent; the modest life that his parents had once had and from which he sprang. It went beyond sentimentality. In passing an empty lot where a building had recently been torn down and carted away, he would experience a keen stab of regret for the loss of what had been there even on those occasions when he could not recall what had been there.

Nor could he imagine a different arrangement for how life might be lived outside of time. Perhaps like a film you could stop, rewind, replay, slow to slow motion, or, at the very least, pause? But what if everybody could do that? What would happen to all those times in the meantime? Time would still have to pass. Of course everything had to pass until … Death. Larkin whispering—*Nothing more terrible. Nothing more true.* A darkness no one sees into or out of. The lights stay on, but not for you. And small consolation that even billionaires aloft in their private jets have to decide what to do with this beloved thing, this pampered thing, this *fleshcase* that we are all walking around in: have it burned to ashes or left to rot in the ground. Gets reworked one way or another. The secret is to live, said Leo O'Boyle to himself, quoting his father quoting Joyce: *Life.*

His mistimed nostalgias were manifestations of periodic bouts of chronophobia, a fear not simply of clocks or other chronometers but of what they represented—time itself and its unrelenting passage from which there was no refuge. Not that he didn't try to find one. Some days were worse than others, afflicting him like an asthmatic suffering a high pollen count. Other days? At best a tenuous normality, but one requiring an aversion to anything smacking of clocks, calendars, dates, references to time. But such that even on good days he would glance around him and wonder why there was no panic. Don't they realize? Time is burning them alive! Yet sane enough to know that everyone else wasn't insane. From which he took a pinch of solace. Better to be mad himself than to have what he feared to be real. He wondered if there was a name for his affliction in that handbook of psychic disorders. Acute Chronophobic Syndrome. ACS. Or Chronic Chronophobic Disorder Syndrome. CCDS. Or Temporal Anxiety Recurrent Disorder.

His peculiar neurosis first appeared during a precocious puberty, a time of facial pimpling and marvelous nocturnal emissions. The proximate cause was an old mantel wind-up clock in the Cassidy house that his mother, along with her siblings, inherited near Crystal Lake in North Chelmsford, Massachusetts. The clock had stopped with its Gothic hands indicating four twenty-three. He took it down and fiddled with it. He wound it up. Nothing. He opened the glass on its face and moved the minute hand. Nothing. He might have taken a screwdriver and examined its innards except there wasn't a small enough one around. Instead he tapped the clock lightly on its oaken head. Nothing. A moment later, the thing began ticking and he nearly dropped it as though some sleeping beast had become alive on his lap.

He had woken up sleeping time. Which he knew to be absurd because he was already acutely conscious of time's ineluctable passage. Still it left him shaken and apprehensive about time always coming and always going. He later surmised his chronophobia began when he grew conscious of his consciousness about time. He grew aware of being aware of public clocks, classroom clocks, digital clocks, alarm clocks, appliance clocks, radio clocks, dashboard clocks. Not to mention watches. Not to mention time checks on radio, on television, at football games. How many minutes, seconds, tenths of seconds left. Then nuclear clocks splitting time down to nanoseconds, to tiny, tiny slices of time. Which didn't slow it down one bit.

Most mornings Leo began his day in denial. That is, he would ignore as best he could the daily dance of the hours even while aware of time's incessant hum, its ticking and its tocking, its chiming and its belling, even its deceptive silences. But that morning, for the first time in many suns and many moons and partly as a counter-phobic exercise, Leo retrieved his dad's wristwatch from a drawer of the desk where he wrote. But only partly as a curative ploy because he had also just risen from a vivid dream of his dad, a dream both reassuring and tantalizing in which Francis X. wanted to tell him something important but never got around to it. In the thrall of that dream, he had wound the watch, set its hands by the digital, truly alarming clock on Annabel's side of the bed, which normally he would avoid looking at, and, with self-conscious fortitude, strapped it on his wrist.

In theory he should have been able to tolerate the watch. Winding its trim little stem gave him a tenuous sense of controlling it. Analog time pieces did not agitate him as much as digital displays, perhaps because the swing of the seconds hand showed distance and motion, linking the passage of time to something if not altogether tangible then at least observable. It helped as well that the face was perfectly round, three hundred and sixty degrees of time, which he took to be emblematic of the spheres circling spheres circling spheres throughout the known universe.

In theory. On previous occasions, strapping on the watch had made him feel manacled to time, convinced the thing had synchronized itself with his heart, which, however slowly, was winding down. He wanted to forget that time was passing, not be reminded of it. So he had not succeeded in his past efforts. His best time in keeping the timepiece on his wrist amounted to just short of half an hour. At that point, with seeming madness looming, he had un-strapped the ticking thing and put it back into the darkness of the drawer.

He glanced again at the street clock in front of the Coop. Then at his dad's watch. 8:40. Still keeping pace. And a faint bell. Then an uncanny, too real sensation: the watch on his wrist was keeping his father's time. Or, more precisely, continuing his father's time. Then another odd thought: he shouldn't be wasting his father's time.

Though waste time he did, musing on his musings.

In his musings, Leo resisted the usual metaphors about time. Time flowing like water under a bridge? What bridge? Did it flow into a larger stream and hence into an ocean of time? Then what? Evaporate, condense, and fall? Showers of time? Downpours? Floods? Perhaps. He would have liked to believe that time circulates. The notion soothed him. But he felt time more as the drip drip of his own blood, his little rill of life slowly, inexorably running dry.

A few years back, jettisoned by a gorgeous young banker named Tyler, who declared, after checking his credit rating, "Sex and talk are not enough," he resorted to an evening of whiskey in the Temple Bar before indulging in some mind-altering weed grown on Mars that left him clinging to the cliff face of chronophobic derangement. He tried to hide from it, pulling the covers over his head in bed that night like a child and lying perfectly still. Only to hear and feel more distinctly the clock of his heart, each beat one less of what remained.

What remained. Midway through his fourth decade, on his birthday, Leo began to keep score of his own time, totaling up what he had left of life like a miser counting his dwindling pile. Having turned thirty-six July 21, he figured another forty years if … ease off the easy life, find a gym, cut out the hot dogs and beer. Forty times three hundred and sixty five plus ten extra for leap years gave him fourteen thousand six hundred and ten days left. That multiplied by twenty four gave him three hundred and fifty thousand, six hundred and forty hours. That came to more than twenty-one million minutes. He didn't count the seconds, not that seconds didn't count.

At other times he thought of time coming and going in a kind of punctuated equilibrium, as though the passage of time disrupted a serene eternal present. Back in grammar school, St. Peter's—For God and Country—the minute hand of the black-banded institutional wall clock remained still until it staggered ever so slightly backward for a second before jolting forward and coming to rest again. A shock, but preferable to the relentlessly mounting numerals on a digital watch. Worst were game clocks showing the whirr of tenths of a second as time ran out. To the point where the only sport he could watch comfortably on television was baseball, a game that, theoretically, could go on forever in extra innings.

Nor could he abide grandfather clocks keeping sentry in some quaint hostelry with their audible time-keeping. After about ten minutes, the tick-tock, tick-tock, tick-tock got to him. On one occasion he and Annabel had to move rooms at a country inn because some ancient timepiece standing in the hallway could not be silenced without resort to violence.

Leo did not need the bearded gentleman in the New Yorker cartoons to suggest to his recumbent form that a deal of his problem derived from a capacious, accurate, and tenacious memory. He could recall in visual, aural, olfactory, and tactile detail events with their accompanying auras reaching back to his toddling days. One of his first distinct memories occurred on his third Christmas when he crawled under the dazzlingly lit and fragrant balsam (his mother's doing) where, pushing aside the neatly wrapped presents (his mother's doing), he discovered that the tree was held in place by a very ordinary stand equipped with an adjustable clamp. Which caused him to sniffle and then cry. Upon asking where the tree came from, he had been told that it grew of its own accord out of the floor. (His dad's doing.) It took him awhile to learn the difference between the telling of untruths and the exercise of imagination.

In other words, Leo's past or large parts of it remained intact, still there and as real as now. But not still there. In fact all gone, gone forever. Time had destroyed them. And yet they remained, vivid, seemingly accessible, creating a void between what was and what is that he could not begin to bridge.

He kept his malaise to himself the way someone with a severe foot fetish might not want it generally known. Annabel knew about it, but she regarded his *mal de temps*, as she so nicely put it, as more of an eccentricity than a condition requiring professional treatment—were such treatment available. Which helped him to feel normal, especially since he had an aversion bordering on the pathological to anything remotely smacking of premeditated verbal therapy. Which did not preclude heart-to-hearts with Annabel or a boozy session in a friendly bar with a pal like Alf. The latter of which might have helped had he been able to recall the next morning more than a few sentences of what had been said the night before.

Alcohol helped, but only in moderation, hangovers being for the temporality-challenged seemingly endless, an inversion of the phobia, pulling and stretching minutes into hours as though to make more time for the deserved misery. Moderate doses of whiskey, on the other hand, helped him to forget about time and, as in any illness real or imagined, forgetting helped. But he couldn't remind himself to forget inasmuch as forgetting is the most involuntary activity of the human mind. But what blissful glimpses of the normality forgetting afforded in wistful retrospect after something as innocuous as the chiseled date on a building reminded him that *tempus fugit*.

In the course of a few severe episodes, Leo taught himself to control his private madness. He had no wish to be enrolled at McLeans, the Harvard of institutions for the differently mental, despite its list of distinguished graduates, including the poet Robert Lowell. Or to have his name affixed forever to a clinical disorder, something like O'Boyle's Syndrome, for which there was no known cure.

Any number of discreet inquiries convinced him there was little in the medical literature about chronophobia other than generalities about phobias in general. Nor could he find among the spin-offs of AA anything resembling Chronophobics Anonymous. Even had there been, he doubted he would have joined with fellow sufferers in the hope and comfort of shared stories in a semi-circle of hard chairs in the community activities room of a local church. Besides, having little inclination to join the growing ranks of those enjoying certified victimhood, he blamed himself for his weird affliction. He blamed himself in part because he wanted to maintain the notion, however illusory, that if it were his fault then he could correct it. Virtue being a fig and within ourselves that we are thus and thus and all that.

To this end, Leo gave himself license to brood endlessly on the nature of time very much at the risk of making this palliative part of the disease. In these broodings, his mind got into ruts, SOTs, same old thoughts. Again and again he pondered whether the future plunged into the past in a circular or linear fashion. That question constituted a major sub-category of his musings, musings he resorted to in his attempts to objectify and thus distance this thing that baffled him at best and terrorized him at worst. As an interim solution to the question of the circularity or linearity of time, he decided it was both and it was neither and it was unknowable in that time would remain the final mystery of existence never to be fathomed.

For a time he had a copy of Dali's *Persistence of Memory* tacked to the wall over his desk. He wanted to agree with the sentiment, but having the right title wasn't enough. With time, the spineless, flowing watches struck him as fakes, cover-ups, making time seem tame, even cute. He would have preferred death heads with clock faces and no hands. Or smashed hour glasses, their fine sands spilled around them. He even thought of writing a letter to the artist to tell him the truth about time. But the artist's time had run out.

In pondering his bouts of chronophobia, Leo noticed they conflated with a hankering for the ordinary, for the repeatability of things, for the steps leading up to the front door of their down-at-heels apartment in Arlington and for its warm wooden stairway which, ascending to the second floor, held time steady in the vestiges of accumulated odors. Of late when he traveled the world, the travel writer L. B. O'Boyle sought out lived-in neighborhoods down side streets. He walked through them, stopping in hardware stores, florists, bookshops, pharmacies, food shops, buying some small item to justify his intrusion. It soothed him to imagine what it was like to live there, to have a house or apartment to fix up, to shop for dinner, to get your clothes cleaned and your car fixed. All of which was related, he considered, to an impulse to experience the time of the place, the time that ticked on, the life that got lived, before he arrived, while he was there, and after he left.

Time as oxidation. Time the fire in which ... And something to find out: How did a New Yorker of the Hebrew persuasion named Schwartz end up with the name Delmore? Maybe it's explained in *Humboldt's Gift*.

The one reliable refuge from his phobia Leo found in reading. Especially fiction but also biography and history. Especially when well written. Before a chance exchange while lunching with Alf at The Potato, Leo had no idea why. It had little to do with the time frame of whatever he was reading. The few hours of *Ulysses* soothed as well as the years of *War and Peace*. On the other hand, *Du Coté de Chez Swann*, into which he periodically immersed himself in the hope of finding something like timelessness, a French-English dictionary at hand, proved disappointing, making him ponder the difference between reading a language you know and thinking in it.

The title of their discussion at the Potato might have been "A Theory of Narrative."

"Actually," said Alf, seldom shy about expatiating on large topics, "*story* is a better word for it." A digression into how the word *narrative* had been hijacked, reduced to a pseudo-technical term, i.e., jargon, in the dubious discipline of postmodernism. "In fact, no one knows why we make up stories, tell stories, listen to stories, need stories. You might as well ask, why do we live?"

"Maybe they figured in our evolution," chanced Leo, writer-to-writer now, pushing one of Alf's many buttons.

A facial shrug. "In early human evolution after the development of language it's possible that the telling of cautionary tales provided a selection advantage at the group level." Then musing out loud. "Stories enlarge our worlds with other places, other lives, other times. We live through others by an act of the imagination, which stories require.

Postmodernism got that much right. Perhaps we are compelled by what happens to others because our own lives are themselves stories set in time."

"From which we cannot escape."

"Ah, but we do. Or we try. Into the lives and especially, into the time and times of others. And not just in stories."

Which rang a bell in Leo's psyche that jarred him awake, but awake to what he wasn't quite sure. It was a bell that continued to ring, sometimes faintly, sometimes loudly. It tolled something about the time of others real or imagined. It tolled with an echo of promise in its reverberations. He didn't delve as perhaps he should have because he did not want to become too conscious of the assuagement that the alternate time of a novel or any other story could provide. He simply indulged. He teased himself with Wilde's *Dorian Gray*, watched more than once the BBC production of *Brideshead Revisited*, having read and reread Waugh's masterpiece, and wallowed in *Love in a Time of Cholera*. At the moment he was deep into the narrative of the still unborn *Tristam Shandy*, a novel overflowing with easy time, but also a novel too large and tempting to carry around like some cumbersome pacifier. Because he was prone to periodic bouts of bibliolepsy with which he eased his phobia even when conscious that he was living the imaginary time of these imaginary people on his own disappearing time.

Which made L. B. O'Boyle think perhaps more than he should have about the novel of his own life. The story of his existence and its inevitable conclusion. Only now it wasn't death aided and abetted by relentless time that stalked him as he went by The Garage that was no longer a garage to the corner of Mount Auburn Street. It was life. Confirmation today. Three o'clock. Without an intervention, Annabel's belly would swell, a swelling act consequent on a swelling act, another new life, a new story, budding, transforming his own life. Unless … For courage, remembering his dad, saying to himself again, *Life*.

At that instant, in a passing car, in the backseat, in profile, in the same figure like the father that's dead, Leo saw his dad. Or a man of middle years very like his dad was then, leaning forward, the face eager, talking to the driver. He glanced at his father's watch with the sensation that it was not only telling his father's time, but was on his father's wrist.

To help gather his scattered wits, Leo reviewed his timetable for the day: Drop by The Grolier for a copy of *Seeing Things*. Then Ferranti Dege for the prints from the two film cassettes he had dropped off from Annabel's point-and-shoot. Snaps of their receding past. Drop by Lamont Library to see what Stratis wanted. Message on the message machine. Perhaps a travel piece for the *Review*. Doesn't pay. But a solid little publication. That piece by Bob Scanlan on working with Beckett in Paris. Brooks-Denny's essay on Nabokov curating and describing butterflies at the MCZ and thereby honing his "high" English. Good company. Then Widener to pick up something on the Nabataeans. Then a meeting of The Committee. Skip the meeting? Mom on the way home.

Mom.

The evening before an employee of The Elms called and addressed him as Mr. O'Boyle in a tone of voice that gave him a stab of concern edged by the expectation that this was The Call, the sorry-to-inform-you call. It wasn't. Mrs. Boyle had been asking for him. Not sleeping well at night. Sleeping a lot during the day. Depressed. Tell her I will be by tomorrow, he said, relieved she was not about to die, relieved not to feel relieved that she might be. No heroic Greek was he. No Telemachus checking back on his mom while in search of his dad.

But still *Ulysses Redux* sang a tune in his head he couldn't silence. A tune yet to be composed. A tune composing itself with off-key dissonance despite his best efforts to shut it up. The illusion being that we think we can think what we want to think and not think what we think we don't want to think.

Across the street the Whitney, old style bar. It used to be near The Tasty. Or was that Harvard Garden? Harvard Garden Grill? Beers for fifteen cents back in the day. Last of the old dives. Not like the chains. Pizzerio Uno. Used to be The King's Men's Bar. Same pizza you get in Chicago. Not that Charlie's 'dog wasn't the same one you get everywhere. Timeless.

He crossed JFK and stood on the opposite corner. An illuminated sign on American Express Travel read "Go Away Often." Leafy, grassy Winthrop Park. Grendel's Den. Was that Armenian Church still there? Down Winthrop Street. House of Blues to the left. Used to be a restaurant with a snug overlooking the street. Then the Galleria. Mini mall.

He turned and retraced his steps. Redbrick under foot and rising around him. Blue sky, muttony clouds, warm, moist air. Could be that June day in Dublin. He paused to regard the stately building housing the Fox Club and the row of businesses down leafy Kennedy Street behind which set the Iruna. Authentic Spanish food. Squid in its own ink sauce. Good dish for writers. Name of the Cafe in Pamplona where Jake Barnes and his friends hung out. Dad hated the book. Said it was a dreary saga of Jew baiting. Fistic Robert Cohn the baited bull, the baited Jew. Cohn's plaint early on, something about his life going so fast he was not really living it, striking a chord. Father and son differed. The man's best work, said the son. The dad softened when told that back in the heyday of Paris, Hemingstein would walk an unsteady or carry a comatose Jim Joyce back to his digs after a night of tippling.

Leopold Bloom O'Boyle crossed back over and went along the south side of Mount Auburn with the traffic. He paused to take a mental image. The travel writer owned a Nikon with several lenses that he used on trips. He also taught himself the knack of framing a view with his eyes and fixing it in his mind. His facility grew to the point where he could call up images and scan them for details as though looking at a photograph. It didn't work as well with the printed page. Too much information.

Now the lens of his mind focused and took in the pre-term bustle that stirred the long vista down to the Lampoon Castle, redbrick trimmed in stone, the inscrutable face with the diamond eyes of its rotund round tower waiting for its audience to get the joke. A sacred ibis, *Threskiornis aethiopica*, perched on the conical point of the tower, its coppery sheen backlit by the rising light. Emblematic of Thoth, god of writing and much else. The same Councilor Vellucci moving in chamber that the building be turned into a public urinal.

Holyoke Center to the left. Ten floors of concrete. Like the second best hotel in a Third World capital, some wag had said. H. L. Sert. Legacy of Gropius. Butt ugly. One of Annabel's southernisms. Big bellied. Would she loose her shape? Her mother Lenoir hadn't. Still a looker at sixty. Harvard Provision. Mostly wine these days. Turning it into water. Would have to drink for two if Annabel ... Up the pole. Where did that come from?

Again he found himself stopping, framing, and fixing views as though seeing them for the first time. Or as though possessed of a second set of eyes. University Typewriter, for example. Laptops in the window now. Back in the day the portables with different alphabets. Cyrillic. Greek. Carriage went left to right on the Hebrew one, return the reverse. *He reads from right to left inaudibly, smiling, kissing the page … Rudy!* His namesake's lost son. Reduxable? Bloom's poignant vision prompted by the memory of a keyboard? Then a pang of *agenbite* in Leo's real world. Would this Leopold collude in canceling his own Rudy before he scarcely began?

J. Press. A blazer on display. Could use a new one. New trousers as well. Could use a nice dollop of cash. An inheritance. Lose a couple of inches first. Prefer the jacket with the herringbone weave. Tweedy. Expensive. Where did all the money go? Not on dry cleaning and gracious living. Not much to begin with. His sporadic checks. Annabel's assistant minister stipend.

She earned that at the Mayflower Congregational Church in Belmington, a seemingly fictional sounding place between Belmont and Arlington on high ground just west of Cambridge. A plain house of worship, it had a clean austerity to it. True to its Puritan origins, no images decorated its pale beige walls and no human form hung in agony from the altar cross. A march of brass pipes loomed over the organ keyboard on the right side of the altar area and a pulpit, a kind of raised gazebo, extended out from the left side. The brethren and sistren around him confirmed a notion he had heard once or twice in Cambridge: the Midwest began in Belmont.

To paraphrase Larkin, Leo could say, though he didn't, that his uncorrected vision continued in church. Because, as the Reverend Chance stood in the pulpit in a black robe and read from the Gospel (how well she invoked the better parts of Leviticus), he would wake to love for her all over again. It occurred to him with a certain amazement that she loved him. Those nights, nudging him, her head turned, her half smile. So that, in the midst of prayer, an erotic expectation would push aside his borrowed piety and persist through the coffee and cake reception afterwards, driving her home.

Pregnant. The word itself pregnant, growing in his head.

If only they might delay the zgotene proliferation into embryo, embryo to fetus, fetus to a being that would destroy forever his dreams of writing. The end of life as he had known it. Morning sickness. Alien invader. Sleepless nights. Sodden diapers the least of it. Was he not *un homme du monde*? Could you be a man of the world and be pregnant as in that awful locution, "We're pregnant?" More like "We're fucked." Could he be a man of the world and walk around wearing one of those front-slung papoose things as though he were about to open his shirt and give suck to … yes, to an infant hanging there with its chubby legs on display? His very own lump of love. Or pushing a baby carriage through the park. Do they have baby carriages anymore?

A man of the world? Really? Was not that character at best a dead cliché found in old movies—a tuxed-up smoothie who tickled the keys at gala parties on board luxury liners or in big houses, who squired sleek women through dazzling nights in three languages and turned back priceless bottles of wine after one sniff of the cork, all the while wielding a rapier wit with which to vanquish any and all comers. Man of the world? In his almost-new Keezer's jacket? Jesus, man, get a handle. More like get a new mirror in which to look at yourself.

Still Larkin whispered, *Get out as soon as you can and don't have any kids yourself.*

The terror, the wonder, the existential angst—as he over-dramatized it to himself—started the day before when Annabel brought home from Walgreen's a small box labeled Clearblue Easy. A private session in the bathroom. The husband pacing in the hallway outside. Floor needs work. Light fixture dusty. Pepperoni does leave a smell. The closed door of his study. The new nursery? The bathroom door opens.

"It's blue," she says, the beam in her eyes if not her voice. "I'm pregnant."

Easier done than said, he almost says. "Really?" Not really a question.

"I think I'll go into Brigham and Women's to get it confirmed." Then falls against him and starts to cry.

Why this outburst he had wondered, holding her gently against himself, thinking, this vessel of new life. Or not. Because they had yet to decide to let be or not let be. That was the question. Making them reluctant little gods of life and death. When the crunch came and soon, they would confer, commune, and pray about it. At least Annabel would pray about it. They might let their ambivalences feed their disquiet, let their disquiet resolve to reluctant decision. D & C.

Then face life wondering forever what if? Or confer, commune, have a drink—her last for a while—and say, Why the hell not? From which prospect Leo O'Boyle could gather no palpable joy as a nebulous but definite anxiety gnawed, an anxiety that he could not grasp, hold in his head, and dispel.

Again it happened again. In the same figure of his dead father, a man turned the corner of Dunster Street in the direction of the river walking in the same peculiarly rapid stride of Francis X. O'Boyle. Looked just like. What could he do about it? Follow the guy? Tap him on the shoulder. Excuse me, are you … ?

It had happened before. Dad sightings, he called them. Though not twice within an hour and with this pertinacity. Time for a talk.

Standing in front of J. Press, his likeness obscurely mirrored in the store's plate glass window, Leo found the prospect of meeting with The Committee brought on an inner snarl of dismissal. The meetings—to plan a swindle to be redeemed by its originality and aesthetic flourishes and based on the plot of The Caper—had degenerated into bull sessions about everything and about nothing. They were a deepening pit down which Leo felt his future plunging into his past with a vacant roar. He knew they would never come to anything.

The meetings certainly did not accord with this shifting image of his mirrored self against the expensive shirts and jackets behind the glass. Musing. L. B. O'Boyle the travel-writer. L. B. O'Boyle the novelist. L. B. O'Boyle? He checked the time. It was 8:55 and counting. What else would it do? He kept walking. His dad saying don't hurry through life. Don't dawdle through it either. Stay on the ground. Let time do the flying.

He should have seen the sorry Caper thing coming that warm spring night when he and Ari and Ari's new friend and probable coke connection, a vaguely Austrian national from Argentina named Fritz, had smoked some mild reefer while parked like high school kids along a stretch of the Charles River adjacent to the Home Depot in Watertown. Ari had been bragging on Leo, how he was a travel writer and a novelist, someone to watch.

They subsequently drove back to the Square and stretched their legs in a walk to the Casablanca where, being a valued customer, Ari and his party were led to a booth where they might converse in private.

His tongue loosened with a large whiskey (they do exist) followed by a beer to go with the lamb and stuffed pepper, the author spoke more than he wanted to about a work barely in progress, *The Caper,* his first attempt at a novel.

Fritz, prematurely balding, reddish, blunt faced, had snorted with a slight accent, "Not another damn book about food?"

Defensively, effusively and with the distortion that comes of truncation, Leo outlined the far-from-original plot: Travel writer in his cups in a Key West bar gets talking to an old salt who just happens to have on him an old chart showing the location where a Spanish galleon loaded with gold, silver, and precious stones went down in a storm back in the seventeenth century or thereabouts. Would the travel writer happen to know any parties willing to buy shares in a sure-fire venture to underwrite the expense of retrieving the treasure from its resting place?

His audience listened attentively. Leo continued, went into details. "The subtext, of course, is that we're all seeking treasure of some kind or another. You know, lost gold, a fantastic mate, the transcendence of nature, the perfect wine ..."

Ari, looking at Fritz, said, "Why don't we make it happen?"

Leo said, "What do you mean?"

Ari was leaning forward wearing his ingratiating smile. "I mean, let's just do it. Leo, you've done the research. Fritz knows some people who could do the documentation."

"Eyah ..."

"And I've got a line into some prospects."

Leo had looked at the remnants of lamb smeared around his plate. As stuffed as the peppers he had eaten, he suffered a spasm of chagrin. They were plagiarizing his novel and in so doing were depriving it of its imaginative freedom. Not that it wasn't, at base, a fairly obvious yarn. But not necessarily a yawn. He had done research, as any story, even a fairy tale, needs a gloss of factuality, needs telling if possibly meretricious detail with which to engage the reader's credulity. That was the easy part.

At the same time he experienced a rare sense of affirmation. His writing had inspired his friends to action. It was as though *The Caper* was going to be made into more than a movie—it was going to be made into life.

Since that evening any sense of affirmation had long shriveled up. Rather than a bright light on the horizon of his existence, he viewed the project through a whiskey glass darkly for what it was—an inner prop, a psychic crutch in that it fostered the illusion that they were doing something interesting if not particularly meaningful or worthy as all of them belonged to that class of people that envision a larger life beyond making a living, raising children, and avoiding as much pain as possible.

The almost novelist crossed Dunster Street and glanced down to the redbrick facade of Kirkland House. No sign of the man in the same figure of his dead father. Kirkland House. Invitation to join the Senior Common Room. Sherry and talk. Brooks-Denny belonged.

He stopped in front of Schoenhof's Foreign Books. Free standing display window. A book in Gaelic. *An Mhaighdean Mhara.* The Mermaid. A Selkie myth. *Asterix* in what looked like Romanian. Or was it Rumanian? Something by Pushkin in the Cyrillic alphabet. *Skazka.* Need to look up that one. The things you don't know. Children's books. Inner wince. If push came to that final shove of new life, dig out his old ones tucked away somewhere on Strand Street.

Strand Street. The apartment already something of a time capsule well before Mom broke her hip and went into hospital and then to The Elms. A lot of his childhood stuff still there. Dad's books and papers and framed photos of Joyce, Yeats, Beckett, and, more recently, Heaney on the untidy walls of the tiny study sectioned off the back porch. The same pots and pans, plates and cups, glasses and silverware in the kitchen with the rustic-looking pine paneling and stainless steel sink. The oddments of crockery with one good setting for eight. A few neo-abstract daubings of artist friends on the walls. A couple of framed posters for some modish and now so-dated cultural event. How quickly the cutting edge dulls. In the living room the LPs in orderly rows beneath the AR turntable. Mom's weakness for show tunes. Old toys. Old clothes down in the basement. Never threw anything away. A museum of lives once lived.

To check the time and a dawning, tremulous equanimity regarding its passage, he looked at the LeCoutre. It read 9:07. Scarcely a flinch.

L. B. O'Boyle entered the emporium of living and dead languages and descended the winding stairs. Just being there made you feel smarter. As if you knew.

The clerk knew. "Aramaic, yes. We have Rosenthal's. *A Grammar of Biblical Aramaic.*"

"That sounds good."

"You might try a Hebrew primer first. It's a bit technical."

"My wife has one of those." And getting in to it. Her assiduous study. Vocabulary cards. Repeating phrases out of a cassette player at the kitchen table. Getting the "keh" sound right. Her way, she said, of going to the Holy Land.

Leo perused the proffered book. If only learning a language was as easy as buying its grammar. In the piece on Petra he would touch on the Nabataeans. Throw in a little Aramaic. Historical filler. Make it seem like he knew. In transliteration and translation, of course. Not cheap. The Div School library would have one. He put it down and smiled dimly, apologetically.

He emerged into the outside world bookless save for the works in progress bumping around in his head and in his hanging bag. *Ice Object 13* nudged him with its exigencies of plot, character, and conclusion. The nudging was associated somehow with the apparitions of his father. Got something to show you, Dad. Finally. A bit pulpy, the characters struggling with the eerie presence of the Object. The skeptical military brass. The huddle of tents amid the cold glitter of glacial ice. The thing itself, with its on-again, off-again presence. A lot of it already done. Or ready for finishing. Time. He needed the time that was ticking on his wrist, slipping through his fingers.

Elsie's across the street. Long gone. That mocha cake. The identical cake each time but each time different. Giving undergraduate L. B. O'Boyle something ontological to chew on with the mustard-smeared bratwurst on a bulky. Repetition did cool the burning of time, if only for a few minutes.

Down Holyoke Street toward the river rose the Malkin Center. Who Malkin? Used to be the Indoor Athletic Building. IAB. No swimsuit allowed in the pool. Until integrated with the fair sex. Ditto naked night at the Adams House pool. Ditto the Forty Foot. Unwashed Stephen Dedalus did not immerse himself with nearly naked Buck Mulligan. Hygienic Bloom bathed in the mosque baths. His floating flower. IAB doesn't work for a redux. Nor was there any snotgreen sea handy for the requisite tightening of scrotums.

He waited on the corner. Archie Epps, the Dean of Students, magisterial in blue blazer and bowtie, came up from the river houses with measured tread. Talk about stately, plump. He smiled his benediction and inclined his head forward.

"Leo, how good to see you."

"Hi, Archie. How are things?"

The Dean beamed benignly, the wave of his pale-palmed hand taking in the busy scene. His domain. For decades now. One of Harvard's Afro-Saxons.

"It's starting all over again. And you, Leo? Where have you been? What are you writing about?"

"Petra. In Jordan. For an airline start-up."

"Indeed. Have you heard from the bard?"

"Seamus? Not in a while." Almost never. Seamus Heaney was Brooks-Denny's friend.

The Dean bowed his dismissal and continued his progress towards the Yard.

Didn't Leopold make Stephen a mug of Epps's cocoa back at Eccles Street? And add the cream meant for Molly's tea? What about Archie as a character in his Blooming redo? His office in University Hall. A favorite spot in the Faculty Club at lunch. What did he do all day?

To Leo's right rose the lofty towers of Lowell House. Bells from Russia had hung and rung there. From the Danilov Monastery in Moscow. Saved from the crushing hand of Josef Dugashivili. Orthodox monks. Were they allowed to marry? Probably not. Need time to pray and self-flagellate. Also that Japanese student Brooks-Denny used to meet on the 74 Bus was at Lowell. He says she may be the next Crown Princess. Masako, that was it.

The story Alf told about the *emeritus* professor of divinity who commuted on the same bus. Wonderful guy, he said. Expert on the Reformation in Bohemia, of all things. Alf gets on the bus one morning and can see the professor is miserable. He tells Alf that he's deeply troubled as his wife of many decades has just left him. Time passes, perhaps a year. They ride together a few more times. The professor tells Alf he is getting used to being a bachelor again. They talk about everything under the sun. Anyway, one day Alf gets on the bus and the professor is there looking crestfallen again. What happened? Alf asks. My wife came back, the man says.

Swears it happened.

Passed the *Lampoon* to the left. Should have tried out for it. Daunted by all those prep-school swells and sharp Jewish kids.

• • •

Variously an ex, a lapsed, and a closet Catholic, Leopold Bloom O'Boyle came in behind St. Paul Church and walked up DeWolfe Street to Bow Street. St. Paul. No apostrophe *s*. Dad knew the history. Inspired by San Zeno Maggiore, the basilica in Verona. Volcanic tuff stone there. Red brick here. The crypt in Verona the place where Romeo and Juliet were married. Says tradition. Francis Xavier O'Boyle, free-thinking Catholic, objected to the quote from Isaiah on the bell tower. *Vox clamantis in deserto.* A voice crying out … Only Harvard Square wasn't exactly a wilderness. Except to the kind of Catholics F. X. O'Boyle could not abide. Their invincible ignorance.

Son Leopold, prompted by the sightings of his dad, mounted the steps to the portico, opened the studded door hung with the *fleur de lis* strap hinges, a touch too authentic, and entered the cool precincts of the narthex. Lots of wood paneling, like the transept at Memorial Hall. The baptismal where he was baptized. The fount of holy water into which he did not dip his finger for the purposes of self-blessing. He pushed through the silent doors to enter the nave.

Romanesque? Barrel vault above a march of columns. Inset windows high along the top. Clerestory? Doesn't that make it a basilica? Those diagrams in *Fine Arts 13*. Darkness at noon in the Fogg. Seymour Slive and his slides of masterpieces. Going on about Saint Theresa's spiritual orgasm as rendered by Bernini. Should have paid more attention.

On this occasion, he took a pew to the left halfway down the center aisle, genuflecting out of habit. He sat, resisting an impulse to check the time and let his eyes adjust to the dimness. He wondered vaguely as he had wondered vaguely before if his visits to this place were not symptomatic of a kind of mild madness, one not without therapeutic value. Because of late, for more than a year, in fact, Leo had dropped by St. Paul Church for any number of reasons: An indulgence in nostalgia. A bolt hole from time's tempo, which seemed to stretch and slow here as it did when he was adolescent and bored and wanting above all else to get out of the place. Also to think, to disengage from by engaging in what troubled him.

Mostly though, Leo O'Boyle came into this hushed gloom to visit his father's shade. It did not occur to him as strange that he should commune with the father he no longer had. Because someone is dead doesn't mean you can't talk to them. Or listen to them. People live as much in each other's minds as anywhere else. Remembered words, glances, and silences echo as plangently as any rumored ghost knocking behind the wall. So nothing really spooky beyond an intimation of a presence, an inkling of something beyond the ordinary. But also a whiff of grace, which Francis X. claimed even the godless could experience.

Technically godless, technically agnostic—even about his agnosticism—Leo settled in. Telemachus in search of his father? Bit of a stretch. Or not. More like Heaney in Jutland: *Lost, unhappy and at home.*

As for communing with Francis Xavier O'Boyle, no other place served so well, not even the inadvertent shrine on Strand Street where artifacts of the man's life—books, papers, and even some clothes including the peaked tweed cap he bought in Galway—formed a display of sorts.

Strange in a way because Frank O'Boyle had not been devout in the liturgical sense. Hit and miss at best. And not even that were it not for Mom, who every Sunday dressed in one of her three if somewhat dowdy good suits, wore white gloves and carried her well-thumbed black missal with red-edged pages. Perhaps more telling, Frank insisted on attending what services he did at St. Paul instead of St. Peter's, their local parish. It was his way of staying close to Harvard. Not that cassock and gown brushed against each other all that much.

Leo O'Boyle shifted in the pew and thought thoughts of his father. Because he might, like his father, become a father. But like his father? As attentive, caring, and, especially, interested in a seemingly disinterested way? All with a deft, definite touch. Feeding him bits and pieces of Latin at the age of five. By the age of eight he had his own globe and an overall grasp of world history—especially World War II, the Japanese, the Nazis, and the spread of Communism. Not to mention words and how words were more than important: how words, beyond being sounds in the air or marks on a page, were living entities.

And powerful. "Be careful about what you put in your mind. Or better, be careful of what you keep there. These will be the words and the voices that you will listen to."

Another time: "It's not what you say, much less what you think, but what you do."

"Where does that leave writing?" young Leo had asked.

"Writing is the word enacted. It is thinking, saying, and acting. "

All for love. Which did not exclude a kind of self-completion on the part of Frank O'Boyle. What he once let slip regarding Leo's exceedingly modest success in the world was the remark, "I wanted to get it right." Well, Dad, you got it right. Though who am I to say you got it right? As he would say to himself whenever he remembered the words. The question, of course: Got what right? All kinds of things, Frank might assure his son, so evidently proud of the letter of admission and those first few travel pieces. But primarily, Francis Xavier O'Boyle had indirectly directed his son to become what he himself had always dreamed of being—a Harvard man.

Secondarily. Well, Francis X. O'Boyle was too subtle and perhaps too diffident to openly urge his son to write something more challenging than travel pieces. His expectations, guised as encouragements, came as gentle nudges. "Have you ever thought of writing short fiction?" Which Leo guessed would be little more, in his father's schemes, than a warm-up for writing a novel. Or several novels. The promptings were oblique except in one instance when one of Leo's better pieces, "Trekking with Jesús," appeared in a well-known men's magazine. It revolved around a high-altitude hike along Peru's Cordillera Huayhuash with a novice guide by the name of Jesús and a mule by the name of Rex. It could have been fictionalized into a short story or even a novella in Frank's view because it turned out that Jesús did not know the way and was far more interested in escaping from and hurrying back to a young woman named Carmina than with guiding Leo on the loop that began and ended in the small town of Llamac.

In badly fractured English, Jesús poured out his highly contradictory feelings about the raven-haired Carmina as they labored up the rock-strewn, barely discernible path. "She beautiful, Senor Leo. She *tetas grandes*. Big tits, what you say, like this. She crazy." Touching his head. "Say she like my cock. Then hit me with cooker." Showing his mangled ear.

Jesús, apparently unable to free his mind from thoughts of the tempestuous Carmina, simply disappeared with Rex late one morning while Leo was off behind a boulder responding to nature. It hadn't occurred to the travel writer what had happened until he climbed a nearby ridge and caught sight in the distance of Jesús mounted on the mule sprightly descending the trail to the green valley far below. A different call of nature. Jesús had the decency to leave behind Leo's heavy backpack and some of the freeze-dried fare they had been surviving on.

Leo might not have survived the hike back or forward had he not, attempting the former, come across a couple of Aussies who let him join their trek onwards. They had two mules and a real guide, Alfonso, who couldn't stop laughing and patting Leo on the shoulder.

To appease the father, the son toyed with the experience as the basis of a short story. It had a nice circularity to it, *Little Gidding on High*. It had comic elements, danger, himself fictionalized into a character named Rory who takes notes. Does Rory continue on alone, coming to terms with his mortality as he climbs up and down to his beginning? Cold and hungry, does he find God in the thin air? Does he lose his way and from on high stare down the void that awaits us all? Or does he scamper back the way he came and wreak his revenge on the betraying Jesús by seducing Carmina? It never got beyond feeling like an incident in the Borges mode much less the basis of a novel. Not that Leo, for all his reading of novels, knew what the basis of a novel should be.

Frank's own sketches for novels were both vague and in the sway of contemporary literary arcana except for the surviving notes of *Working Class Hero*, which appeared to emulate, however haltingly, the spiritual and artistic transformations of Stephen Dedalus as portrayed in *A Portrait of the Artist as a Young Man*.

Leo did not hold it against his father that he had ambitions for him. Far better than abuse or neglect. But it led him to rephrase Larkin about your mum and dad: They give you all the *dreams* they had and add some extra just for you. And dreams thwarted can cling and corrode with as much tenacity as any faults. As right then, there in the twilight of the church, the urge to work on his ice object novel was on him with compulsive force.

He sighed. He leaned back. He needed an ending. A finale. A *dénouement*. Trying to think. Thinking. Thinking that time did warp in these holy places. A different kind of dilation.

A figure kneeling near the altar that he hadn't noticed rose from the pew, blessed himself, genuflected, and walked up and out. Praying. Prayer. What do we do when we pray? Talking to God or one of his deputies. Hail Marys. Numbers count. Or does God value originality? Dear God, I need a miracle. I need to finish my novel. Is there a patron saint of novelists? Someone from among those numberless scribing monks put out of business by Gutenberg. St. Kevin and the Blackbird. Heaney again. But that's about self-transcendence. So about writing.

Well, if you're going to write, write. Take out your tools. Get it down on paper. Words. Then more words. Yes, but would it be disrespectful to take out a notebook or even the three-ring binder, and begin to edit, organize, write, rewrite? Monks of old wrote in holy places. Indeed, they made those places holy by writing in them. Okay, they scribed, copied. Is there a patron saint of writers to petition? Say a seventeenth-century Spanish monk, worldly, literate, given to a glass now and then, maybe martyred for resisting the editing sword of the Inquisition. Someone other than the Kinchite Jew Jesuit James Joyce? Could always call on Thoth. He wouldn't be very busy these days. All the same a bit of a wince, not wanting to offend the God he couldn't know by having strange gods before him.

With or without God's help and whatever his own praxis, the writer L. B. O'Boyle dearly loved the idea of writing. The seeming freedom and mastery of it all. Last stronghold of the heroic loner. The English language at the tip of his mind, the tip of his tongue, the tips of his fingers. The only limit being his imagination.

In theory.

In reality, at the desk in the corner of the spare room, the nearby magic casement opened on the faery lands forlorn of the Donnellens' chain-linked backyard with its vaguely sinister hooded barbecue thing, scattered plastic toys, straggling lilac, over-grown sand box, unkempt grass and, occasionally, Mrs. Donnellen herself, bikini naked, sunning her abundance of pale flesh on a collapsible chaise lounge with an iced drink to hand while reading a paperback. A voyeur of the ordinary, the author would sit and smolder with the recurring realization that

Mrs. Donnellen, Mary, not a bad sort, was his target audience, that, with any luck, millions like her, though more like thousands like her, or perhaps hundreds like her, would end up reading what he was writing.

Or not reading what he was not writing.

Brooks-Denny saying don't write unless you have something to say. But how do you know you have anything to say if you don't write, writing being the discipline of putting into words what you think you want to say? Or Alf saying the words have to rise off the page like fumes you inhale into your imagination. Yes, but Christ, man, you have to get the words on the page first.

What drove Leo close to drink before the noontime whistle was the vision, just within his reach, of a moving, well-paced adventure yarn, the ensuing film with enough raw-boned, big-jawed action stuff for the mall-dwelling mouth-breathers (and the Hollywood types who catered to them) coupled with living, developing characters and profound philosophical inquiries into the nature of time and being. It was all there, in him, real as granite, if only he could get it … expressed.

He glanced around the pews. He had the place to himself. He took out the small notebook from his inside jacket pocket, opened it, and on a fresh page under the heading all caps ICE, he wrote, "Either find a way to use space-time or ignore it. Or go over *A Brief History of Time* yet again and allude to it, but peripherally."

A taste. Now he wanted more.

Risking desecration however minor of this place holy to others, he opened his satchel and quietly fished out the three-ring binder. Just enough light. Scanning early notes. Pidgin English picked up among the emanations coming from the Object. No. No time. We need own time. Must escape, go back to own time. Own time waiting for us. Need energy. You come?

Too crude, he had decided. Why broken English if the Object is capable of getting here from another solar system or another galaxy? From their, its, perspective, we are little more than evolved apes, little more than metabolizing, hydrocarbon life forms still sharing genes with ancestors from the Precambrian.

He looked around. Still virtually empty. In the name of propriety, he decided he wouldn't write, only review what he had written. He turned to the opening page of the latest print-out, an amended note that read:

The Object exists and doesn't exist. It is sighted visually on the Hubbard Glacier on the Alaska side of Mount St. Elias by the crew of a C-130 on a routine flight. But the Object does not show up on radar or satellite reconnaissance photos, making its existence mysterious and officially tenuous even while classified top secret.

Scientists at NASA determine that the Object is able to switch back and forth between solid and various forms of plasma. They theorize that it travels as a kind of photonized energy, hence speed of light speeds. Need to work in all of the above.

He called this narrative scaffolding—the author telling himself what to tell the reader. It was a kind of verbal staging, an integral part of the disorderly order in which L. B. O'Boyle composed fiction. He tended to write longer passages in a fast, barely legible scrawl, the better to catch his tumbling thoughts. At other times for important notes he used block letters, which obviated the need of having to decipher them later. He spent a deal of time organizing, labeling, and including his notes, his notes on notes, and then including those into the scaffolding which he reworked into first and second drafts, the latter of which he entered into his ThinkPad before printing them out and defacing them again with marginalia, Post-its, stapled additions and, occasionally, smears of raspberry jam.

Thus, a note in the margin, block lettered read:

OBJECT HAS TROUBLE GETTING BACK TO IONIZED FORM TO ESCAPE/IN AND OUT/NOT TIME TRAVELERS BUT EXTRATERRESTRIALS THAT BRING THEIR OWN TIME WITH THEM/NOT LITTLE HOMINOIDS OF ALIEN LORE BUT A KIND OF COHERENT PLASMA/THE MACHINE ITSELF BEING THE BEING (OR THE LIFE FORM)

He turned to a section labeled POSSIBLE OPENINGS.

At his ranch north of Boise, Idaho, retired Navy Seal Cam McInally takes an early morning call from his old commander, now Vice Admiral Dale Hurst.

"Cam, this is Dale. You got a minute?"

Yawning, rubbing an eye, aware of the emptiness on the other side of the king-sized bed, Cam says, "At this time of the morning, I've got the rest of the day. What's up?"

"I've got you on scrambler. You know the Hubbard Glacier?"

"Too damn well."

"That's right. Forgot. Sorry. Look, a National Guard Herk on a routine training mission the day before yesterday got a visual of an object right next to the glacier where …"

"Okay."

"No one can identify it."

"Not the first time."

"Yeah, but that's not the news. They've been back and used everything from radar to infra-red without any effect."

"You mean … ?"

"I mean that except to the human eye and then only sporadically, the thing is invisible."

"Landsat?"

"Nothing."

"Metrics?"

"Estimates at best."

"Electronic signatures?"

"Like nothing we've ever measured and too powerful to approach."

Cam McInally, tall and lean with the ruggedness that comes from working his three-thousand acre spread from horseback and only occasionally a four-wheeler, feels a familiar jolt of fear and expectation.

In the right margin, the author had noted in all caps,

GIVE THE RANCH A NAME. CHECK TO MAKE SURE THERE IS RANCHLAND NORTH OF BOISE. ANY RIVERS, MOUNTAINS? LOOK UP SCENERY. GET FEEL OF PLACE. GET REAL.

Real? He glanced up at the stain-glassed saints, at the statue of Christ, at the shrine to the left for his virgin mother, holding him, her sacrificial son, crowned and a bit pudgy, on her lap. The holy family. Again that word. How real was any of this? A thought: Religion had prepared the mass of humanity to tolerate, even need, visions of other realities including all the zombie stuff. Is the Bible the first sci-fi thriller? Because God, when you get down to it, is an extraterrestrial. But not his son. He was both. Should ask Annabel.

He read another bit of verbal scaffolding.

> Cam, known for his mountaineering—Everest twice, K-2, and several others—is called out of retirement and asked to assemble a crack crew consisting of fellow mountaineers and Navy Seals. Question. Mountaineers and Seals?
>
> It is haunted territory for Cam. In this same area he had lost his beautiful wife Daphne while skiing on this same glacier.

A note on the side:

> THIS HAPPENS IN FLASHBACK IN THE NOVEL (AND SUBSEQUENT FILM) OR PERHAPS THE OPENING SCENE?

He glanced up to see a very pregnant woman in a light dress, her breasts seeming to brim over her pronounced bulge, come down the central aisle and let herself into a pew on the other side close to the altar. Dark-haired, round-faced, her dress dark blue with white polka dots, the woman didn't kneel, but sat and bent forward in prayer. A wondrous sight. Like an apparition of reality in this unreal place. Not to mention in the frozen wastes of Leo's conjuring mind. Would Annabel look like that? Some women hardly showed. Some looked pregnant all the time.

The praying woman reminded him that he had come into this place to talk to his dad, to tell him in so many words that Annabel was with child. More than likely. To this end, he quietly closed the binder, marking his place with the small notebook, and sat back.

Leo slouched and with an effort familiar to those who meditate, emptied his mind the better to summon his father. To summon recollections that rose as images from the rich store of his memories. Some of an aging and failing self-disappointed teacher of high school English. More were of a man in his late middle years, a man of medium size with ginger hair and a focused face, green blue eyes, sharp nose, and pursing mouth of which, even in repose, had a hair-trigger intensity that was more apparent than real. He controlled his temper, letting his silence growl for him. He deplored arguments over politics and culture as "rituals of disagreement" even as he succumbed himself to the disputatious.

A teacher, a scholar, and a walking library, especially about subjects that interested him, Frank O'Boyle balanced a jumble of what he called "consistent contradictions." Thus was he a fervent anti-Communist and as fervently anti-McCarthy ("The fact of witches does not justify witch-hunts."); a practicing Catholic and anti-clerical; a Democrat and a conservative in the mold of Daniel Patrick Moynihan; fastidious in his personal predilections while tolerant about the peccadilloes of his pals, a tolerance that included an active sympathy for his gay friends when the AIDS scourge savaged them.

Leo's invocations of his dad went beyond filial piety. Hearing in his head the certainty in that Boston voice, its impatience to get to the heart of things even as it drifted far and wide, he felt time palpably slow. Remembering, which was his special gift, came close to reclaiming time and times. Those times when, nattily dressed in tie, Oxford shirt, tweed jacket—he bought several in Ireland—and exuding a red cedar aftershave, Francis X. would leave the first floor apartment on Strand Street, descend the porch steps, and drive off in the red VW, later replaced by a black Volvo, and finally a small Ford. Drive off to Arlington High to bring the living word to a bunch of smart, smart-ass working-class kids.

The times Frank would sit at the kitchen table, *The Best of Myles* opened before him, his voice grabbing you by the lapel, quoting: "I might as well be talking to the wall, of course, though this phrase has always seemed strange in view of the belief that walls have ears." Or quoting from *The Third Policeman*. "Listen to this ..."

Leo could hear the man talking in his memory. He would also talk to that same man. The irony being that he could tell his dad far more in death than he ever could in life. He couldn't tell him personal stuff in life because Francis X. O'Boyle wouldn't begin to presume to advise someone else, especially his son, about what to do in his private life. Private meant private. Frank's private life had been so private as to seem in retrospect non-existent. Leaving his son to ponder: Had Mom and Dad ever gotten extravagant with each other, Kama Sutra-ing into the night? Unlike Big Dan O'Boyle, his own dad, Frank O'Boyle did not dally with other women nor did he joke about it. In life he would have been embarrassed—while trying to hide it—to hear Leo telling him about his vacillation regarding Annabel's condition.

Condition. Inner cringe at the euphemism even as he voiced it to himself.

Indecision hovered. Lots of time to decide. Though the sooner the better if they decided to terminate ... To terminate what had scarcely begun. But surely better than in the tri-semester. Bloody work then. Full term. Late April. *O, to be in England.* O, to be anywhere than in this sink hole of indecision.

The pregnant woman, who had most obviously decided, rose from the pew, gestured a genuflection toward the altar, and gave Leo a glancing smile as she passed.

He checked the time. 9:39. A sharp stab of his phobia. The curse returning, hovering just when ... He opened again the binder on his lap and poised his pen.

A second beginning of the novel began:

> The choppers, two four-rotor Bell 412s with snow-rigged skids, circle carefully before landing in a dust-up of snow high on the Hubbard Glacier on the American side of Alaska's Mt. Saint Elias. One by one, the team of five descends from the first machine into the chilled, high-altitude air. Their leader Cam McInally fills his lungs and moves to the second chopper to supervise the unloading of gear. The first bird lifts into another cloud of snow dust, bends forward, and roars off.
>
> Tall, with a sharp face and mineral blue eyes touched with tragedy, McInally hesitates, holding up a hand to the on-board crew chief. The exposed firn of the location has more of a slope than he had expected.

"Best you're going to get," the pilot yells at him over the chop of the rotors. "We can't get any closer. A lot of risk as it is."

They knew that coming in. Any closer than a thousand meters from the Object and the avionics start to go haywire.

McInally nods grimly. They unload the boxes and bags of gear—all-weather tents, portable latrine, fuel, food, communications, sensing equipment. A few moments later, it's thumbs up. The chopper lifts and leaves. They are alone with the thing, a thing that is and isn't, a thing that can be seen and can make itself invisible. McInally's orders: Make contact if possible. Assess threat potential. Recommend course of action.

While the team begins to rig the tents, which include a larger one for operations and mess and five smaller for sleeping, he takes a moment to view the Object through a regulation pair of 8x50 binoculars. The thing is located on a narrow ledge of rock and ice about thirty feet above the surface of the glacier. The shamble of strewn rocks is alive with runoff from the deliquescing ice and shrouded in drifting tendrils of white mist. When visible, the Object is roughly spherical, seemingly solid but indefinite at the same time, achromatically ice gray, more like a high-tech modern art installation than an extraterrestrial thinking thing. Already Cam McInally can feel its presence in his brain, like a program in a computer that hadn't been there before. Or maybe it's just the thin air.

Despite his resolve only to review the copy, L. B. O'Boyle made a few changes and noted in the margin:

THIN AIR IF COMING FROM SEA LEVEL? HOW
FAR UP THE GLACIER TO GET TO THIN AIR?

Strange, he thought, writing in church like this. Not that God would care one way or the other. God, who created a universe that gets bigger and more complex by the day, which is beyond the imaginable, surely has more important things on his mind. If that mind exists.

Thin air. And dim light. He put the binder aside and tried again. He had come into this place to talk to his dad, to listen to his dad should he speak. Which meant clearing his mind of extraneous thoughts, a discipline he was not good at. He tried. He rehearsed what he might say about *Ice Object 13*. I'm working on something to show you, Dad. I'm not sure you'll like it. It's not especially literary. But ...

He drifted. He contemplated the statue of Christ dead ahead. Two fingers of right hand up in blessing. Finger of left hand pointing to the monstrance on his chest. It was a likeness (or an unlikeness) with which he had been acquainted for three decades and more. Under the influence of the Reverend Dr. Chance, DDV, his wife, the mother of ... Leo O'Boyle had begun to have doubts about his doubts about the man called Jesus. Said he to himself with a touch of defensive sarcasm as his glance at the presumed likeness became mindful. Annabel had left behind Barth's austere theology and Updike's clinical sex (left them to those fussing with her thesis for publication) to open a new seam in the well-worked vein of that Christology devoted to Christ in the World. Not the idealized Christ, the one who didn't smoke or swear, but Christ as a significant event in the moral evolution of the species. In this she assented to Brooks-Denny's dictum that no philosophical system, no theology, no perception of reality, made sense if it did not take evolution into account.

Some knotty problems. Hadn't the twentieth century—Hitler and Stalin's millions of murdered innocents—made specious the idea of man's moral improvement? More problematic: modern evolutionary theory did not recognize judgments such as improvement or direction in evolution, settling for the term "derived" in charting any measurable increase in complexity or capacity.

The notion of Christ as a significant evolutionary event had begun to appear in Annabel's homilies and, in a more forceful and explicated form, in the application she was making for a grant to fund a post-doctoral niche at the Divinity School. Her husband refrained from wisecracks about Christ being alive and well in the competitive craft of grant writing.

For all that, she had moved her husband to think about Jesus the man, the guy who wondered if he shouldn't give up this all-but-hopeless task of redeeming mankind and go back to making cabinets with his stepfather Joe. The guy who might have been tempted to take advantage of Mary Magdalene or one of the younger apostles. Who worried about his mom. Who wondered about his real dad. Who wanted to hang with some literate, liberal-minded Romans and talk about stuff with a goblet of decent wine to hand.

Alf, sipping a glass of decent gin, talking how he had done a sketch of Christ resurrected, come again, in contemporary times. No big announcement. Guy just shows up. Goes by the name Christy or Theo. Theo better. Shaves his head but keeps the beard. Buys a vintage Shovelhead Harley in Oakland from an aging skull-scarfed biker with a bad limp and starts off cross country, gathering pals as he goes. Twelve in number. The Holy Rollers. Skirting the Burn, they growl into Vegas. They clean out a couple of big casinos and give the money to the poor. At a truck stop, Theo meets and picks up one Maggy de Lena, a free-lance hooker working the truckers. Maybe they start ... *a relationship*. Anyway, she rides pillion on his bike as they head for a rambling old commune somewhere between Los Alamos and the holy city of Santa Fe. Some soul-swelling fungi and heavy hash going around under the cacti. Spiritual, man. Near Amarillo, Texas, they come upon a bad accident involving a cattle truck and a hatchback. Theo revives a geezer everyone else had given up for dead. In Missouri Theo steps between the Mothers and the Fuckers, an association of motorcyclists riven into warring camps, each about to use deadly force on the other. Theo achieves peace aided and abetted by some significant amounts of valuable contraband. So on and so forth. Until they reach Jersey and run afoul of a mobster named Pauli "Punch" Pilato. Perhaps over issues relating to said contraband, Theo gets whacked but somehow survives and then disappears. The legend grows after four of his pals get gigs consulting for a TV series based on the life of ...

"You can have it," said Alf with a laugh. "Call it 'The Second Coming.' Or call it 'The Second Coming and Going.' Hell, you're married to an authority on the subject."

So he was, but his in-house divine had not been enthusiastic when he broached the idea. "Christ should be emulated, not mocked."

Dad ...

But Leo could not keep his mind from wandering. Wasn't this place stranger than strange? When you thought about it. And he was married to the ministering angel of another strange place. And yet it is the stuff dreams or at least memories are made of. Not just real memories but memories of imagining all those other palaces of God through all those centuries. An old fantasy of reverence, of pomp and circumstance, of monkish self-severity and the fragrance of incense rising with the heavenly music. Even as he could hear Larkin: *a vast, moth-eaten musical brocade.*

With time and gurus like Larkin, his faith unraveled strand by strand such that Leo O'Boyle would join the more erudite Joycean scoff when the occasion arose. Jesus of Nazareth, King of the Jews. *Iesus Nazarenus, Rex Iudaeorum.* INRI. Iron Nails Ran In. The taunt by the crucifying Romans still echoing millennia later. Not to mention the ritualized cannibalism, *Hoc est enim corpus meum.* Brooks-Denny lifting his gin glass like a chalice, asking, "Exactly what part of Christ are we eating when we eat Christ?" Starting on a blasphemous riff. "Is it muscle meat? Or is it organ meat? Certainly not his sacred heart. Or especially his sacred heart? Or a little bit of everything? A kind of holy hot dog?"

The mockery of it.

Alf, who tended to enjoy his apostasy, tempered his sacrilege with a touch of the anthropological: "Communion exemplifies the atavistic belief that we can literally ingest and make part of us the essence of a god or of a great leader. The old adage—we are what we eat."

Then back into it, touching on the genealogy of God.

"If Christ the son is a Jew, doesn't that mean that God the Father is a Jew?"

"Not necessarily. Jewishness comes matrilineally. Perhaps the DNA would tell."

"That God is a Jew?"

"Until he became a Christian."

Connecting that somehow to Stephen Dedalus holding forth on the consubstantiation of the Father and the Son in the library scene of *Ulysses.* Bits and pieces: *He Who Himself begot ... and Himself sent Himself ... was nailed like bat to barndoor ...*

The Ballad of Joking Jesus. Dad had it off by heart though it made him frown.

But did our Lord and Savior ever tell a joke? In Aramaic, perhaps, the mother tongue of Hebrew? What was that one about what happens when you cross a Mormon and a Unitarian? You get someone who goes door to door but doesn't know why. But, Christ, was there one funny line in the whole Bible, old or new? Plimpton should do a take-off on the wedding feast of Cana. Shows up as a pal of the groom. Or even a friend of Christ. He does know everyone. Wine running low. Jesus steps up. The original transubstantiation. Plimpton sniffing and sipping. A wettish nose and a bit thin on the palate but with undertones of the miraculous and an everlasting finish. Work in Wilde's witticism about the Brits and wine into water. Go a step further. Wine into blood. A positive? Wouldn't do for a transfusion. The Buck: *A little trouble about those white corpuscles.* Could try writing that one himself. Needs the antic touch.

Was blasphemy an inevitable part of piety, of remembered piety? Even a form of piety? Can't let it go. Had been a good boy until a different, usurping deity had raised its knobbed godhead on the ramparts of his corporeal temple and the Latin turned vulgar. *Masturbationen*, of course, then the dream of *fornicatio* turning real. *Fellatio* from the mound, *cunnilingus* on the mound. "Yeah," said Alf on an occasion when the talk had gotten scholarly, "what Seamus calls the oral tradition." But no real temptation for *peccatum sodomiticum*, however heterosexual. Too many sins to confess. The rope of faith unraveling to a few strands of frayed fiber. Something had gone missing, a rich, ancient fold in the texture of life. Because the world did need a larger vision than Darwinism, even the grand Darwinism of Teilhard de Chardin.

Moth-eaten.

For Christ sake, Philip, leave us some illusions. Living and dying is bad enough. Life isn't just one long moan. Even when it is. Besides, Malcolm Muggeridge was wittier when he said he'd like to show Christ around the Vatican. See what you have wrought. Speaking of which, take Orville and Wilbur for a ride on the Concorde. Or sail with Columbus around the Caribbean on one of those gigantic cruise ships. Or send Marx to North Korea.

Leo refocused. He picked up the binder from the seat beside him and turned to a section, one labeled TEAM AND SET UP. He had followed his own advice. It wasn't just the exigencies of plot: He saw a screenplay and a film in the making as much as a novel. If for no other reason, the team of five would constitute a demographic cross-section. The communications guy, Dash, short for Dasheen, Ledyard, is a civilian, black, self-deprecating, and culturally solid being given to saying things like, "That thing is one strange motherfucker." But also, "I doubt I'll ever be in a position to exercise false modesty." How to capture the black gift of laughter? Dash not only keeps them connected with the outside world, but he assists Air Force Lieutenant Marvis Bently, who is slight, blond, perhaps gay, in setting up and maintaining the sensitive monitoring equipment. They both report to Tina Larson, a Ph.D. in physics from Stanford. Petite, tough, and sexy, Tina is a possible love interest of Cam's. Love interest. Talk about the decay of language. Finally, there's Air Force Sergeant Piko Ramos, all around handyman and guitarist. In the Shackleton mode, everyone on the team shares in the chores, including the daily firing of the burn-out latrine.

He skimmed over:

> They spend most of the first day setting up the camp. A gasoline-fired portable generator supplies power to the operations tent which opens into a small mess and social tent. Marvis has priority to get the monitoring equipment on line. It being May and so far north, darkness doesn't fall until late. Cam, outside his tent and looking through binoculars, notices that the Object gives off an eerie, pulsating light unlike anything he has ever seen before. Tina joins him with her own binoculars.
>
> "I've been timing and counting," she says. "It might be trying to communicate."
>
> "Can Marvis pick it up?"
>
> "It's worth a try. Send it on to Langley. If it's in code, they should be able to break it."
>
> Cam shook his head. "Maybe, but this is like nothing else the world has ever seen."

Too many *ever seens*, he noted. Crossing out first one and interpolating with carrot, "unlike anything he had ever experienced." Then a post-it note:

TINA: "ARE WE LOOKING AT THE VEHICLE?"
CAM: "DO YOU MEAN ARE THERE LIFE FORMS INSIDE?"

TINA: "YES."
CAM: "I THINK IT MIGHT BE THE LIFE FORM
ITSELF. IT SEEMS ALIVE."
TINA: "YOU MEAN IT HAS CONSCIOUSNESS?"
CAM: "I DO, BUT IT WOULD NEED A WHOLE LOT
MORE THAN CONSCIOUSNESS TO GET HERE FROM
WHEREVER IT COMES FROM."

The author lifted his eyes from the page after securing the Post-it.
Could make a habit of writing in church. Nice sense of sanctification.
But not too obviously. Due respect and all. Small notebook only. A form
of meditation. He wondered what Annabel would make of it.

He wondered even though he knew she would say would something like, It depends on what you're writing. And he might counter,
I think it depends on how well I'm writing. It was the kind of distinction they could spar about with a humor that belied a seriousness that
confirmed deeper, unspoken bonds.

Early on in their courtship, Leopold had asked Annabel, "So you
really take all of this God stuff seriously?"

"Yes, I really take all of this God stuff seriously," playing back his
words, letting him hear their banality.

"I mean God in Heaven, sinners in Hell … ?"

"You don't have to believe any of that."

"Really?"

"Really. I'm a Christian. I believe in Christ and what he stood for. I
believe that Christ exemplifies what Nietzsche called the moral genius
of the Jews, even if he meant it in a back-handed way."

Into his silence an elaboration: "You and your daddy and Alf and
thousands of others made or make a fetish out of the works of Joyce,
Proust, Heaney, Nabokov, Hemingway, Shakespeare, whomever. What's
wrong with my doing the same for Christ? You say there's moral force
in great works of literature. Why are the words of Christ so different?"

"Well, he wasn't exactly a writer. Except in the as-told-to mode."

"Listen to yourself."

"I do."

"Who wrote down his words is not relevant." Her drawl shortening
into something more academic than southern. "They are the words of
Christ and it's the words that count. That's what you always say."

Which brought back his dad who had said the same thing in another way: "I don't worship God, I try to follow Christ. We should worship nothing but life itself."

Reminding himself to focus on un-focusing his mind on anything but a vivid recollection of Francis Xavier O'Boyle as he was in life. Futile. Something else nagging. Like wondering if he were there with the tatters of faith for an answer he would not heed? Bowing to strictures of the Everlasting who had fixed his canon 'gainst self-slaughter. Because wouldn't dilation and curettage amount to self-slaughter? Because half of what was growing in Annabel's moist womb was he and his. A sin against God and Nature, the latter of which surely existed. To let be or not let be remained the real question. Was Annabel secretly happy? *But, Ellbee, it's our decision.* Too damn ethical by half.

The advice he was there to seek from his departed father came down at first blush to a binary yes or no in relation to Annabel's condition, there being no in-between state, no *in vitro* limbo where life might be put on hold while Leo pondered the larger contextual question: To have a child that would encumber him or to remain relatively free to write novels and, as writers do, live the over-examined life? To which question rose yet another question: How much time do you actually spend writing, which does not include the time spent fretting about not writing? Meaning? Meaning the possibility of having neither a real life nor a life of the imagination. Meaning the continuation of what felt like a gray, abortive existence.

Thus did Leo O'Boyle perch on the edge of a dilemma sharpened by ambivalence and conducive to convolutions of thought such as: Had Annabel already decided to … terminate? Have it yanked? (Language does fail.) Which is why she has gotten so emotional, which I mistake as a state of joy. She has already decided and in some insidious, subtle way she wants me to persuade her to do what she has already decided to do? Or wants to do. Because she has always been more than a staunch believer in the reproductive rights of women. But to persuade her, I would have to first persuade myself.

To do what?

From which conundrums he lapsed into a kind of default nihilism. In the cosmic scope of things, did it make any difference? With time, all of this would pass, all of these borrowed molecules and atoms off somewhere else. The promiscuity of matter. The ephemerality of form. Being and nothingness. The nessness of ness. The *endlessnessnessness*. Unto madness.

Okay, Monsieur Joyce, so *No one is anything*. One still must decide to decide to decide. D&C. An office visit. Everyone polite. Everything hygienic. Post-procedural counseling. For both of them. This way, please. Wasted on Leopold, he being therapy-proof, he would explain to the therapist he would avoid by SOTing on about his selfish genes, the genes that simply want to make more of themselves. Making Leopold Bloom O'Boyle suffer, if only sporadically, a nag about disappointing his more recent ancestors, especially his dad, by failing, so far, to continue significant parts of their genomes into an uncertain future. Just who, he asked the grand jury of himself, were these aging or no longer extant people to whom he felt beholden? Other than his dad, dead these four years, and his fading mother and a couple of scattered aunts and uncles. What were these genes that he should want to propagate them? (Quite aside from the fact that he was, as a palpable expression of them, a decent enough human specimen, that is, rather handsome, smart enough to get into and out of Harvard, a lover able to go the distance, kind to animals, a potential novelist, and a faithful husband—so far.) Wasn't this impulse to continue your own kind—kinder—kin—the root of fascism? Because if you favor your own kind more than others, will you not also value the lives of those genetically closer to you than the lives of others? Hence tribalism writ small and large.

But also kindness.

Then, back-tracking along the same track: If Leo O'Boyle was in fact the last in that branch of the family—no more O'Boyles in Ballyboyle— and if he didn't perform his Darwinian duty, it meant that genetically and therefore evolutionarily the lives of all his immediate ancestors had been in vain. Because he did not have a fecund sister or two doing the selfish gene thing or a philandering first cousin propagating any number of brilliant bastards in good families. But surely there were still plenty of O'Boyles left in the world. Surely somewhere, in the reaches of New South Wales or in the frigid wastes of Manitoba or in a row house in Liverpool, there was a crinkly-haired, Dying Gaulish young husband begetting a whole new tribe of O'Boyles on some sturdy colleen named Fiona from, say, Dungarvin.

And if not? Could explain a dawning fascination with the Nabataeans. A lost people. Disappeared. Extinct. Death beyond death. But then, even if they did survive in name, would they be the same as what they were? Are the Greeks? The Italians? The Jews? The Chinese? Maybe the Chinese.

Who was San Zeno anyway? Must look him up. Did he come up with the paradox? Wasn't that a Greek? Doesn't work unless you stop each time. Step, stop. Step, stop. Step, stop. Each step smaller and smaller. Pregnancy the reverse. Each step bigger. No stopping.

But it could be stopped. His mind SOTing again. D&C. Merely a cancellation of possibilities, true enough, but there was flesh and blood involved, his flesh and blood. A crime against nature. Brooks-Denny said capital punishment was a form of delayed abortion. An attempt at perspective. But Leo O'Boyle had no perspective. It was trivial, a few cells. It was of a significance words like *enormity* could not encompass. It was his life. It was the end of his life. As he had known it.

Then a disturbing thought: Would he bring any conceived, any conceivable child into this place? Because this would be at least part of his or her heritage. In temples like this your ancestors worshiped. So now as what? A museum of faith? Because his own faith had been lost. Lost along with a recollection of wholeness. In this very pew he had stood between Mom and Dad, scrubbed clean in his Sunday clothes, the world with everything in its place. And able early on to read the old-fashioned bilingual missal. *Sursum corda.* Let us lift up our hearts. Stations of the Cross during Lent. Incense wafting from the swinging thurible. From the choir, *Tantum ergo sacramentum.*

Tantum Ergo issuing from the simple fane besides the waves as Bloom on the rocks performed the Rite of Onan.

Well, it wouldn't be his decision alone. Annabel would have a very articulate say where as to where their child would worship. Should their child come to pass.

He chanced a glimpse at his watch, his time. 10:13. In less than five hours, Annabel would be … Why did that bother him? It wasn't like some last-minute appeal to the Supreme Court. Stay granted. Stay denied. An inward half smile. Better than worrying about time. Or was it the same? That phrase, real time. Was there imaginary time? Hawking mentions it. Nice concept. Would solve his problem. Slip out of real time into imaginary time, do imaginary things, and slip back in.

Dad, you there?

Leo waited and waited. Until, finally, images of his father came to him with the slow deliberation of memory. The hair graying in later years, the voice emphatic in the Kennedy way. The way he listened to you at the kitchen table and then raised a finger to respond. The way he said in the middle of a heated discussion, "I will listen to you if you will listen to me." Then lapsing into a cold silence when people hadn't listened to him about listening to him.

Dad regarded himself as a thinking Catholic. He struck a balance and bargain with Holy Mother the Church. Not quite *non serviam*. It's the faith of our fathers, including the bad guys. People died for it. It's what we have. It's what we are. The inertia of history. Even so, he would voice a neat heresy: Had Ireland joined the Reformation, it would have been united, Gaelic speaking, prosperous and independent early on. Big ideas about church reform. Pope for a day. Bring back the Latin Mass. Get out of the birth control business. Let each parish choose its own priest. Worship Christ by following him. Infallibility? Prove it. Let parish priests marry. What next, a lady Pope? So what?

It's like grammar, Francis X. would say. You should know the rules if you're going to break them. Also, if nothing else, the Church will give you a moral vocabulary, he would add, just a bit defensive. Not allowed to despair of salvation or to presume salvation. Damnation, yes, but redemption as well. Each soul precious. The Seven Deadly sins. Forgiveness. Doing unto others ... Heaven, Hell, and Purgatory. Limbo.

Limbo.

The word a resonant chord. One of Heaney's great poems. Leo O'Boyle scanned the pages of his mind but only came up with the odd phrase or paraphrase: The woman who drowned her illegitimate spawning. Hauled in with the salmon. *A cold glitter of souls. Some far briny zone.* Where Christ's unhealed palms cannot fish.

Is that where the aborted go?

Dad, he reminded himself. Reminded himself that, whatever his Catholicism, Frank O'Boyle had prayed most fervently in the Church of James Joyce. Died on the good couch reading *Finnegans Wake*, the book open on his chest, spine up. His funeral Mass here. Church crowded with friends, ex-students, Cambridge officialdom. Wake at Keefe Funeral Home. All kinds of flowers. "Your Dad looks good," someone said. "Not for long," sputtered Tim Logue, in his cups, in his tears, one last bad joke.

The recollection brought on a muted grief, a love and longing and sorrow for what no longer existed, a pity mingling with self-pity, a futile regret for not having somehow grasped and held what was. None of which he had particularly felt at the wake, the funeral right here, and the internment in North Cambridge. Not so much out of shock as a kind of callous acceptance of death. It had been gradual. For some months, Frank, the old Frank, had begun to slip away, able to remember whole passages from Joyce but forgetting what he went to look for in the kitchen.

More same old thoughts, more SOTs. Though in this case, conjuring his dad's obsequies made Leo realize anew that he would not have gone to him for advice about his angst over Annabel's condition. What would he say? Like you, Dad, I yearn for a world larger than the one I have and have not found in traveling to distant places and writing about them. Explaining how an exploration of the Bordeaux wine country, however subtle and accomplished, bore scant resemblance to, say, living in Paris and hanging out with Hemingway, Joyce, Fitzgerald, Picasso, and that crowd. True, that world had passed. But what about some current equivalent? How to explain his hankering for what no longer exists, for what would still no longer exist whether or no he was responsible for a small, dependent creature called a child? Well, if not the Paris of the 20s, then some contemporaneous equivalent thereof. Where? More and more writers grazed the high meadows of academe (all the while looking for holes in the fence). How many English departments today would sanction bullfighting let alone celebrate it?

An old couple walked by him arm-in-arm to the front pew, genuflected, knelt and prayed. For what? To stop time? The eternal doesn't mean endless time as much as the end of time. You would think.

On the altar, Larkin's holy end, a figure in a soutane emerged and crossed from left to right stopping to genuflect. Was that the Reverend Bryan Hehir from Chelmsford? Maybe not. Looked like him. An internationalist. Academic. Friend of Stanley Hoffmann. Mom knew the family. North Chelmsford. No issue, legal, anyhow, if you're a priest.

Celibates not practicing what they preach telling people to have kids. More souls for God.

Dad?

He scanned the manuscript on his lap. A thing on the edge of a glacier. Paltry stuff, he could hear Frank O'Boyle think. Frank, who told his students that a great novel like *War and Peace* unfolded like an awakening to another view of the world. Well, Dad, this doesn't pretend to be a great novel. At this point I just want to get it finished. Get it published. Besides, you said you have to write for yourself.

They give you all the dreams they had …

Leo lowered the binder to his lap and settled back against the corner of the pew. Comfortable enough. Distractedly, he pulled his left sleeve back and let his dazing eyes follow the seconds hand as it minutely ticked down the right side, touched bottom and started up the left side. Conceding to it, half musing about how nice time can be, how handy, how productive … Till he slid into a semi-conscious reverie, his mind unclenching, half aware of its half awareness.

His dad appeared as though he had been there all the time, a continuation of Leo's morning dream, but only the face, a face mobile with life, an intent, listening face. But different than it had been in ordinary life being a distillation of his ages and his goodness of which there was much. But now disturbed, not holding, shadowing off, returning, the same, disturbed. Leo not asking, the asking assumed. Somewhere a door slammed in the sacristy next to the altar and in his dream. Leo opened unseeing eyes to see the seconds hand counter-clockwising in time to a line of Aramaic text neatly typing backwards a caption under his father's face frowning at the question of being and not being, remembering for Leo his own funeral that would now happen again in exquisite miniature, the microscopic coffin holding the future, Christ's maimed palms helpless to retrieve what would never be again.

Leo O'Boyle came to with a start to the clatter of the binder sliding off his lap onto the cramped space in front of him. A sound started in his mouth he couldn't unmute. Where? He thought for a second before normal awakeness made him squint at the LeCoutre as though its silent ticking might anchor him to when it was. 10:27. Though it moved, time was a place, at least right then as the dream lingered, brightening and darkening his mind.

Then a second, better confusion. He found himself in the sway of a small miracle: A sense of timelessness enfolding and suspending him for a time out of time. A momentary transcendence. A touch of grace. Something like a conciliation with the inevitable. Not a Road to Damascus sort of thing, but an epiphany, the significance, the very form of which, eluded him, but an epiphany nonetheless. Such that, after a moment of wonderment, Leopold Bloom O'Boyle stood in the grip of a resolve that had no object, but one that made him move.

• • •

Emerging into the ordinary light of day, Leo felt again the better for having visited this place holy to others and no longer altogether unholy to himself. Not that he knew why. Beyond engaging the ghost of his father and the descent of grace. Nothing decided, not consciously anyway, but recollecting Larkin in the positive mode:

> A serious house on serious earth it is,
> In whose blent air all our compulsions meet ...

Though tempted to, Leo did not dip his finger into the holy water and bless himself on his way out. He would need more than holy water to get right with the Lord. He would need to be baptized again. Shriven within an inch of his soul's life. He would need the faith he didn't have. But he clung to his moment of grace, the memory of it like grace.

Which did not keep him from musing again, as he stood on the church steps on Bow Street just below where Arrow Street notched in, where might their possible child be baptized and as what? Probably Protestant. And might have entangled himself with thoughts of possibilities had not Alf Brooks-Denny's ancient Land Rover with its spare tire on the hood come down from the avenue with rattling authority. The vehicle pulled over and the front window slid open.

"Leopold Bloom O'Boyle as I live and breathe. Been a while. What's happening?"

Leo came down to the curb. Awkward handshake through the window's small opening.

"Nothing much. I was just in the house of God." Might as well admit it.

"Anyone home?"

"Very possibly."

"Don't tell me you're returning to the fold?"

"A lamb to slaughter."

"Been anywhere lately?"

"Not really."

"Anything planned?"

"Jordan. Theoretically. Know anything about Petra?"

"Ha! You're doing another un-traveled piece."

Alf laughed. A good laugh with a touch of mockery to it. Life a serious joke. Life one long safari. A new species every day. Brooks-Denny had himself a sweet gig. Basement office in the MCZ, Museum of Comparative Zoology. Bones and stuffed beasts. Glass Flowers. Running up-market natural history trips. Antarctica. Galapagos. Tanzania. Up the Orinoco. Down the Amazon. You name it. For the snowhead set. Getting to be a bit of snowhead himself, was Alf.

Leo O'Boyle smiled back into the ruddy face, the thickish nose, the self-amused hazel brown eyes.

"I was thinking about it."

"There's a decent hotel, the Rest House Hotel, if memory serves. It's right next to where you pick up the horses that take you to the opening of the siq. That's the narrow gorge you walk through. It's played up in one of those Indiana Jones things. Pretty spectacular. It leads into what looks like a Hollywood set only real. Greco-Roman stuff mostly, some Egyptianate ruins. But, hey, it's been done to death."

"Sounds good." Alf did know his way around the world.

"Talk about the Nabataeans if you want to sound the authoritative note."

"Right. Heard about the Nabataeans."

"Traders. A whole culture. Disappeared. How's the writing going?"

"Fits and starts. Mostly fits. How about you? You've got another one coming?"

"Yeah. Who doesn't?"

"Heard from Seamus?"

"Sassie heard from Marie. Stratis mentioned something about him coming for the spring semester. I'll keep you in the loop."

"Speaking of Stratis, I'm on my way to see the man. I don't know why. He called and left a message."

"Give him my best."

A long pause.

Leo said, "I need to talk to you."

"Nothing serious, I hope."

"Could be."

"Sure. This afternoon. I'll be around. Come by. We'll do a tour."

Then off with a roar, like the U.N. going through.

To forestall sessions at one of the taprooms on Massachusetts Avenue up towards Porter Square where they might waste themselves and a good bit of an afternoon, Alf and Leo had taken to walking the glass-encased exhibits of the museum during the latter's visitations. The last time they ended in the Romer Room sitting on a bench within view of the fossilized skeleton of the forty-foot *Kronosaurus*, the name making Leo think "chronosaurus." Time lizard.

L. B. O'Boyle continued along the lower part of Bow Street, past the back of Tommy's, the scene of all-nighters when there had been time to waste. Something else he missed—time to waste even as he wasted the time he might save to waste. At the ass-end of the Lampoon, he turned up Plympton Street. Could be Bowstring Street with a bit of a stretch. Up past Adams House on the left. The Heaneys in I entryway. That party in the common room. When was that? Meeting Seamus and Marie for the first time—thanks to Alf. The two of them together. Like visiting royalty without the ceremony. The literary life as one might dream it. Just the way Seamus spoke, a freshness to everything. The voice, Irish, the Ulster burr, confiding. Utterance as art, creating a force field of language. People standing, sitting around with their drinks, getting their literary batteries recharged. Because Seamus had been granted the wish he voiced in "Oysters"—that he be "quickened all into verb, pure verb."

A few years back, Dad still going strong, there had been a party after the party in Belmont. Mom, Dad, Alf, Sassie, Leo, Annabel, Seamus and Marie. Dad in a kind of hellish heaven, a bit too much of an agenda of asking and by asking showing that he shared the same green field as the great wordsmith. In pursuit of the ever-posed, never-answered question: What is poetry?

Alf saying that Larkin was too simple and too negative.

Seamus saying simply, "He's neither."

Or the Catholic Protestant thing in the North, Dad siding just a tad with the Orange, mentioning birth control and divorce.

Right enough, conceded Seamus, his acquiescence more tentative than skeptical, of a piece with his gift of listening, of inclusion.

So that Dad held his own, basking in the seriousness with which Seamus took his sallies even as Dad suspected and was charmed by the *noblesse oblige.*

Then the party after that party, a taxi having been called to take Marie and Seamus back to Cambridge. Still under the stars, the night tender with warmth and the scent of roses. One last small one going around among the men, a bottle of single malt Bushmills available for the occasion. The ladies in the kitchen washing up. Typical.

Frank led the hagiographical elevation, his eyes blurry with moisture. "He's a great poet and a great man. And Marie … my God what a privilege. I felt like we were at the very heart of literature. Wordsworth, Yeats, Dickens, Shakespeare himself could have walked in and the chat would have gone on and on …"

Alf picking it up. "Indeed, had William joined us, Seamus would have shook his hand, you know, with that deference edged with incipient humor, and asked him, 'How are you getting on?' you know, with that Ulster lift to the final word."

Leo prompting them. "But what would they say to one another?"

Alf, who claimed he could speak Shakespearean, lifted a finger, paused a moment to think, and gave it a go. "William first. 'I see, Irish Seamus, that thou doth our royal English wield uncommonly well.' Then our own bard. 'Aye, sir, our tongue is indeed a gift, but one not so royal with us.'"

A round of clapping. The bottle lifted. One more small one?

"Whenever I see Seamus," said Leo, "I want to draw or paint his face."

"Aye," said Frank, echoing the echo. "To me he looks like something carved on a burial tomb, you know, archaic, archetypal, the podded eyelids, the oblong face, big nose, and jaw all but set in a smile."

Then Frank again, lifting his glass. "He's like a gift from the gods. And Marie. A corn goddess." Smitten he was.

Alf with the final word: "Seamus has a great gift that he takes for what it is, a gift, however intrinsic to himself, that he shares with seeming ease with the world."

Final because Sheila appeared on the side porch beseeching her husband. "Frank, I have to go home or I'll drop."

L. B. O'Boyle paused in front of *The Crimson* offices. Should have tried out for that as well. Maybe have started a career in real journalism.

Plympton Street rose gently. Five hundred years before a wooded slope easing down to the estuarine stretches of the long-channeled Charles. Lots of wildlife. Indians. What tribe? Had some brave paused in his hunting to wonder what would be here many, many moons into the future? Or was the future a western concept? Had time been timeless then? Could have been even though they counted. Had to. Wampum. Aztecs certainly did. Higher math. Calendars. Had time been the snake in the garden? Not time but measuring time, chopping it up into little bits, doling it out, timing it?

Then remembered why he thought what he thought. The five-hundredth anniversary of Columbus loomed. October, 1492. A month away. Now a day of mourning. Now a day of virtue-mongering among the moral classes. Susan Sontag: *The white race is the cancer of human history.* Later apologizing to cancer victims. For what? Giving cancer a bad name by associating it with white people? One of the best minds of a generation.

He shook off the inner rant about his betters and stood in the warming day to muse about that hunting brave. Must look into those Mayan calendars. Would they see time as circular or linear? Probably circular. Worth a travel piece. Worth a whole book.

As a result of his particular phobia, not to mention fears about the early onset of middle age, L. B. O'Boyle let gnaw at him the question: How did time occur? That is, was time circular or linear? Was it, like the face of his father's watch and the progress of the earth around the sun and the moon around the earth a matter of circles within circles *ad infinitum*? Time didn't move, it merely repeated itself. The Great Circle. Metempsychosis. Reincarnation. Former lives. *Its time come round at last … etc. etc.* It might have helped to believe that.

But Brooks-Denny the evolutionist claimed time to be linear. "If the overriding mode of time is circular, evolution could not occur.

Evolution makes a muddle of the Great Circle, past lives and all that. How far back could past lives go? To when we were bipedal australopithecines with brains smaller than those of chimps? Do those wise men of the East recall their past lives as hairy brutes learning to walk on their hind limbs in the Great Rift Valley back in the day? There are new things under the sun. We are the new things under the sun."

Then adding: "A wheel on the ground turns repeatedly in traversing linear space."

Was it a mistake to figure time as either a circle or a straight line? But how else to conceive it? As a triangle? A cube? Perhaps a form of energy. Would researchers at Cern one day detect a time particle, something so small and fleeting as to be almost non-existent. But real, real enough for theorists to trace its origins to the Big Bang which, along with everything else, created time. Presumably.

Circular or linear? What difference did it make in the end? Either way, he wasn't coming around again on some big wheel of time. Nor did he want to. Leo the dog? Leo the frog? Leo the ladybug crawling up the window pane?

He stopped to glance down at his and his father's watch. 10:42. No fear. Perhaps because he closed his eyes and recalled with clairvoyance the face he had seen in the church. What time are you now, Dad? he asked. Is your time now my time?

• • •

He opened his eyes and gently climbed to The Grolier. Black-trimmed windows and heavy door. Venerable. All the poetry fit to read. Another refuge from the tick-tocking of life. Another kind of church. A temple, actually, one of the old ones on the Parnassus of Harvard. Louisa the reigning votary.

The volumes were slender on the shelves. Brevity the soul of poetry. Making each word count and more than once. Form follows nature in that—all the things the mouth can do, including the speaking of verse.

The framed photos on the wall. Immortals, writers. There forever in shades of gray—Auden, Cummings, Frost, Lowell, Moore, Bishop, Williams, and who …? The faces, from a click of time out of their lives, seemed studiously ironic to L. B. O'Boyle.

Larkin's *Collected Poems* on display. No refuge there. "Aubade" off by heart. Death. *No touch or taste or smell, nothing to think with,/nothing to love or link with …*

Louisa Solano welcomed him with a small smile and an old dog named Pumpkin. Pale of face, auburn of hair, her mind an archive of poetry and poets, Louisa was very much of her books, not of herself.

"Been anywhere lately, L. B.?"

"Arlington."

"Oh?"

"Yes. I travel a lot in my mind these days."

"That must be interesting."

"Indeed. It makes the Gobi look like a rainforest." You had to get there first with Louisa, who had a nose for guff.

"What can I do for you?"

"Do you have the latest Seamus?"

"*Seeing Things?*"

"The very one."

"Just in and running low. Hardback or paper?"

"Hardback."

"So where are you going next?"

"To Jordan. To Petra and surrounds. Theoretically."

Louisa did not pursue it. She took his money with another small smile. He thanked her and moved aside for another customer looking to buy some words.

Leopold Bloom O'Boyle stood back with his prize. Annabel, who had a knack for pithy truths, told him that Heaney was his antidote to Larkin. He leafed through to "Squarings," number *xli*, which he had already read in Brooks-Denny's copy.

> Sand-bed, they said. And gravel-bed. Before
> I knew river shallows or river pleasures
> I knew the ore of longing in those words.

L. B. O'Boyle lifted eyes from the page and sighed inwardly. He could hear the poet's voice. He could taste it. Like the first sip of a rich wine. You let the words warm the tongue and throat on their way to the head, to the heart. Nay, to the soul. Then a larger tipple.

As I took squarings from the top of bridges …

Yet another customer came in. More talk. Leo stepped back into the September sunshine, book up to his face, pausing, starting again.

> As I took squarings from the top of bridges
> Or the banks of self at evening
> Lick of fear. Sweet transience. Flirt and splash.
> Crumpled flow the sky-dipped willows trailed in.

The sky-dipped willows his High Windows, his Tolstoyan infinite blue. Only Seamus might subdue with words the inevitable flow. It is crumpled. And it is sweet.

Walk, stop, read, walk, stop, read. *Sweet transience.* The words a bulwark against the Larkin already in his mind's blood. "Aubade" again: *The sure extinction we travel to.* Then, *Not to be here,/Not to be anywhere,/ And soon; nothing more terrible, nothing more true.*

In the warmth of the day, his jacket off and shouldered and clutching his purchase in his oxter like a scholar of old, Leo O'Boyle proceeded up Plympton Street to Massachusetts Avenue. Flow of people and cars, crumpled flow. Here he paused. On the other side of the avenue Widener Library lifted its bulk behind Wigglesworth Hall, a redbrick wall with windows and rooms. The library more and more a monument to books. *Causal nexus* a Greenland iceberg. Somewhat *remotus*.

He stopped and moved aside, a thought about *Ice Object* surfacing. He placed the book of poetry in his satchel and took out his small notebook. In block lettering, he wrote under the heading ICE:

THE LATE SPRING STORM ON THE GLACIER
ERUPTS AS THOUGH OUT OF NOWHERE. IT
INTERFERES WITH COMMUNICATIONS. WHAT
THEY LEARN FROM THE STATIC-FILLED SPORADIC
EXCHANGES WITH THE BASE CAMP (WHAT BASE
CAMP? WHERE? NEED TO ESTABLISH ONE) IS
THAT THE STORM IS REMARKABLY LOCAL AND
SMALL, ONLY TWO MILES IN DIAMETER AND
UNRELATED TO ANY WEATHER PATTERN (OR
SYSTEM) ONGOING. IT HAS HIGH GUSTING WINDS
THAT MAKE THE TENT WALLS BILLOW AND SNAP

LIKE SAILS. AT TIMES THE LIGHTNING FLASHES
DOWN ON THEM THROUGH PELTING RAIN AS
FROM A CORONA. A CORONA LIKE A RAINBOW
GONE FULL CIRCLE ONLY MORE VIVID, OMINOUS,
THREATENING.

Already had some of that in the text, he mused. Threatening
rainbow not bad. God's promise inverted.

Harvard Book Store on the right. *Ice Object 13* would look good in
the window. Local author and all that. What for a cover? Try to work in
Mount St. Elias in the background.

He turned left. Briggs & Briggs, purveyors of all things musical.
Scores by the score. Records. Instruments. *Just buy you a guitar and put
it in tune ...* Could set the Sirens scene there. If he knew anything about
music. If he could play something beside the record player. Compact
disks now. Perhaps better to set it in the Longy. During a rehearsal.

Impossible! Stupid. A redux cannot be done. A pallid imitation at
best. Only it did get in his head like a tune that wouldn't go away.

The One Potato Two Potato. Literary goings on. Professor Fleming at
lunch. His lectures on American intellectual history. In Sever. One of the
great courses. Must tell him sometime. Cross the top of Linden Street.

Another quick glance at their watch. 11:06. Almost soothing. Was
it a flow, circulating, circular? Or an arrow? Or Delmore's fire?

• • •

Then Ferranti Dege, black-painted window frames framing a
display of used cameras. Leicas. Hasselblads, a Burke and James eleven-
by-fourteen, Schneider lenses. Buy that B&J and do the Ansel Adams
thing. In Ireland. In Wicklow. In the mountains. Take it up on a donkey.
Just above Luggala. Loch Dan. Loch Tay. Glint of the Irish Sea to the
east. Shades of grays. Zone system. Shadows. Stunning, slanting bril-
liance. Wait for the exact instant. The art of light.

He entered into the distinct chemical smell as into another medium.
D-76 developer. Fixer.

Cave of the Cyclops? Not really. Cameras are benign, only capture
what they are aimed at. More than benign. Another shelter from the

leakage of time the way they trap and hold moments. Each click stopping everything or the illusion thereof. What happened just before? Just after? Those Civil War generals posing for Mathew Brady in front of their tents. Hold it, sir. Thank you. Then, back then, in that instant of life, those still forms resuming the reading of dispatches, the giving of orders, the scratching of britches. That instant happened. It still lived, somewhere, somehow. Old photos look like pictures of old times. New photos, especially slides, give the illusion of retrievability, make what they capture still seem accessible as though there was nothing between you and what you looked at even though what you looked at would never be again.

And yet, this professional place provided the promise of an aperture—many apertures—into other worlds, the promise, however illusory, of grasping and keeping the motionless flight of a hovering hummingbird, the smile of a child, the full moon on a cold, cloudless night, a Vermont landscape in October, a dandelion puff against the light, the very time of that time.

Yes, his photos were ready. L. B. O'Boyle paid for the two packages of four-by-six snapshots and stood back from the counter out of the way. He undid the first package carefully and took out the reassuringly heavy wad of images from his recent past. More like Annabel's recent past. The church youth group on a field trip to Gloucester. Snap, snap, snap. Mostly girls, teenagers, one or two boys who were there for the girls. Snap. Snap. Seashore. A couple of seascapes. Where the Boston School painted. *Epi oinopa ponton.* Wine dark? More like champagne with all the surging foam. Snap. Snap. One of Hopper's houses. Snap. The fisherman at the helm, steady as a statue looking out to sea. Snap.

No sign of assistant subdeacon Bernie Lusk, the hovering, hankering divinity student, ubiquitous volunteer, Annabel's would-be lover. Would be? Cause for thought was Bernard Lusk. A small factor in the equation, parenthetical perhaps, but there. Because might he not be Annabel's Blazes Boylan? Another reducing stretch. Sub subdeacon Lusk might visit of an afternoon with the hymnal program for the Sunday service, but no tan-shoes-shod, straw-hatted, garter-snapping dandy was he. Wouldn't work. Because? Because unlike James Joyce, said Leo to himself, I take no pleasure in fantasies of my wife bedding all and sundry. And even if I did, I could not render such fantasies with the flair of the master.

"Really, Ellbee," Annabel protested when he alluded one evening to the need for pest control, "he's my only tutee, he makes my link to the department ... legitimate."

"I'm only saying ..."

Saying that no one wants to be cuckolded by a jerk or anyone else. I have my pride. Unsaid on the tip of the tongue.

More snaps. Early August at Chebeague Island, Maine, for a long weekend. Casco Bay from the Cousins Island dock. Snap. The crowded ferry over with Alf Brooks-Denny and lovely wife Sassie. Snap. Their friend Tom Rothschild waiting on the stone wharf, Chebeague Inn in the background. Snap. Tom pacing. Could have been Alf's brother. Of course he remembered us. All smiles as he helped with the luggage. Piled into the Mini Moke. Snap. Arrival at the upper house. Modern in an old-fashioned way. Snap. Tom's wife Peggy with welcoming words and smiles. From the Midwest and not very Jewish in a Jewish sort of way. Asking Tom if he stopped at Earl's for the rat cheese. Growing boys in evidence. Politely met. Names. Luke a young man. Sam and Adam. Alf saying something about how they had the Old and New Testament covered. Luggage down a sloping lawn to the red, clapboard lower house. Worthy of Hopper. Settling in. Upstairs bedroom redolent of old, warmed wood. A few more snaps.

Chebeague Island. It happened here.

Lobsters that night. Bugs, Tom called them. Peggy busy with Sassie at the stove. A flood of friends for a pre-dinner glass in the long living room with the picture window facing northeast across the spill of islands. The rat cheese off a round much too good for rats.

Next day Tom holding expertly the curving tiller of the Ensign. The *Lyra*. Snap. Greek sailor's cap. Where are we? Check the chart. Crow Island. Sail luffing. Hard to lee! Coming about. Blue white water. Cold enough to shrivel your privates. Sea air. Bangs Island, large rock with pine tree quills. Snap. Then Stave. More of the same. What's that in the chop? *A sleek brown head, a seal's ...* Snap. Need a longer lens. Then Eagle Island, summer home of the explorer Robert Peary. Snap. Anchor. Row ashore in the tender. Historic site. Another refuge from time.

Memorabilia. The great man's knick-knacks. Pictures on the wall. Ice and snow. Mathew Henson, his black man Friday. More like his black man Saturday, Sunday, Monday, and probably half of Tuesday as well, said Alf, explaining how Henson did most of the navigating and his share of the heavy lifting. Now they say they were off by a few miles and the Brit, whatshisname, got there first.

Then the story about the Harvard guy, Allen Counter, how he went to Greenland a few years back and found these two old guys in their eighties, one half Inuit and half white, the other one half Inuit and half black. Peary and Henson had not slept alone through those long Arctic nights. How Counter brought the two old guys back to Cambridge for a high-table dinner and how the two of them kept marveling at the sycamores along the Charles and touching them.

Leo saying, "I hope they took them to Widener and explained it existed because a big piece of ice fell off their homeland."

"Not a bad place to start the novel or the screenplay," said Alf, definite with the definite article, going on about the perilous reach for the geographical abstraction. The imagined scenes. The parting as Peary and Henson head out for the farthest north. Sled dogs. Snow-filled wind. Wintering over with their Inuit ladies.

L. B. O'Boyle, donning his author's cap, pondered *Redux* possibilities. Peary and Henson had been at sea albeit a frozen sea. The North Pole their Ithaca? Nah. Doesn't work.

Alf said, "It would be a kind of Nanook of the North meets Lolita."

Tom Rothschild laughed.

"How so?"

"Peary's winter wife was only fifteen."

"*Fruit vert*," said Tom, who read Nabokov. "So to speak."

"But remember what Humbert Humbert said—something about nymphets not occurring in polar regions.'"

"Actually, the young women in *Nanook* are quite attractive."

"It was just more lepidopteral wordplay because nymphs ..."

Sassie rolled her eyes. Tom guffawed. "You Harvard guys."

A dear man, Tom Rothschild. Vulnerable, a certain hunger for life, in tentative love with everyone, with the very air.

A young family out on the grounds. Mom, dad, two little girls. Annabel framing. "May I?" Snap.

Leo paused over one picture taken by Tom of him and Annabel on the couch together in the upper house, a picture of married bliss. A few snaps of the boys taken by Annabel, her camera's eye doting on them. Is that what led to what happened the next day, the next day when Annabel begged off the sail and nudged her Ellbee to stay with her?

Because carefully careless was Annabel Chance that afternoon in the gabled, wood-lined, sun-warmed bedroom. "I want to play Russian roulette with your better part." Announced the Reverend Doctor of Divinity in a manner that a gentleman could not disoblige.

"I'm not shooting blanks."

"Neither am I."

"Off the pill?"

"Off the pill."

"Shouldn't we talk ...?"

But she was splendidly naked and demurely bending over the suitcase looking for nothing and Leopold Bloom O'Boyle experienced the ineluctability of the all-too-visible to the degree that his body language grew unequivocally eloquent in what grammarians call the cohortative modality.

No Kodachromes of that memorable time out of time. Except in the Technicolor running film of the mind remembering. Did the possibility of creating new life give their junctures a keener edge of feeling and significance? Making time. First inkling that when you create life you create time even if, in retrospect, time had slowed to dozy intervals between the engagements that left time behind.

So that he wondered idly, self-stirred standing in the busy store, about species of time. Elevator time. Airport time. Death-row time. Love-making time. Library time. A natural history of time. Time as a social construct. Gag on that stuff.

Morning at the upper house. Smell of bacon. Tom hovering over the stove. Snap. Tom and Alf, peas in a pod. Alf and Tom going on about a TW breakfast. From the same described in *Look Homeward, Angel* or one of the other novels of Thomas Wolfe. Didn't time haunt him? Because, snap, the instant is captured the instant it disappears, shutter speed, the click, provoking and easing Leo O'Boyle's fear of time. Shutter speed. A thousandth of a second. In that instant, right then, around the world, how many people dying, right then, or giving birth right then. Or eating an apple. Or falling in love. Now all gone. As though that instant never existed. Except for its consequences. The womb of time. Annabel's womb, its accreting life.

A crack of light between two eternities of darkness …

The problem with ransacking the future, another Nabokov phrase—quite aside from the inconvenient truth that every future leads but to the grave—was that such ransacking vitiated the present, this right now, this breath, this blink, this spasm of spending. Which is all we have. Because where does the time go? Not into some handy bag. You can't ransack the past, but we all try. Language deceives us. You can't keep time. You can't save time. And you are going to lose time no matter what you do with it. The womb of time. Easy now. Annabel's womb. *Blessed is the fruit of thy …* Time will tell.

Alf saying somewhat pompously you can't escape time without escaping life. Still it touched a nerve. The question Leo kept askance: Was his fear of time a fear of life? Was he afraid to vest too much in something he might lose? But, of course, you could lose your life or a big chunk of it and still be alive. Or half alive. By wasting it. By half living it.

There were, among the snaps, a few of his own artsy attempts. The close-up of the boiled lobsters. The log-stacked corn on the platter. Tom at the head of the table. Snap. A view of the lawn sloping down to the lower house, the boat house beyond, cove, moored boats, almost hear the jangle of their rigging. Snap. He did have an eye. Borrow the Burke and James. Bring it to Chebeague. Must wrangle an invite for next year. With a baby?

Another *Redux* nag: where might Chebeague fit into his Harvard Square Bloomsday wanderings? What had it to do with the ancient Mediterranean or not so ancient Dublin? But it didn't have to. It is his Ithaca where, as Odysseus, he reclaimed his Penelope.

Leo repackaged the snaps of his revisited and receding life and placed them carefully in his satchel before stepping into the warm light of the avenue. As he walked he told himself to forget the *Redux*, to work instead on *Ice Object 13*, which was alive, glowing in the smithy of his soul, waiting for the hammer strokes that would give it shape.

A sudden thought had him moving out of the way of pedestrian traffic, stopping, taking out his Moleskine notebook, and readying his hammer-like pen for writing a note. To wit:

DOES CAM HAVE HIMSELF IONIZED (TEMPO-
RARILY) THE BETTER TO KNOW THE OBJECT? BUT
HOW TO DESCRIBE THE INDESCRIBABLE? POSSIBLE
SUBPLOT. HE IS TEMPTED TO LEAVE WITH THE
OBJECT IN A SEARCH TO FIND DAPHNE. HOW
WOULD THAT WEAVE WITH THE OTHER THEMES?
DOES IT HAVE TO? THE NAME DAPHNE HAS TO GO.

He crossed the busy thoroughfare and turned right along the rounding wall to Quincy Street. Brick upon brick upon brick. On the other side of the street was the rotunda that attached to the old Union where in the high-ceilinged, dark-paneled commons, Teddy Roosevelt's hunting trophies once recalled a Hemingwayesque manliness. Slated for offices according to Brooks-Denny, who kept an eye on such things. Then left into the upper yard, the Moore statue bestrewn with a young scholar reading in the mild sunshine. Then the redbrick box that was Lamont Library. Form follows function. Who advocated that? Horatio Greenough? Louis Sullivan? From Fleming's course.

In the sunshine in front of the entrance to Lamont Library, Leo O'Boyle stood and pondered. Stratis said any time between eleven thirty and noon. Leo held up his left arm to look at the watch on his wrist. 11:31. Nearly half an hour. The seconds hand, with barely perceptible ticks, moved towards the twelve o'clock bar. He found himself anxious but not particularly fearful. Something was changing. This anxiety was an ordinary fretting about time, about wanting more of it. More of it right then to write his novel. Among other things. It was an anxiety he had felt before but usually as another chord in the dark music of his phobia. Which had attenuated to the point where he suffered a liberating disorientation he didn't entirely trust.

Because he couldn't explain it to himself. Was it the watch, acting like a magic talisman warding off the monsters of his fear? Was it the visit of his father's shade in the church, an apparition that in short retrospect had begun to assume meaning and substance? Francis X. had been there. Or was it Annabel's situation? Their situation.

The actual time was thirty-two past eleven. No, it was now thirty-three past eleven and eight seconds. No, it was … So what? What did he expect time to do? It's what time did. It came and it went. It passed. You couldn't stop it. And this was now his watch, his time. His dad had left him the watch, had given him his time.

Leo sat on the stone bench to one side of the main door, a glass affair showing the lobby within. He looked again at his ticking watch. Enough time to dig out his novel and get down to real work? He usually needed a few minutes of preliminary dithering and even then ...

Or did he? Because he was thinking again without planning to think that the name Daphne would have to go. Too stage British. I say, Daphne dharhling ... Samantha? Would be Sam. Martha? From Martyr? Claudia, feminine of Claude. You need a sliver of significance. Michelle? Barbara? Barbie. Alicia. Nice. Rhymes with delicia. No one would get it. Rosamund? Rosalie. A rose by any other comes out Rosie. Philippa? Katherine. Almost too royal. Clare better. Clare Quilty, Humbert Humbert's nemesis. Quilty, County Clare. Spell it Claire, nice fresh ring. Claire ... Savoy? Touch of class. Claire Lorraine. Maybe. Zeke Cameron and Claire Lorraine? Substitute later. Find and replace. Maybe.

He made a few notes accordingly in his notebook.

Brooks-Denny tended to go on about names for characters. Had to resonate. Uriah Heep. Stephen Dedalus. Buck Mulligan. Oliver Twist. Polonius. Norman de Ratour. Falstaff. Guttman in *The Maltese Falcon*. Iago. Leopold Bloom. Scarlet O'Hara. Arthur Dimmesdale. Humbert Humbert. Sherlock Holmes. Isabel Archer.

What's in a name is that naming something gave that something a reality it might not otherwise possess. Even talking about naming something conferred a status that the unnamed did not have. Careful here. If naming things made them real ... And you can't get more real than another human being.

He and Annabel had discussed names in a hypothetical mode well before there was any necessity to do so. Chance O'Boyle. A bit Darwinian. Leopold Bloom O'Boyle, Jr. would not make the cut. Another F. X. O'Boyle? Doubtful. Francis might do, but not the Xavier. Molly Bloom O'Boyle would be coming it a bit rich. Not for Annabel. She was not a devotee of the master. One exchange on the subject going something like—"You may be my Moldy Poldy, but I'm not your Molly Polly. Really, Ellbee, do you want me to fart in bed?" Then launching into a parody that rather unmanned him. Something like, "He licked my bum, yes. I made him spend on my bare foot, yes. And there were two dogs out the window doing in the street, yes. And I made him breakfast, yes ..."

He had muttered something like, "She was a liberated woman ... for that time."

"Screwing everything in trousers is not women's lib. Women want to get paid more, not laid more." Sly smile. "Or both."

He paused to watch a shapely woman of color approach and go by in jeans and medium heels. He smiled at her. She smiled at him. Appreciating his appreciation. Another callipygian wonder. Then gone. Forever. Not that he would have stood up and launched into some line about having met her before, embarrassed at the obviousness of his ploy, half amazed how well it worked, until ... But now he was married to, wedded to, practically welded to the Reverend Annabel. Wife. Wife and ... Especially the and dot, dot, dot closing down the possibilities of romance with another, meaning an adventure with another person, another person's mind, another person's person. All of which would take energy, interest, generosity, and, in his case, deceit.

Not that Leopold Bloom O'Boyle, like his namesake, did not have a keen eye for feminine beauty in its myriad forms. He was susceptible in particular to what a Frenchman might call *pensés derrières*. Today especially. Not just *ciao bello* in The Tasty. That very morning, gliding along next to the pavement a winsomely latex-clad cyclist standing on the pedals above her suggestively erect bicycle seat. Three blond Scandinavian demi-goddesses checking the map and peering around. Oh, let me help you. A sweated up joggeress with dimpled water bottle in need of an after-run rubdown. All forsaken. Forever.

A like phenomenon had occurred just prior to their nuptials in the Deep South. The shortly-to-be-forever-forsaken seemed to be flowering everywhere. But especially Annabel's cousin Violet, down from Opelika, a regular good old girl, a most willing maid of dishonor had he succumbed to the all but engraved invitation to see the view in her room just doors from his own in that unmemorable motel. He forsook not only because he found regret preferable to remorse, but because he loved his Annabel Folsom Chance. Because it was the right thing not to do. Not that he didn't have regrets on that happiest of days, his face sore from smiling as he chatted around, far more aware of Cousin Violet than he should have been, intellectualizing his unseemly attraction by pondering the curious role curiosity played in the workings of lust.

But this would be very different if Annabel proceeded to parturition. Because, while it was naughty to betray your espoused, there was at least the possibility that he or she would be better off without you. It's quite another thing to endanger a child's wellbeing. Not that half the population didn't do just that. Not that he judged. But he would judge himself. As Annabel said, he had a gift for guilt. Or, less nobly, he strived to avoid at all costs the pain of guilt.

Then there was Dad telling him that to hanker after what you don't really want is the avarice of a fool.

Dad.

He opened his satchel which lay on his jacket on the smooth stone bench beside him. Something he wanted to look at.

Visiting 68 Strand Street shortly after his mother had been wheel-chaired from the hospital into The Elms, Leo had chanced upon a collection of his dad's files in dire need of curating. Or of that final curation, the recycling bin. They included a lot of teaching materials—conferences, notes on kids, books for assigned reading, class plans, that sort of thing. One fat folder titled "LIT/BIOGRAPHIA" held notebooks of various sizes and shapes wherein Frank had kept a haphazard diary, more a running commentary on the life around him. There were also attempts at short stories; sketches, very vague, for novels; a few still-born poems. Some of it could be sorted, edited, arranged with a bit of connective tissue and privately printed? For whom? To what end? To revive them, to bring them and their time back to the time that is? To make an act of filial reverence?

Amid the clutter, Leo had found the small bound notebook with lined pages labeled "Working Class Hero" and put it in his satchel to take home. In part because a yellow Post-it on the front had the word "BURN" in block capitals done with a black marker. A renewed qualm about privacy. Did the dead have rights? Especially your parents. A kind of respect or at least something more than a queasiness to be kept at bay by ignorance. Well, he would only glance, not pry.

Roughly a third of the pages in the front had been ripped out. The remainder contained but a few scattered entries, if that's what they were. Mostly notes about the novels he was reading. A shame, thought son

Leo, disappointed and relieved not to have to confront the possibility of violating his dead father's privacy.

Leo assumed the missing pages were about his dad's flirtation with the Communist party in the late thirties. Frank had gone to a few meetings in Cambridge and Brookline. Had met what he called "a Brattle Street beauty" and been rejected.

That came out one memorable night in the kitchen when the bottle of Paddy remained on the table instead of up and down from the cupboard as customary. Frank wanted to tell his son about being a son himself. Not really private stuff but more personal than Frank had been before. The dad borrowed one of the son's Camels. They fumed together but the dad did most of the talking, setting the scene of his involvement—the middle class and even upper-middle class milieu, the pipe smoking, the educated voices, the blend of seriousness and tenuous self-importance.

Frank leaning forward, his eyes remembering. "One minute I was just another human being. The next I'm working class, I'm Irish, I'm Catholic, I'm in all their little pigeon holes—and expected to act accordingly. The best part, listen to this, the best part was that, as a member of the proletariat, I was assumed to have some profound grasp of the class struggle." Pause for a grimace. "Though you can be sure I was coaxed and coached to make my views line up with the party line. How many times did I hear, 'What you really mean is ...' Little did any of them know that Big Dan got me on the maintenance crew at Boston Consolidated, you know, the gas company. Meaning I spent most of my time standing by, reading novels lying down on the bench in the locker room. But I know how blacks feel when some well-meaning white liberal starts nosing around for sensibilities and vulnerabilities that may or may not be there."

He pondered a while, looked at his cigarette and put it out. "There was a woman at the meetings. A girl, actually. An undergraduate. Her name was Veronica Tamworth or something like that. Skin like white porcelain. I took her out a couple of times. I took her to see the *Wizard of Oz*. I thought it was great. She told me it was a bourgeois fantasy meant to lull the revolutionary classes into accepting their lot. She was in favor of free love, but not, alas, with me. She ended up with a guy from Beacon Hill who had a really nice Packard."

He laughed at this memory of himself. "I'm not sure I blame her. I was a rough piece of work, I mean compared to the others. People actually wore suits or at least jackets and ties to the meetings. I think I was the only one who had a pair of overalls. Not that I ever showed up in them."

A sip of Paddy, a swallow of water. Frank got up and turned on the fan in the window. He came back, took off his watch, and put it on the table. He rubbed the red band it had left on his wrist.

"But what really made me see the light …"

"Other than this porcelain doll … ?"

A laugh of assent. "Right. What really made me walk were the meetings right after the Communists and the Nazis became allies against the British. The Hitler Stalin thing. The verbal gymnastics were something to behold. Comrade Stalin knew what he was doing. Hitler was not the monster portrayed in the reactionary press. It was a non-aggression pact, not an alliance. Then word came down. Every effort was to be made to keep America out of the war. Even industrial sabotage. Which they sponsored. It made the Bund types in the Midwest look like patriots. I almost bit. I was ready to be duped into duping myself. Around me all kinds of smart people were nodding and knocking back the Kool-Aid. A lot of them had gone to college." Another sip of Paddy.

"Not all of them swallowed. I had these friends, Ike and Naomi. A nice Jewish couple. When they finally got up and walked out, I followed them. We went to their apartment in Brookline and had a few beers and a long talk. They lent me *A Portrait of the Artist as a Young Man.* Reading that was like a kick in the head. I had no idea. It was like something I had been looking for all my life."

A tattered edition of *Portrait, ex libris* Issac Felderman, was among his things. But Leo had yet to find the thumbed and re-thumbed copy of *Ulysses*, which made it into his duffel when he shipped out for Europe with the Yankee Division. In later years Frank was given to paraphrasing bits from a poem by Auden: "More than ever life is goodly, miraculous, loveable, but we won't, not since Stalin and Hitler, trust ourselves ever again: we know that all is possible."

"You wanted to tell me about Big Dan," Leo had prompted.

"Yeah, Big Dan. And he was big."

The black-and-white snapshots taken with a Brownie box camera showed a large, well-made, good-looking man with a knowing truculence in the set of his eyes even when smiling.

"I think I fooled around with the Reds to poke him in the eye."

"He knew about it?"

"He suspected. But he suspected everything. He hated everything and everyone. He never used the word Negro. It was nigger this and nigger that. Same for Italians. Wops. And Jews. Watch out. Kikes or Yids. He would listen to Father Coughlin ranting on the old Philco every week. 'The Jews are taking over, Frank my boy. Roosevelt. Rockefeller. Carnegie. What kind of a name is Carnegie?' Then Eisenhower. 'Have no doubt about it. You'll see.'"

Frank at the table pondering another disclosure. "To tell you the truth, Leo, I was embarrassed by my father, I was ashamed of him." The pale eyes turned vulnerable as the shame returned and lingered like a stain in need of removal. "Because I did want to love and respect him. Hell, it's in the Bible, it's one of the Commandments. It's part of nature. But I couldn't. I began to hate him instead. I was glad when he was away, which he was a lot. Not just the business of being a union rep but another woman it turned out. I hated seeing him return with his fake good cheer as though nothing had happened."

Picking up his watch, looking at it, putting it back down as though they didn't have the rest of the evening to themselves, Sheila being out visiting.

"It wasn't just that. By then I had friends, a few Italians, people like Ike and Naomi, and even a black guy, a janitor at the plant named Lewis who liked to read and talk about it. Not that Big Dan ever let on in public what he thought about other kinds of people. Always glad-mouthing, glad-handing, which was almost worse. At least the Nazis ..." He looked away.

"What about the Nazis?"

"They weren't hypocrites."

"More's the shame."

"Right. I think Orwell said something to that effect."

He kept going. "So we woke up one morning to Pearl Harbor and we were at war. I enlisted in the Yankee Division. Japs or Krauts, take your pick, we were going to kick their ass. And we did. After basic training, I came home for a couple of days. Like a bloody hero. That night before supper Dad got half in the bag and started in on Mom. Maybe my uniform set him off. When he lifted his hand to her I stepped in. He tried to hit me and I shoved him into a chair that tipped over and he landed on the floor. I stood over him and I told him that if he ever hit her again, I would come home and break his head open. That August I shipped out to go fight a much bigger bully."

Picking up his watch and putting it back on. Nodding. Another sip of whisky. Another Camel, turning the fan back on.

"You want to know what the real bitch is, Leo? I'll tell you. My mother never forgave me for defending her. Big Dan went into decline and died a year and a half later in an alcoholic coma. And Mom said, in so many words, that it was my fault. She had a point. He might have slapped her around and had other women, but he did provide for her and my brother and sister."

"Did he ever hit her again?"

"I don't think so. But you know what I really learned from Big Dan?"

"What's that?"

"That a bad role model can serve as well as a good one. It helps to know what you don't want to be."

He used to say that the rest of his professional life fit into a paragraph: He came back from the war an old young man. He kicked around for a while and then went to Salem State Teachers College on the GI Bill even as he yearned after Harvard, his Christminster. Graduating, he moved to Cambridge where he taught fifth graders and attended the Harvard Graduate School of Education where he earned a Master's Degree which allowed him to intimate he had gone to Harvard and qualified him to teach high school English, which he did the rest of his working life.

Leo's outer gaze shifted again to the LeCoutre. 11:40. Still time for *Ice*. Getting to be a habit checking the time. Reveling just a bit in the apparent release from his fear. Testing it. Not quite trusting. Wondering if you could become a chronophile, a connoisseur of time? Choice slices out of the day. Morning best? Cocktail time? Happy hour? In bed dallying? Drifting off to sleep at night? Best part of the week? Friday. If you were a nine-to-fiver. Best part of the year? June? June nights in the country. Best time of your life? Falling in love. Or having a child?

Leo put the notebook back in his satchel. He resisted a sense of futility about his father's life. About all life. Can't judge. Futile to whom? Frank had his students. Friends. Mom. Joyce. His Harvard man. A trace of well dissembled disappointment toward the end. A travel writer? Well, yes, but … Had he expected Leo to provide some kind of generational payoff? By being and doing what?

By writing a novel worthy of his name.

Moving the author to extract the three-ring binder from his satchel and open it on his knees. Opening to where he and Tina are speculating on the nature of the thing. After a few more paragraphs of this, the author turned to a section titled EVENTS AND DEVELOPMENT. A lot of this was standard playbook stuff. In the scaffolding mode, he had written:

> There are tensions. Dash is just a touch homophobic and lets it show in a remark or two. Marvis doesn't like Piko's guitar playing and puts on earphones to listen to classical music when the Air Force sergeant starts strumming. Piko doesn't like taking orders from Cam, who is a civilian. Tina and Cam, after a few meaningful exchanges, teeter on the verge of a romantic interlude, held back only by professional restraint.

In the margin, he block-lettered:

> CAN'T JUST TELL, NEED TO SHOW. NEED INCIDENTS. INCIDENTS HAVE TO BLEND. DIALOGUE HAS TO MOVE ACTION THROUGH INDIRECTION EXCEPT WHEN DEALING WITH OBJECT.

Then more scaffolding, scribbling:

> A brutal, late-spring storm descends on them. (PLACE HERE THE DESCRIPTION OF THE WEIRD STORM FROM THE MOLESKINE.)
>
> They are closed down for nearly five days. They go into survival mode. The glacier surges with crunching sounds

under them. On the fifth day, they find they are on the edge of a crevasse opening deep into the blue ice of the glacier.

Later they find that Marvis' tent is gone. They find it in the crevasse. Miraculously, Marvis is still alive. They pull him out alive.

Pausing. Stuff barely legible. Switching to all caps:

THEY DIG HIM OUT AND EVEN PULL OUT HIS TENT. THEY HAVE TO MOVE CAMP. DURING THIS TIME, THE TEAM BONDS INTO A UNIT. INCIDENT: IT IS DASH WHO RAPPELS INTO THE CREVASSE AT GREAT RISK TO HIMSELF TO RESCUE MARVIS WHO IS BARELY HANGING ON IN THE WEIRD BLUE LIGHT OF DEEP ICE. INCIDENT: IN A MOMENT OF STRESS, TINA CLINGS TO CAM AND THEY BREAK OFF JUST BEFORE THEY KISS. OR DO THEY KISS? BUT A LOVING KISS, NOT ONE OF THOSE HOLLYWOOD MOUTH-SUCKING THINGS. (FALSE NOTE FOR A BEREAVED MAN?) THEN, BACK ON TRACK, THEY COMMUNICATE WITH THE COMMAND POST IN ANCHORAGE (RIGHT, COMMAND POST OR COMMAND AND CONTROL, DIG OUT THE JARGON) THEIR MISSION RESUMES.

Leo checked the time. 11:59. Scarcely thinking about it, closing the binder and placing it back into the satchel, thinking he should color code the stick-ons. Red for characters. Yellow for dialogue. Blue for plotting. Pink for action. Lemony green for odd thoughts. Still no ending in sight. *Deus ex machina* wouldn't work. Or might it? Bereft of his Daphne does Cam decide to let himself get vaporized so that he can join the thing before it gets nuked and heads at warp speed into deep space? The ending would be the literal start of a sequel. He could see his dad's averted frown.

· · ·

Lament, he used to call Lamont. Lots of polished maple wood. Its own bookish smell. Comfortable armchairs. Hard not to doze as time circled the wall clocks back in the day. He showed his library card to the gentleman at the desk and climbed two flights to the Poetry Room.

Leopold Bloom O'Boyle pushed open the door and entered the room of poetry. The Woodberry Room. Designed by Alvar Aalto, a Finn. A touch too woody for Leo's taste. Wood. Wood-kerne. More Heaney. Escaping from the massacre of time. Into words. Into language. Seamus speaking in his mind again: *Do not waver into language./Do not waver in it.*

He could hear Stratis on the phone in his office where hung on the wall the image of Marilyn Monroe. Haviaras had known her. Taken her out? Must have been like consorting with a goddess. Greeks used to that sort of thing.

He paused outside the office door glancing around. A young man with shaggy hair appeared leashed to one of the consoles with earphones and cable. The spoken word. One of Leo's favorite places. He came here not so much to escape time as to recapture it. Here he put on earphones and listened to tapes from the library of recordings. Nabokov in Sanders. Lowell in Emerson. Heaney in 1975. The voices lifting the words off the page, the poetry as voices in your mind. Another dimension. Not always edifying. Yeats' Anglo-Irish enunciations disappointed, not up to his poetry. Lowell with a Brahmin honk.

Of late Leo had indulged himself in Tennyson. The man's voice, reaching out of history—the tapes taken from the scratchy wax recordings more than a century old—came through strong and rhythmic.

> Theirs not to reason why,
> Theirs but to do and die:

The voice the living link to what had happened in the Crimea in the Battle of Balaclava. Lord Cardigan leading the charge of the light brigade on the orders of Lord Raglan. Dad's gentle mockery of the haberdashery overtones. Son Leo letting his fancy flow back to the event itself, to the men and their horses as they charged into a fortified line of cannons. Could go there and do a piece touched with history. The Jews of Odessa. Kalinnikov's final years in Yalta composing his two symphonies as he died of tuberculosis. Now part of the Ukraine but mostly Russified. Had the Wehrmacht taken it in World War II? Must have to besiege Stalingrad. Roosevelt, Churchill, and Stalin at Yalta, Roosevelt visibly ailing.

Check to see if they had Wilfred Owen on tape. Antidote to the doing and dying. Man does hand on misery to man. Larkin sounding upper crusty, at home among the swells of Oxford.

At the same time a resistance to voices from the past, the illusory comfort of hearing a time where and when time no longer moved? The illusion of timelessness even as the present came and went second by microsecond, one's own game clock whirring away.

You could waste a lot of time trying to hide from time, thought Leo O'Boyle sitting there, biding his time. He had spent a lot of time thinking about how he might have lived his life in a more timely fashion. As though, in being less conscious of time passing back then, he might have been able to have used it better, done more with it, and in some way kept it from passing so quickly or passing so carelessly. As though much of his life had been a wasting of time that he would never retrieve even as he knew the whole time that all time passed was *temps perdu*. Not even Proust in his reveries of memory could master time, though his little cakes provided Marcel a kind of time out from time.

We all have our madeleines, said Alf, whose incense of memory was turf smoke, recalling with uncanny poignancy a boyhood year in the County Roscommon. Annabel kept a small antique bottle of *flor de naranja*, a scent her mother used years ago. Every once in while she took a dab and rubbed it between her hands before holding them up to her face. Leo's was the lowly hot dog. The snap of processed meat when you bit into it through the soft fold of bread dressed with yellow mustard and plain relish provoked an un-beckoned collage of sensations—lake water lapping, lake water clogging your nose, lake water muffling the voices around you and the shouts from the bleachers where the Pony League games played out through summer evenings and dreamy Sunday afternoons. Un-beckoned, welcomed, savored, making a future memory so that years later the taste of a thrifty hot dog with all the fixings would bring back both The Tasty and the memory of remembering those other, fossilizing memories.

Sounds did the same thing. The tunes you danced to back when. Love's old sweet song. Or bird song. The cry of gulls. Pigeons cooing. The bawl of penned cattle. The fog horn off Chebeague. Everyone, consciously or otherwise, must have their madeleines as an indulgence in and momentary refuge from time.

Yeah, his inner skeptic interrupting—what about those scents and sounds that brought back sadness, regret, even horror?

Lawn Tennyson. Joyce's jibe wasn't fair. Young Dedalus calls him a rhymester in *Portrait.* Because of the poet's passionate regard for Hallam? Joyce a homophobe? Could be even if he defended Wilde as the poet of *Salome.* Or less than straight himself and casting nasturtiums.

Alf, as big a Joyce nut as any of them, had a theory based on Brenda Maddox's recent book about Nora Barnacle. Alf, figuratively grasping the lectern: "It's subtitled *The Real Life of Molly Bloom.* If such is the case, and she makes a strong case for it, then why did Joyce make Molly an accomplished adulteress in fact or in Bloom's head? The list of her lovers goes on and on, starting with one Mulvey based on Mulvagh, a young Protestant suitor from Nora's Galway days. Or was it pure prurient fantasy as Nora Barnacle did not wander from the marital bed even when it got decidedly rocky or non-existent. Then why the list? Because, through Molly, James Joyce vicariously slept with the men listed as Molly's lovers? Mention is made of young Jim wrestling with homosexual feelings. Or, much more likely, was it a kind of defilement? Defilement, self-defilement, and love being all one to Joyce. Read his letters to Nora. Or, perhaps most likely, Joyce suffered from and gratified himself with the exquisite pain of the green-eyed demons of his own imagining.

"The novel was moving toward and should have culminated with a three-way involving Leopold, Molly, and Stephen in that big, brass-quoit-jangling, violated bed at Eccles Street. A mollified Bloom—hey, that's not bad—would have abetted the younger man's bedding of his wife to go with the Italian lessons. At one level it would have been the father and the son sharing the wife and the mother. Odysseus and Telemachus sharing Penelope. Or, given who was standing in for whom—Joyce being both Dedalus and Bloom, and Nora being Molly—Joyce would have been committing adultery with his wife in the presence of her husband."

Lawn Tennyson, gentleman poet. Maybe the gentleman part. Because there is the undying elegiac eloquence.

> Twilight and evening bell,
> And after that the dark!

The dark.

The telephone talking stopped. Stratis appeared in the doorway. Squarish head. Moustache. On the small side, smiling, a quiet hubris. The Attic touch. Greeks the genuine *ur*.

"Leo! Thanks for coming by. How are you doing?"

L. B. O'Boyle smiled back, shaking hands. "Getting by. Your summer go well?"

"I'm still here."

"Have you heard from Seamus?"

"I just had a card. He may be reading for us in the spring. I have a call into Archie about using Sanders."

"He could probably fill Fenway Park. The last great poet. Present company excepted."

"You're too kind. Have a chair." They sat and regarded each other easily across the desk.

"I don't think so. But Seamus is the only one still worth memorizing. I think it's cadence. And the imagery. "'Our shells clacked on the plates/My mouth was a filling estuary …'"

"That's from …"

"'Oysters.'"

"He does have it."

Stratis had it. *When the Tree Sings* a classic. Each vignette jewellike. The starving doctor seeing patients from his bed. The same doctor telling the boy that the invaders ran a motorcycle during beatings to cover their own silent cries.

Stratis could be touchy. But big minded. Holding that reading for Nicholas Gage when he came out with *Eleni*. On the other side of the Greek divide.

"I just ran into Brooks-Denny. He sends his best."

"His best is pretty good. He has the life."

"I'll see him again this afternoon."

"Give him my best. Actually, I should call him."

"You left me a message?" Leo O'Boyle dissembled any note of expectancy.

"Yeaasss …" As though remembering. "Let's go into my office."

Which they did and sat facing each other across the busy desk. The curator in his unnamed chair opened a file and withdrew a manila envelope. From it he took a thin sheaf of paper-clipped, typed pages. He looked the sheaf over and then passed it across the desk.

In twelve-point typewriter typed lettering, the title page read,

SCYLLA AND CHARYBDIS IN *ULYSSES*:
THE WHIRLPOOLS OF JOYCE'S PATERNITY

Farther down the page flush left:

Francis X. O'Boyle
68 Strand Street
Cambridge, MA 02138
ALL RIGHTS RESERVED

The opening line read:

So much light has been shed on this linchpin episode in the novel *Ulysses* by James Joyce that one needs step back to see the obvious in all the glare.

Leo looked up. "This isn't bad."
"I know."
He read on. By the second page, his dad is quoting from the chapter:

"*Amor matris*, subjective and objective genitive, may be the only true thing in life." A mother's love.

Then:

"Paternity may be a legal fiction. Who is the father of any son that any son should love him or he any son?"

Leo glanced at Stratis. "Any date on this?"
Stratis, watching him, shook his head. "None that I could find."
L. B. O'Boyle read on. More stand-alone quotes: "A father is a necessary evil." Then something about how a ghost can be someone, like his father, who has faded into impalpability.

When challenged regarding his views on fatherhood, Stephen Dedalus, who is Joyce impersonating himself, utters the strongest language in the whole scene: "I know. Shut up. Blast you. I have reasons."

Then:

> Whereas a mother's love may be the only true thing in
> life, what links father and son in nature? "An instant of
> blind rut."

The piece contained more in this vein including Buck Mulligan's jibe, "The aunt is going to call on your unsubstantial father." Then playing with the word "consubstantial," the God the father and God the son. He quotes in full Stephen's mocking take on God the Father and God the Son.

> "He Who Himself begot middler the Holy Ghost
> and Himself sent Himself, Agenbuyer, between Himself
> and others, Who, put upon by His fiends, stripped and
> whipped, was nailed like bat to barndoor, starved on cross-
> tree, Who let Him bury, stood up, harrowed hell, fared into
> heaven and there these nineteen hundred years sitteth on
> the right hand of His Own Self but yet shall come in the
> latter day to doom the quick and dead when all the quick
> shall be dead already."

Then an allusion to the paternity of Hamlet and the nature of his father's ghost. Then, abruptly, the tone of the article becomes something less than scholarly.

> It's all a smokescreen. Joyce through Dedalus foists his
> pain about an absent, wastrel father whom he wants to
> love and admire on a schema invoking the Trinity and
> the family life of the lesser god Shakespeare including
> Anne Hathaway's infidelity. When asked by John Eglinton
> whether he believes his theory, Stephen responds "No." It
> is a smokescreen Joyce wants the reader to see through.
> It's a case of cover your eyes and see. In this instance, the
> ineluctable modality is his father's unsubstantiality.

Leo read on, moved by hearing his father's diction in the words. In drawing from autobiographical sources on the family of young Joyce, the declarative tone Frank O'Boyle used when on sure ground came through.

Circumstances, chiefly the fecklessness of his father
John Joyce, forced James at an early age to become his own
father. Which he did, but never without ceasing to try to fill
or explain this void in his life. To seek the approval of one
that one cannot approve of can drive one to despair. As the
portrayal of Simon Dedalus in the body of the novel shows,
this ambivalence is damning.

L. B. O'Boyle said, "I'm assuming this was submitted for publication in *Erato* and turned down."

"Not rejected as such. Filed."

The tone Stratis used made Leo attentive. He said, "My father Frank was his own father. I mean his dad was a no-show and worse. Until he got sick and died. By that time, Dad was overseas in the war."

"So he knows what he is talking about."

An involuntary smile. "You could say he was foisting his own experience on his reading of the scene." At which point Leo O'Boyle recalled that Stratis Haviaras had lost his father at an early age.

"How old were you when your father was killed?"

"I was nine. He wasn't killed, Leo, he was murdered."

"So you, too?"

"Right. I was my own father."

They were silent for a moment as though out of respect.

Stratis said, "I'd like to publish the piece in the *Review*."

"Really?"

"But it needs checking."

"What do you mean?"

"I mean there's so much written and being written about Joyce, I don't want to duplicate what's already been done."

"You want me to search the literature?"

"That's what I need."

Leo O'Boyle felt inadequate to the generosity of the man behind the desk. He nodded his thanks. "So I can keep this?"

"I've got a copy."

"Many thanks."

"Thanks to your dad."

The son who had had the benefit of a father gave a rueful laugh. "I only wish Frank was around. Just to be seriously considered would have ..." He looked up into the face of Stratis. "You knew him, right?"

"I did know him. He showed up for readings. He had the look of a pure scholar. Bubbling with knowledge and sensibilities he didn't know what to do with."

The curator glanced surreptitiously at his watch.

"Need anything reviewed?" L. B. O'Boyle was a hit and miss reviewer.

"Caballos has a new Belmont Park murder mystery." He handed across a glossy jacketed book, something about a dark horse. "Why don't you do it with an overview of the others?"

Leo held the book in his hand. Nice heft. The weight of words. He frowned dimly and returned it. "I hear they're good but I haven't read them." Then he asked, "What do you know about the Nabataeans?"

"Not much. They were a trading people. Probably wiped out by the Turks."

Haunted by the Turks. By the Germans, too. It was the Nazis who executed his father. Another stiff-necked Greek.

"Are you writing about them?"

"About Petra. And maybe Jerash. I'm scheduled to do a piece. I'd rather go to New Jersey at this point. How about you? How's the novel?"

"I need time, Leo, I need time."

Time the fire in which we write.

"At least you do it. I mean not just talk about it."

A wry smile. He rose. "So what's your listening pleasure today?" He knew Leo's habits.

L. B. O'Boyle smiled back. "Nothing today. Kind of busy." He did want something but did not know what.

They went out into the main room and its wood upon wood. Leo glanced around. The night at the writer's group, guest of Brooks-Denny. Newspaper covering the door window so they could smoke. There, reading each others stuff, wine going around, sat Stratis, Estevan Caballos, poet and novelist; Kerry Marr, memorable memoirist; Ferdinand "Ferd" Ambling, a poet in history; Steve Littlebirch; critic and essayist; Willy Tigerman, teacher and poet; Chuck Melnakov, late-blooming novelist; and Romana Klee, the name twister.

Leo had every intention of asking to join. Once he had something to bring to the table. No body of work. No book of poetry. No short stories. No novel. Travel writing did count, but only at a level he wasn't interested in pursuing.

The phone rang on the outer desk. They shook hands. Leo said, "I'll get back to you on this." Stratis nodded and picked up the phone.

L. B. O'Boyle exited the reading room. Out among the stacks of books, he felt a familiar prompting in his fundament. The Tasty's coffee finally working. Libraries were conducive somehow. Thus musing he made his way to the men's room.

Floor-to-ceiling doors on the stalls. For privacy. Gay influence? For close encounters of the homophilic kind. Gay sex not his thing. Not that all sex isn't, in the end, whichever end, sublime and ridiculous. No accounting for tastes. He subscribed to Alf's take: It is of little or no consequence to anyone but themselves what consenting adults get up to in private. Nature's real pansies are those big strong guys who don't acknowledge and care for the children they engender. Full stop.

Where might he fit in all that? One of nature's real pansies?

Leo settled in. He considered opening the three-ring binder. Check out some notes. Wouldn't need words this time. A few at-stool SOTs would suffice. Are the words *proctor* and *proctoscope* related? *Rectum* and *rector* and *rectitude*? Still need to look up. Tight-arsed, say the Irish. What Henry James would have thought of Joyce's depiction of Bloom in the jakes. Could take notes for scene in *Redux*. The new Bloom at stool. Dad squeamish about Joyce's scatological enthusiasms. "I skip those parts." Here now, almost. The three states of matter. Or Alf's aphorism: Prejudice is like excrement: we tend to think that of others smells worse than our own. An intervening thought making him fumble out the Moleskine notebook and pen for an *Ice Object* note.

IS CAM CHRONOPHOBIC? NO. DO NOT MAKE
NOVEL INTO AN EXERCISE OF SELF-THERAPY.

Back to the business at hand. Have to maintain a kind of concentrated non concentration in these matters.

Another thought, block lettering:

NEED MORE BACK-STORY FILL INS ON CAM &
DAPH. TELLING SCENES AT THE RANCH. RESCUING
NEW-BORN CALVES DURING AN EARLY SPRING
SNOWSTORM. DANGER. FACE TO FACE WITH
A MOUNTAIN LIONESS DEFENDING HER CUBS.
WINTER LONELINESS. CLOSENESS. IN FRONT OF
FIRE LATER ON WITH A BOTTLE OF GOOD WINE.

Ah, here it is. Ah … easy. Nice. Wait. And a small encore.

Curious stuff when you think about it. One moment so intimately part of you, so uniquely your very own creation; the next expelled, disavowed, flushed out of sight, and reduced to an expletive for what is false, ugly, and odious. When it's only matter, the necessary residue of nutrition, only molecules that will get recycled into newsprint, wood paneling, Chinese take-out, the brain cells of writers, etc. etc. Could write an essay or a small book: *In Defense of …* Or a nineteenth century parody: *The Virtues of Ordure*. Or *Night Soiling in the Perfume Garden and Other Poems*, a translation from the … Not that far-fetched. Winthrop House Master David Owen orated a defense of Scrooge every Christmas and masterful it was. All the same a moment of grace when you think about it. Should be a short prayer of thanksgiving as before a meal. Praise the Lord, for I have shat. Billions of people every day. All of those toilets. That ancient communal defecatorium in Ephesus, marble, men only.

Then a parenthetical thought among the brain cells of this writer: Have philosophers confused the recycling of matter with the recycling of time?

Lighter, hands washed, Leopold Bloom O'Boyle hesitated near the entrance after showing the contents of his bag. Stop and write for a spell? He could feel another, more elevated stirring within. *Ice Object 13* kicking again, clamoring to be fed. Or just sucking its thumb?

He came down past the bunker that was Pusey Library. Books underground. Petra. Research. Had to face it sometime. Fake travel writing had nearly be better than the real thing. A touch of history never hurts. Check a few travel guides. Sound the off-hand note.

• • •

He climbed the wide steps of Widener toward the stolid march of Corinthian columns. Was it the mountainous piece of floating ice or the faulty architecture of the *Titanic*? In irreverent moments he wondered if Gaudi might have modeled the building on an iceberg had he gotten the commission. Or Gehry on the doomed liner as she slid bow first under the waves at an angle. A monument to a mother's grief. We'd love to have your late son's library, Mrs. Widener, it's just that we don't have any place to put it. Harry Elkins did have a lot of books. Not cheap to accommodate them. How many millions did she sign for? Back when a million was a million.

The names on buildings. An attempt to stymie time, that is, to persist if only in name, the name the relict of a flesh and blood being that walked and talked, a being that no longer exists except in a name that could have been another name as what's in a name? Not to mention that almost no one remembers who the hell you were. Because where the hell did everything go? And if everything did just disappear and it did, with time, what was the point?

With sudden trepidation, he glanced at the watch on his wrist. Nearly one of the clock. More than a wince. Was his reprieve over? Would time ever leave him alone? A bell rang. Memorial Church. And this thing strapped to him like a bomb. Find a trash can. Or hide it somewhere. Come back and get it when it stopped. A couple of deep breaths. Steady.

Past the check-in desk, his pulse still throbbing noticeably, he walked in to the colonnaded main lobby of white marble. A double grand stairway led up to the grand door opening into Harry Widener's collection of books. Should check the titles sometime. Might there be some classic erotica? The door was flanked on either side with murals by Sargent. Put up after the Great War. Harry sharing his memorial with the thousands of American dead.

He checked his wrist like checking his heart. Better.

Leo had seen the murals hundreds of times. The one on the right, facing, depicted an army of identically faced young men, doughboys in Sergeant Preston Mountie hats and with shouldered rifles heading off to war, the leading one reaching for a young blond woman demurely breast feeding a child, the whole thing surmounted by the Stars and Stripes and a soaring eagle.

The panel on the left, facing, bore the inscription in all caps engraved in the marble, "HAPPY THOSE WHO WITH A GLOWING FAITH IN ONE EMBRACE CLASPED DEATH AND VICTORY." The spirit of a doughboy is depicted rising from his corpse. He has one arm around the waist of a dark, shrouded figure that seems to be pulling him downward. His other arm is around a blond, bare-breasted Brunhilde with great feathered wings who appears to be pulling him upward.

Happy?

The depiction disturbed Leo O'Boyle, not only its content or message as how it betrayed so graphically the limitations of art. Art reduced to figments of the national psyche current at that time. Upscale propaganda, so to speak. Was the heroism and sadness of a soldier's death simply too profound to be shown without mawkishness? Was it beyond art? Like time or timelessness?

Questions as answers that had never quite appeased him, they being SOTs of long standing. Now it was as though he were trying to explain the image not only to himself but to someone else as well. Explain it or criticize it with something besides the usual anti-war rhetoric, which, though he agreed with it, didn't require any thinking. Something like: the idiocy of industrialized war and the mass slaughter it entailed had yet to sink in.

Now, looking at the Sargent mural to the left by itself, he saw something different, something more basic, more profound. The painting clearly transcended its caption. In it big-winged life lifted the dead soldier's form upward, toward the light while dark, fearsome death tugged downward. Sargent was depicting nothing less than the struggle between light and darkness, between life and death.

Leo smiled with just a touch of self-congratulation. Until, in thinking what to say to this other, inexplicable presence, the significance of his perception rebounded on him with unexpected force. Wasn't he, that very day, struggling with the question of life or death? And was that choice the same as between light and darkness?

Too disturbing. With deliberation and a measure of cowardice, he escaped into thoughts of *Ice Object 13* and, as he ascended the remaining white marble steps, into thoughts of a building created because a very large drifting piece of ice collided with a ship with less than water-tight compartments. Or blind bad luck. He escaped into more thoughts about Harry Elkins Widener. But did anyone other than paid curators know who he was? Who was the Logan of Logan Airport, the Storrow of Storrow Drive, the Devens of Fort Devens? At least honorific. Not like the *vanitas* of the rich. Proclaiming I made enough money by hook or by crook to have my name plastered here or chiseled in stone to remind everyone that they don't know who I was. No one is listening or remembering. Ted Williams didn't need a tunnel to be remembered, nor Longfellow a bridge, though that probably helped. SOTs.

The banks of card catalogues stood neglected. Everything on computer now. Pretty soon put the whole thing on a disc or a few discs. Words on a screen. Come and go. Like thoughts.

Leo B. O'Boyle sought and found Eddie Doctoroff, doctor of books and mixed and unmixed potables. He loomed shyly in tucked white shirt. He loomed tall, dignified, friendly, his noble circumference worthy of a character out of *Casablanca*. He worked both sides of the street being called to the bar at The Potato in the evenings.

"Been anywhere interesting lately?" Eddie asked Leo.

"I have traveled far in Harvard Square. And how goes your double duties?"

"More dry than wet. You've heard The Potato's closing."

"Aye. The ship deserting its sinking rats. What's going in there?"

"Slate's expanding. Have you heard from Seamus lately?"

Leo patted his hanging bag. "I just bought his latest."

"So what brings you to fair Widener?"

"I want to know something about Petra and the Nabataeans that no one else knows."

"You won't find that in a book."

"That makes sense. Actually, I just want to know something about them."

"Jordan? Are you going there?"

"In a manner of speaking … I'm writing a travel piece and possibly … not traveling."

"A new genre." The smile was encouraging. Then, "The stacks should have something."

Down they went into the bowels of the place, down through floor upon floor, row upon row of steel shelving. Not bowels exactly. Analogy off a bit off. The bowels of libraries are in the heads of scholars—a sampling of them bent in study in the monkish carrels ranged along the stack ends—ingesting, digesting, excreting words. Still off a bit. More like a giant womb. Books breeding books. Still not ... More like making sausages, most books being bits and pieces of other books or documents or reports all chopped up, blended, re-seasoned, reconstituted, and, above all, reordered. Never know whose thoughts you're chewing, thought the original Leopold. But you have to know whose words you're chewing. Can't copy without attribution. Because in academia you can steal a colleague's spouse with impunity, but if you steal his ideas or her words, you will have your insignia ripped off and be unceremoniously drummed out of the corps .

They went down to CE, C East, one floor up from D, the lowest. They went to the stacks labeled M.E., Middle East. A short shelf dedicated to the Nabataeans. After thanks and a handshake, Eddie Doctoroff left L. B. O'Boyle to browse on his own. He browsed several before alighting on *Deities and Dolphins* by Nelson Glueck. Good heft. Thumbing. Lots of pictures.

He took his prize up the rattling elevator and emerged from the stacks. He checked the book out and took it into the vast, barrel-vaulted Reading Room. Would that iceberg have fit in here? Probably not. He made himself glance at the clock and checked it against his, his dad's, watch. 1:11. How time flies! But what a luxury to simply check the time without wanting to hide from it, deny it, curse it.

On one of the substantial tables amid yet more scholars, real scholars, he opened *Deities and Dolphins* to Chapter 1. *They Began as Bedouins.* "The mystery that once shrouded the past of the Nabataeans has been much modified in modern times by numerous and rich archaeological discoveries."

A spasm of conscience. To go or not to go to Jordan? Because he was about to indulge again in a fiction, not a real fiction, but a fictive fiction, that is, a fiction passing itself off as non-fiction.

Quite by chance, L. B. O'Boyle had begun the new—to him—craft of virtual travel writing or, more accurately, the craft of writing about virtual travel. *Gourmandizer Traveler* "sent" him to Dublin to do an atmospheric piece on the city of Joyce, Behan, Kavanaugh, to mention a few. More of a knock-about piece, the restaurant scene such as it was. No more Jammet's. He was able, with a touch of research and a few calls to friends, to cobble together an impressionistic account, mentioning what was playing at the Abbey, at the Gaiety, at the Gate, throwing in that the latter was started by Hilton Edwards, that "Fenian Pouf" in the words of the Reverend Ian Paisley. A night at Neary's drawn hazily from memory. From an *Irish Times* bought at Out of Town News and perused at leisure, he referenced a show jumping and equitation event at the Royal Dublin Society in Ballsbridge. A horse race at Leopardstown. Beckett's definition of genius: the horse trainer Vincent O'Brien. An allusive allusion to tea with the Boormans in Wickow. For those in the know. The Martello Tower in Sandycove, of course. The bully-bag-shrinking, runny-nose Irish Sea.

Ethics aside, was it not a violation of basic journalistic standards to imply you had traveled to the place you are writing about as though you had traveled there though you had not? What if you had been there before? What about those reporters who call in a story from, say, Cairo, about some atrocity in Syria? Can you not experience something at a remove—on the phone, for instance—and still experience it sufficiently to claim a certain presence? Is the implied presence of the writer a form of mendacity? Or is it more akin to phone sex which to some, in its freedom of fantasy, is more arousing and satisfying that the in-the-flesh variety? That is to say, is writing about virtual travel a form of literary masturbation?

Yes.

In a state of mild agitation, aware of the creeping clock and his watch keeping pace, the travel writer put aside the scholarly tome and took the folder with *The Caper* material out of his satchel. Notes and jottings. *The Caper*, slowly shriveling, lay strewn around in pieces in the cluttered workshop of his imagination. Or remained in a suspended, fetal state, not quite stillborn, not quite alive.

Meeting of The Committee at Giannino's scheduled for one thirty. Could skip it. Could call in healthy. Real work to do. Writing. *Ice Object 13.*

Because the meetings went nowhere. They called themselves, with a certain officiousness, "The Committee." The Committee met irregularly and schemed—if endless, usually pointless talking can be described as such. To which Leo should have objected. He didn't. He went along with increasing reluctance, frustrated that their machinations, however sketchy and feeble, had taken over the story. Worse, for all their talk about making a killing, they had usurped his dreams, more like fantasies, of a cash windfall from book sales, movie rights, and whatever else ensued in the form of franchises, sequels, prequels, genuine reproductions of whatever.

These had been important, sustaining fantasies. Though Leo had never tested the equation, he believed that, under many conditions, time did equal money, and, more certainly, that money equaled time, the latter with a necessary qualifier. To wit: the possession of sufficient funds with which to live allowed one to use one's time for purposes other than the acquisition of sufficient funds with which to live. Though far from a universal solvent for his complicated fears about time, a sufficiency of disposable wealth would allow him more time or at least "free" time. Not to mention the purchase of some decent clothes.

Thus, the authoring of *The Caper* was to have been a quickie money maker, perhaps even under a pen name, a maker of enough money in any event to allow Leo to achieve a masterwork, not that he had any idea at the time what his masterwork might be. *Ice Object 13* had come along in the meanwhile and now *Ulysses Redux* was making a pest of itself.

Then The Committee expanded to four with the recruitment of Graham Crocker III, a man of modest demeanor who knew, or appeared to know, anyone who was anyone. Ari had enlisted Gray, as he was aptly called, in part for his name and for the patina of respectability it gave the enterprise. He was also a valued customer in the line of nose candy and a potential source of capital their enterprise would need if it were to advance beyond the verbal stage. An attorney, Gray, the "III" added by Ari to give a certain burnish, administered trust funds, mostly his own very sizable one. That was all but a full-time job given the number of committees he served on within the vast non-profit world where his largess was, with subtle flattery, courted and anxiously awaited. In which respect, this committee, The Committee, existed, Ari assured him, not to take his money but to make him more of it.

Around Gray they downplayed any open advocacy of law breakage as he, a member of the Massachusetts Bar in good standing, might object. However, other than evince a studied obliviousness, he never did object, perhaps because he sensed that the others, wallowing in prolonged adolescence, were merely indulging childish fantasies. Perhaps he knew better than they did that their hypothetical talk and creative thinking about a scheme to relieve people of their money under false pretenses had yet to become conspiracy, an infraction punishable by fines, imprisonment, or both. Perhaps he knew how a well-fee'd lawyer could plead their use of the subjunctive or future conditional, the "if we were to ..."

So that with the advent of Graham Crocker, Esq., the aim of the project evolved from a quick killing to a slow fleecing. Olden Golden Holdings or some such was to be incorporated as a limited liability, not-for-profit entity with generous salaries and expense accounts for its directors and with virtually endless tax relief for its well-heeled subscribers inasmuch as any recovered art or artifacts not retained for research purposes would be distributed among the subscribers for the express purpose of donation for tax purposes to other not-for-profit entities or for their own private collections. Their project, in short, had the moral underpinnings of art.

The irregular meetings came to order or disorder as ordinary citizens might conceive it at various venues—Giannino's, The Potato, and the Regatta Bar. Not for the variety of it, but because Ari entertained the illusion that more than one of the nation's multifarious law enforcement agencies were taking an active interest in what they were conspiring about.

Leo was appointed the writer, the idea man. He was to come up with names, dates, and copies of original documents for Fritz, who knew people who knew people who knew how to fabricate realistic facsimiles from the original copies, a matter about which The Committee remained appropriately vague. Ari assumed the chair of The Committee as a matter of course and acted as the moderator—or immoderator—as Leo liked to joke. Leo was to take notes but in a hypothetical way or as source material for a book he was writing such that no hint of wrongdoing might be extracted from them. Gray, with a wide acquaintance among people of substance, would help Ari recruit the "subscribers," as their prospective marks were called. They would issue a hundred shares, each share selling for $100,000.

Ari claimed they would only need three or four to "seed" the thing. "Okay, people who invest in this kind of stuff like to talk, brag discreetly, you might say. They recruit without knowing it. Tainted money has its own appeal. Word gets around. You end up with people begging to get a piece of the action." He paused. "Another thing, when you're talking about found treasure, sunken stuff, the possible pay-offs run into the tens of millions. It's like an investment and a lottery rolled into one."

From its inception, the project teetered between garrulous fantasy and unconvincing glimpses of distant wealth. Things were backwards. Instead of some reality triggering an idea for a novel, an idea for a novel had triggered this reality, a reality that sagged and sank in a whirlpool of words going round and round. But so convincing on the surface. A distinct note of competent bravado marked their meetings. No expense would be spared for whatever it took to further the operation. Of course, they would need an office in Key West. And perhaps one in Boston or Cambridge. And antique parchment for doctoring could be gotten and damn the cost. Etc. Etc. The fact that The Committee possessed not one nickel to defray costs did not deter them in the least.

L. B. O'Boyle avoided looking at the clock on the wall. He looked at the clock on the wall. 1:19. He closed the folder. He took out the three-ring binder with the manuscript of *Ice Object 13*. Opening chapter. Overview. He mused. Make some notes. Time. Restless again. Something dawning. Gnawing.

He stood up and went for a stroll along the book-lined walls. Musing. Place big enough for a football field. A punt might bounce off the ceiling. Or break one of the three great windows that allowed in light at either end. Would have to do something with the floor. Artificial turf maybe.

Dad's article. Could start checking the literature now. A few key words. *Ulysses. Scylla and Charybdis.* Father and son. But the part about Joyce being his own father sounds original. Might be able to do a computer search. Almost too easy.

Clock again. 1:25 Five minutes gone. Time ticking. Those cells dividing inside of Annabel. More and more. Probably every second. Every minute. Takes billions of them to make a human being, even a small one.

He settled into his chair. Across from him at an angle, a scholarly woman of about forty, blond hair, nice eyes, reading and taking notes from a volume of the *Journal of Physical Anthropology*. And slowly, discreetly consuming a package of Fig Newtons. Temptation. The fig things, not the scholar. He mutely craved to have one, just one. The way the tiny seeds crunched between your teeth when you chewed the softly chewy cookie surround. She had plenty left, almost half a package. Strange how you couldn't just ask for one. Whispering, "Hi, you know, I'd love one of your Fig Newtons." How to do that without annoyance. How to intimate it wasn't a come-on. Or only enough of a come-on not to be insulting, there being something disproportionate in being nice to someone for the sake of a Fig Newton.

The question Leo O'Boyle had to ask himself: How badly do you want a Fig Newton? Badly enough to cadge one off this reader of anthropology? Badly enough to get up, go to the Square, to Sage's, and get a package of the things. Wouldn't be the same. The moment would be lost. He would walk back stuffing the things into his mouth and remembering when he wore a size 30.

Remembering now how, starting at the age of 30, his waist size began to keep pace with his years. And then to outpace his years. He was determined to hold the line at 36. Meaning push back the line to 34 as though in losing weight he might regain some years. It took some doing. He found there were sizes and there were sizes. There were small 38s that he could barely get above his crotch. There were regular 38s that gave him bladder problems. And then, there were more commodious size 38s that he could wear more or less comfortably. He owned as a result an odd assortment of trousers including a kind of plaid worn by golfers and a new pair of jodhpurs he found at Keezers for two dollars that made him think of Hermann Goering. Tomorrow he would start his diet with coffee, blueberry muffin and OJ for breakfast. Salad for lunch. And tomorrow, he would exercise, walk, work out. And tomorrow, Annabel would be ...

The novelist, having distracted his craving for a fig roll, turned to where he had left off in the latest print-out of *Ice Object 13*. Real. He had underscored it. *Real*.

The real reality was all around him, distracting him. Real scholars bent to real work, absorbing words, sentences, paragraphs and perhaps making a few of their own. Or not so real. A table over, a bit of subtle flirtation was coming to fruition. An older, donnish man in whispered exchange with younger, somewhat fey Adonis. Edging now toward the exit. Coffee first or a quickie in the men's room? Was everyone below a certain age just plain horny most of the time?

Another distracting thought: what about straight quickies in Widener? No place to go. A kind of discrimination? Could put that in a suggestion box. Item on a committee agenda. Small, discreetly placed cubicles with wash basins. Precluding horizontality? What about wheel-chair access?

He shook it off. He made himself focus. He reconsidered again point of view. First person too restrictive. Better an omniscient narrator or disguised first person with the camera poised over Cam's shoulder. Openings very important. Snag the reader. But which opening? Start with the action. Then backfill with the first opening. Change the tense. A little repetition okay. Readers get lazy.

He would make the changes at home, on his IBM. Amazing how much easier. Block off section. Hit copy. Cut. Paste. A bit of verbal stitching.

He flipped to one of the back pages and a section titled "NAMES AND CHARACTERS" and resumed working on names. He had printed out:

Cam McInally. Short for Cameron. Mac Cameron? Mick Cameron? Too Scottish? Too white bread? Need an added flavor. Cherokee maybe. Grandmother a Comanche. Explain his stoic courage. What's a typical Cherokee name? That joke about two dogs fucking. Something Spanish or Native American. Just a touch. Diego. Diego Cameron. Shorten it to Deke. Deke Cameron. Mother from an old California family. There before the Anglos. Blood royal. Like the family in One-Eyed Jacks. So possibly Deke Cameron.

He added,

IF CAM IS WRITING THAT NOVEL, THEN HE HAS TO BE PART MEXICAN, MAYBE DECAYED MEXICAN ARISTOCRACY, ON HIS MOTHER'S SIDE. OR DOES HE? MAYBE HE SIMPLY WANTS TO BE OF OLD MEXICO. NOTES ARE SOMEWHERE.

He went over notes on the main characters he made in church. He had decided early on that he couldn't have only muscle-faced climbers on the team. Needed technicians. From the Air Force. He had put in Dash, a black guy. Why? Because black guys are here. If they don't belong, who does? But not one of those counter-stereotypes, the tweed-clad, resident intellectual, perhaps with a Ph.D. in psychology or some other ology the idiot public thinks is deep and difficult. Evokes the stereotype. So make him real. Why not a black woman? Need specific skills. He had assembled a motley crew. Careful not to make them too close to real people. Daphne only a tad like Annabel. Cam a kind of inversion of himself. Everest twice. Sure. The Cordillera Huayhuash notwithstanding, the backstairs twice on a hot day was more like it.

He looked at the Lecoutre. He closed his eyes. The dream face he had seen in St. Paul appeared on the screen of his mind. He spoke to it again with silent thought. Actually, Dad, this novel isn't half bad. I'd love it if you'd read it. If I ever finish it. Not that far off. Okay, it's got some pulpy themes and situations and a few stock characters. But it does reach for a kind of transcendence.

He could imagine his twisted smile of skeptical encouragement.

He flipped to another section labeled BACK STORY/CAM AND DAPHNE SKIING TRAGEDY. He had written, typed, and printed out:

> The sky is a dome of turquoise, rare for this area where rain, snow, and fog flare up at a moment's notice. The day before, coming into Yakuta Bay aboard their small excursion vessel, Mt. Saint Elias, only ten miles from the water, rose more than eighteen thousand feet into clear air, a vertical lift of three miles, an astonishing sight, one worthy of the Himalayas. Mike and Myra Joplin, friends from Boise, both expert skiers, had decided at the last minute to join them on this optional activity, as the cruise director had called it. Also along was Nate Curling, a local guide hired by the tour company.
>
> Since no civilian helicopters were allowed in the Wrangell Saint Elias Park, they take a bush plane with skis and land up close to one of the sources on the west side. In some respects it's a bit tame compared to some of the

routes they could have taken. But not entirely. Along with crevasses, there was always the danger of avalanches from the snow piles along the ridges lining the ice. DOUBLE CHECK

It's not just another heli-skiing trip for Cam and Daphne; it may be their last for a good while. She is now closing on thirty-four and her clock is ticking. (OR IS SHE ALREADY PREGNANT?) Back in Idaho where they raise free-range Belted Galloways on their four-thousand acre spread, (REPEAT?) they are in the pleasant preliminaries of starting a family. It's not an easy decision. They both have busy, fulfilling lives. Daphne works to include other ranchers in a conservation project designed to help preserve some of the area's large predators. Cam not only raises prize-winning stock with a couple of hired hands, he is writing his memoirs or, perhaps, a novel based on them. (NOVEL WITHIN A NOVEL?) They love this kind of travel. Indeed, they had considered joining their Florida friends Jack Manning and his wife Adelaide Warren on a sail to Antarctica on *Long Reach*, their forty-five foot-ketch. Couldn't risk that with an infant on board.

L. B. O'Boyle paused in his perusal. He had forgotten that he had written this part. Easy to confuse stuff in your head and what's been put to paper. Easy to have fictional characters do great things! Not that conceiving and having a child hadn't been done before. Had he been foreshadowing his own small destiny? Or was he creating a surrogate life—adventure, larger-than-life characters, global significance—all that was lacking in his own proscribed existence?

As for the possibility of a novel within the novel, he came across a patch of small, numbered pink stick-ons labeled "DEKE'S NOVEL." A note on a page from a notebook in block lettering read,

> (FOR ANY NOVEL WITHIN THE NOVEL, CAN'T
> JUST TELL, HAVE TO SHOW. MEANS ANOTHER
> NARRATIVE, ONE THAT SHOULD PARALLEL,
> IF ONLY IRONICALLY, THE MAIN PLOT. OR
> SHOULD IT?)

The remainder in a reasonably legible scrawl:

(1) Bernardo O'Higgins O'Malley, who plies between his sprawling Russian Hill penthouse overlooking San Francisco Bay and a commodious shack overlooking Tomales Bay on the Point Reyes side to the north, has time on his bachelor hands.

(2) In his early thirties, love life languishing, but sitting on a pile of money from the sale of his dot-com start-up, Bo, as he is called, receives a letter one morning that changes his life. It appears oddly formal, written with a typewriter on expensive paper.

(3) It is from Benita Porfirio (or the lawyer of Benita, who is an ancient aunt of his long dead mother Felicia Dias.) In fact, it's from the side of the family that he had lost contact with though he knew it to be once prominent in the (area) though impoverished.

(4) In stilted English the letter informs him that he has inherited the Hacienda don Carlos, a vast old land-grant ranch, debt-ridden, its buildings falling down, etc.

(5) Possibilities: Bo hones his Spanish and drives south. He spends time with Benita in her town house going over old photographs, letters, family history. He camps one night in the old hacienda and hears a mountain lion screaming not far away.

(6) He has a run-in with a local gang. He meets and falls for the ravishingly beautiful Esmeralda, his first cousin once removed. She is no pushover nor is her boyfriend, one Juan del something. What happens? It doesn't matter. The quest is everything.

He put the stick-ons aside. Probably not. Did he really want his main character writing a novel which would start a whole new narrative and need all kinds of attention and even some research? Wouldn't Bo O'Malley have to be working on something as well? Nesting dolls.

He flipped back to the fatal scene on the glacier and read:

Daphne and Cam start off together, ahead of the others. The surface is mostly fresh snow with patches of firn—granular snow in process of turning into ice. It's not very steep, but nearly as fast as they want it. The vistas all around them are ethereal. What Cam feels at that moment is a heady sense of privilege and luck. He has everything. Especially Daphne. Up ahead of him, her striking form sashays leaving a plume of virgin white snow. Though he is an expert skier, she is better, having qualified for the slalom in the last Winter Olympics.

He should have seen it coming. He notices the angle of the snow-piled slope to their right: It is neither steep enough to shed the snow as it accumulates nor shallow enough to hold it indefinitely. But he had stopped to adjust his right boot. Tearing after her, frantic, calling out. He is too late. His own shouts may have triggered the swift, deadly avalanche that explodes onto the glacier with pluming speed, blurring around him and burying his beloved under twenty feet of the suffocating stuff.

!!!SINCE THE ACTION IS IN THE PAST, SHOULD SWITCH TO SIMPLE PAST HERE AS MAIN ACTION IS IN PRESENT. ALSO WORK INTO SCENE MORE SUSPENSE. CAM HAS FOREBODINGS AS THEY GET OFF THE PLANE. HE REMARKS TO HIMSELF THE RIDGES OF UNSTABLE SNOW ALONG THE GLACIER EDGE. HE FEELS AND FAINTLY HEARS THE INITIAL RUMBLINGS OF THE AVALANCHE.

To that note he added on a Post-it:

THE NAME DAPHNE REALLY HAS TO GO. CAN'T USE NICKNAME DAPH OR DAPHY. DOESN'T WORK.

Then another Post-it:

THE PLACE WHERE THE OBJECT HAS BEEN UNCOVERED IS VERY CLOSE TO WHERE THE AVALANCHE TOOK DAPHNE'S LIFE. WORK IN CAM'S EMOTIONS EARLY ON AT THE COINCIDENCE. OR IS IT A COINCIDENCE?

Not bad for a polished-up first draft. Not bad was not the same as good. There was more to be had, not just the cold details, but something he couldn't quite translate from the vivid screen of his imagination to the clean page or the blank screen of his aging laptop. How to insinuate the theme of time? Something about the slow-moving glacier and the speed of the loosened snow? How the hope arises that this object may be able to breach the implacability of the lost past, to reorder events such that he is able to sweep Daphne to safety before the cascade of snow buries her.

An appended note:

> PARALLEL UNIVERSES A POSSIBILITY? AN
> INFINITE NUMBER OF BIG BANGS BANGING
> AWAY? OBJECT 13 FIRST TO CROSS FROM
> ANOTHER UNIVERSE? IN AN INFINITE NUMBER OF
> UNIVERSES, CAM AND DAPHNE ARE STILL ALIVE.
> HOW TO FIND THEM.HOW TO RECONSTITUTE
> THEIR LOST LIVES. NAH. DUCKS THE WHOLE
> DILEMMA OF TIME.

Why the theme of time? To add the appearance of *gravitas* to what otherwise would be little more than a Tom Clancy shit-kicker in the sci-fi mode? (Not that he would object to having Mr. Clancy's readership.) Or to exorcise his own demons about time and death, as the shrink he didn't go to might imply with his silence? Easier thought than done. Time could not be imagined as anything more than what it is.

From the onset, the novelist Leo O'Boyle faced a formidable problem in dealing novelistically with this most elemental of mediums, if that's what it was. Though a graduate of Harvard and thus admitted to the company of educated men and women, he believed in absolute time or, more accurately, Newtonian time or, more descriptively, universal time. That is to say, he believed that the instant it said one o'clock on the digital readout on the Cambridge Saving Bank building in Harvard Square (however theoretical that instant was), it was exactly the same instant on some pale pink planet circling a small sun in some distant nebulae and throughout the known and unknown universe. Though obviously not numerically the same time because other places, even on Earth, had their own afternoons. But the same instant of time. Because time was time was time. Time machines did not and could not exist. Nor was there any possibility of distorting time down black holes or worm holes or any other kind of holes. Dilation was a hoax.

Or was it? If he couldn't quite grasp the concept of space-time emotionally, if he couldn't feel it, he was smart enough to know that people such as Einstein, Poincaré, Heisenberg, Hawking and others were a lot smarter than he. But to him they were like the priests of another religion talking about another god, a god quite as inconceivable as his own truant deity. More than that, he knew that, without a whole lot of mind bending, he couldn't use what they had discovered. Or created.

And more than that, more than that—his mind stuttering just a bit, thinking about thinking—he agreed with Brooks-Denny that evolution was time's arrow, that over billions of years, the pulsing, expanding, swirling universe–with its innate swerve towards complexity–had created the elements, the molecules, the compounds that led to this thing inside his skull thinking about this thing inside his skull.

Questions kept interrupting. Had time evolved … over time? Was a second shorter or longer now than ten billion years ago? And if the speed of light is such a constant constant, how did the universe get so big in a microsecond after the Big Bang? Did light have to catch up?

Or, if time is so real, could you not, applying the logic of Zeno's Paradox, divide it down to shorter and shorter units? The agreed upon shortest natural time is one Planck Time or ten to minus forty four of a second, shorter by a relatively long time than the Zeptosecond which is ten to minus twenty-one or one sextillionth of a second. Is time, like space, infinitely divisible? Or, at some point, does time disappear? Leo could not stretch his mind that small, but he suspected that the present didn't exist, leaving nothing but the past and the future, neither of which existed because the past was past and the future hadn't arrived. (Even while musing parenthetically one Sunday morning that time had to have been because in what other medium had he just carefully shaved off the ginger bristles on his cheeks and chin? And if the future did not exist, why was he hurrying into respectable clothes to get the Reverend Chance to church on time?)

But even if you could objectively quantify it, as seems to have been done, how did you get to its essence? In *Ada*, Nabokov reels his hooked reader into murky depths for a disquisition on just that. "Maybe the only thing that hints at a sense of time is rhythm; not the recurrent beats of the rhythm but the gap between two such beats, the gray gap between black beats: the Tender Interval."

Leo reached in vain for the Tender Interval.

Leo ended where he started: Time itself was little more than a necessary fiction about which to think too much was to court madness.

Leo courted madness.

To the point that, the year before, in an attempt to deal with his obsession, he decided it was time to deny the existence of time. He reasoned that only space, objects, and motion existed, that time was an unproven, unprovable *a priori* concept and little more than a futile attempt to establish relations between and among these three basic entities. Utterly arbitrary. A human imposition. An artifact of intelligence. A way of ordering activity. A (shudder) social construct.

Thus did he spend a week in blissful denial, at least initially. Clocks of any kind represented little more than an agreed-upon convention. Born again into timelessness, he shrugged when Annabel asked him what he might want for dinner. Because dinner came at dinner time and he was above all that. Yes, he would put out the garbage for pickup, scheduled for the next morning, but only because garbage began to smell and attract rats, raccoons, and the like.

It didn't last long. He found to his chagrin that it was easier to deny the existence of God than the existence of time. He began to sense that if time didn't exist, neither did he. Except for the dazed and the clueless sprawled about the redbrick pavilion in the middle of the Square, everyone else lived in time the same way they breathed air. He couldn't pretend time didn't exist if Annabel needed a drive to the Divinity School for a nine o'clock meeting. Or feed the parking meter quarters for what amounted to buying time. And not just time, but timing, whether attempting a witticism or boiling an egg just right or making love. He might as well have pretended he was Superman, able to doff his street clothes in one of those disappearing phone booths and fly off to fight evil in its many forms.

He had returned to time as chronophobic as ever if not more so and inclined to waste more time thinking about time. Again the question: Was it circular or linear? How could it be both? That is, could time go in circles, be continuous but not exactly repetitious? Was time finite with a beginning, a middle, and an end, like a novel? No, time was absolute, as real as granite. And listen to this—grabbing his inner doubter by the lapels—estimates put the age of the universe at around thirteen billion years, give or take. But what's a year? A year is the time it takes the Earth, spinning on its tilted axis, to circle completely around the sun. But given the trillions of stars, suns, and other heavenly bodies, there must be many kinds of years, some longer, some shorter, some even erratic. The point being that to measure the duration of the universe from the instant it blossomed into being, it is necessary to use Newtonian time. Not only Newtonian or absolute time, but time as measured by the revolution of a smallish planet around a middling star that evolved long after the Big Bang banged. Absolute time absolutely proven.

At the same time, for novelistic purposes, Leo O'Boyle toyed with the idea of employing space-time, which would afford an elasticity to his narrative that a commitment to absolute time would have precluded. For this, he read and reread Hawking's *A Brief History of Time* before deciding that he would rely on the ignorance about relativity and space-time among his millions of potential readers if he resorted to black holes and the like with singularities down and through which, like Alice, his Object might plunge into another universe on its way back and forth … In time. Okay, it smacked of a cop-out. But it would go with the idea of Cam being transformed into a plasma or even into photons so he might hitch a ride with the Object back through time to the fateful moment on the glacier just in time to save Daphne from the avalanche.

Talk about weak.

He had written himself into a corner. In more ways than one.

Because, given his initial aspirations to high literary standards, the author wanted his novel to contribute to what, for want of a better term, he would call the literature of the unknown. Because he yearned for, if not greatness, then at least significance. He wanted his novel to be considered significant because he wanted to be considered significant or more significant than he was. But he no longer knew why he wanted more significance. Other than for the sake of a fading careerist SOT: In the wake of a successfully published significant novel, he might be asked by *Vanity Fair* or *Rolling Stone*, for instance, to do a piece on Cannes during the festival. He might get to hang out with George

Plimpton at a Red Sox game, even though baseball and especially the Red Sox made him want to gnaw his hands. In truth, the prospect of interesting, exotic, manageably dangerous assignments had begun to pall. Been there, done that. Partied with an Italian count in a terraced garden overlooking Lake Como—along with four hundred other guests. Shown around the White House gardens by Nancy Reagan—only twenty-five other guests on that occasion. Supped with the Knight of Glin at Glin Castle hard by the mouth of the Shannon. Trekked with Jesús in the Andes. Sipped on location the poor wine produced at Harvard's Villa I Tatti in the hills of Tuscany (and not all that impressed by Berenson's own collection). Swum, very briefly, in the midnight sun to the far north of Norway. Galloped sore-assed with local tribesmen on the steppes of central Asia.

What he really wanted, what he thought he really wanted, was something like what Brooks-Denny had. Some real literary friends instead of the losers that hung around with Ari. A couple of published novels. Being a kind of outsider/insider. Life as a long safari. Being able to claim halfway plausibly to need quinine water cut with gin for a lingering case of malaria picked up on the Zambezi. Even some of Alf's memories. That story he told about a dinner party with the Heaneys at a house in Cambridge. The dishes cleared, the coffee poured. Seamus in a lull saying, "Marie, give us a song." And Marie sang.

"I'll never forget it," said Alf. "It was a sound ancient and fresh, the ages come alive."

"What did she sing?"

"I don't remember. I wasn't listening to the words."

• • •

The reader of anthropology and her Fig Newtons were gone. The big clock said 1:43. He would be late. A ten-minute walk. A touch of normal anxiety about lateness, his mind already drifting to the school-room scene in *Ulysses*. One of Dedalus' students had a bag of fig rolls. Armstrong. Talking about Pyrrhus. Yeah, but how do you connect that to a researcher reading a journal of physical anthropology? Well, you give her a book about the Nabataeans to read. Why? An allusion to the Pyrrhic essence of their history, all history? Weak. Later.

He went back to the thing on the ice, to the storm, the glacier surge, the rescue. On a Post-it, L. B. started to write in block lettering until the notes turned into a first-draft narration he continued on a lined, five-by-eight notepad.

WHILE THEY ARE RECOVERING IN THE AFTERMATH OF THE STORM, A FULL BIRD COLONEL NAMED JACK FARLEY OR HARLEY OR MARLEY (NAME!) CHOPPERS IN WITH A LIEUTENANT IN TOW. THE COLONEL, WITH NO MENTION OF THE STORM (WHICH IS REMARKABLY LOCAL AND CAUSED BY THE OBJECT), CARRIES OUT A VERY CURSORY INSPECTION. (CONT.)

At a meeting in the large tent, he turns to Cam, "You were sent up here to carry out a mission and all you've done is make a mess as far as I can see. Explain this situation, sir."

"Mother Nature, sir," Cam says with unfeigned hostility. "Or the Object interacting with Mother Nature."

Piko pipes up, "Sir, with all due respect, we're lucky to be alive."

The colonel rounds on him. "Sergeant, when I want you to speak, I'll let you know."

"Excuse me, sir, you don't understand …"

"Sergeant, if you don't shut up I'll have you busted to …"

But he gags on the word as Cam's big left hand grabs the colonel by the front of his shirt and all but pulls him off his feet. When the lieutenant accompanying the colonel moves to intervene, Dash blocks him.

His face close to the sputtering face of the colonel, Cam hisses, "No one talks to these brave people like that. Bust? You're lucky I don't bust your face right now."

He releases the flustered officer.

The colonel, gaining composure, says, "You'll be hearing from me, McInally."

Cam looms over the man. "I'm really scared, Colonel. Why don't you go back to your comfortable desk and tell the brass you lick up to to send someone who's been briefed and who honors courage. You certainly don't."

When the colonel hesitates, Cam says to the lieutenant, "Get him out of here before I find a crevasse deep enough …"

The author leaned back. Not bad. Make rebuke more subtle. Not bad at all. Storm needs more explaining. He notes down:

> IF THE STORM, WHICH IS LOCAL, IS CAUSED BY THE OBJECT HOW? BUT WHY CAUSE A STORM IF IT NEEDS HELP FROM THE EARTHLINGS TO ESCAPE? TO SHOW THEM ITS POWER? OR IT TURNS OUT THERE WAS A HIGHLY LOCALIZED METEORLOGICAL IMPACT WHEN THE OBJECT DEPLOYED ALL BUT INVISIBLE SOLAR MAGNIFIERS IN THE ATMOSPHERE OVER THE IMMEDIATE AREA. THE OBJECT NEEDS THE FOCUSED RADIATION TO ACHIEVE A STEADY PLASMA STATE IN ORDER TO ESCAPE THE EARTH'S GRAVITATION.

Note to the note:

> ICE OBJECT INFORMS CAM DURING ONE OF THEIR INTERACTIONS THAT IT HAD A GRAVITATION-NEUTRALIZATION MALFUNCTION AND, UPON LANDING, DE-IONIZED TO SAVE ENERGY. THEN THE SNOW BUILT UP AND IT/THEY WENT INTO A DORMANT MODE AND REMAINED IN THAT STATE UNTIL THE AVALANCHE EXPOSED THEM ONCE MORE TO THE SUN'S RADIATION WITH WHICH THEY BEGAN TO RECHARGE THEIR ENERGY SUPPLIES BUT NOT ENOUGH TO ESCAPE.

The author resumed scanning what he had written before, another passage that started as scaffolding and was worked into a plausible first draft.

> After regrouping and another night of strange dreams, Cam decides to take Dash with him on a mission to

approach the Object as closely as possible on foot. Tina, who was with Cam in Desert Storm, wants to be part of the team. She convinces him that monitoring the Object is necessary. Cam agrees, but both she and Dash are to keep a safe distance as he approaches the target.

It's a clear, windy day, the sky a crystalline blue, the Object both visible and invisible by turn as they approach. Their plan: Get within a hundred meters, stop and assess. They cover the ground from the camp to the hundred meters from the Object in about an hour, stopping to take various measurements. These include assessments by the naked eye and through binoculars. Their instruments show nothing. Closer in, the reality of the thing is even more strange and illusive than from a distance. It is more ovoid than spherical, seemingly visible when it's all but invisible. And it gives off the distinct impression of something trapped.

About a hundred and fifty meters away, Dash is the first to falter. He stops suddenly and clutches his head. "Man, this is like some kind of LSD shit. I don't feel good." Cam, feeling a bit weird himself, looks to Tina. She's shaking her head. "I'm getting the same thing."

Cam senses it as well, but apparently less than the other two. He says, "Let's establish a post a few yards back, out of the range of whatever's happening. I'll continue as far as I can."

Which he does. Like the others, he begins to feel an effect on his thought processes. At the same time he is both clear-headed and confused. Something is happening inside his skull. Instinct tells him to retreat, but he plods on.

Then, within twenty-five meters of the Object, which he guesses is about five meters high when visible, he finds his own consciousness reprogrammed. Only in this case, it's more like another voice. No, not a voice, but thoughts running through a second mind in his mind. Inside his head, Cam forms the question, *What are you?*

There is an answering thought, distinct from his own: *We are what you would call a life form. We are from a nearby galaxy. Tell us what you think you are.*

• • •

The large clock read 1:58. L. B. O'Boyle collected his things. Reluctantly. Their last meeting at the Wursthaus began with Fritz bullying in German a waitress wearing a dirndl who smiled idiotically at him and read off the specials in Boston English. Then the same old same old and more of the same old, Ari officiously officiating unconsciously aping his father's management style—as described by Ari.

So why not skip it? Because he was Ari's crutch and Ari was his crutch in the loserly way their lives were unfolding. Because he and Ari went way back. Their capering continued a conspiracy of superiority they shared since rooming together in Winthrop House in their undergraduate days. They had conspired then not so much to achieve Cs and Bs as to rise above the driven, grade-obsessed over-achievers surrounding them. It was a pure superiority, one based on nothing but its own assumption. As such it was inviolable, unquestioned, at least by them. Nothing, except their disdain, was above their disdain. They failed with time to outgrow their juvenile posturing even when reality in its many guises slammed them up against the wall. They did not outgrow each other. They remained like Siamese twins joined at the ego. It was as though neither might quite exist without the bonding that, negative at best, toxic at worst, held them together as each other's alibi, disabler, default fallback. Neither could deny the other's validity without facing the possibility that he, too, was a delusional loser.

Such that, years later, they were still talking about how to make a million. Or ten million. If not overnight then painlessly. And not necessarily ethically. They pondered such ponderables as why two such sterling fellows as themselves, Harvard graduates, for Christ sake, worldly and traveled, could not do what (to judge from the stories on the business page and the magazines found in waiting rooms) very ordinary guys did every day—drop a line into the great roiling pot of American enterprise and come up with enough moola to warrant a couple of Brinks trucks. Speaking of which, they had considered robbing a bank and dismissed it; unless done exactly right, it involved high risk and low returns when they wanted it exactly the other way. Besides, they were in agreement with Oscar Wilde that crime was a form of vulgarity and vulgarity a form of crime, not that both were not fascinating in their way. So that banks, despite Mr. Sutton's irrefutable logic, were out.

They had the occasional flutter of a business idea. Organic condoms, L. B. suggested at one of their bouts when drink was being taken.

"They already have them," Ari sniffed. "Lambskins. It says right on the package."

"True. But are they appropriate for everyone? I mean, could a vegetarian, in good conscience, pull on a condom made from sheep gut or a pig gut and go at it?"

Ari nodded more affirmatively. "Come to think of it, wearing one of those things is equivalent to buggering a sheep."

"A dead sheep at that."

"Or a dead pig."

"Yeah, but we eat parts of dead sheep and dead pigs all the time. You can't get more intimate with something than eating it. I mean part of that part becomes part of you. Speaking of which, do condoms have to be Kosher? I mean, if you're observant?"

"I don't know. Depends on what you do with them. Don't ask me. I don't keep up with that stuff."

Which did not leave out considerations of condoms made of organic natural rubber from certified organic rubber trees. Lubricated with processed mucilage derived from, say, organically grown okra.

Their enthusiasm soon shriveled. Such an enterprise would entail the dreary real work at the heart of those stories about how Randy and Sue started with only three hundred dollars in her parents' garden shed making prosthetic devices for crippled pets and now have their corporate headquarters in Van Nuys, CA.

No. As they reminded each other, they had already put in their time. They had done their stint in the daily grind. Albeit it took some eloquence on the part of L. B. O'Boyle, his *nom de plume comme un écrivain voyage*, to convince people that flying all over the world to sample the food and fetes, museums, old castles, glorious operas, views to die for, etc., etc. could be considered a grind. Believe me, he would protest, when you are obliged, professionally, to appreciate things as you are as a travel writer, it can be a job of work. It can become a tiring blur of sensation from which you might seek release in a Jane Austen novel or a bit of decent porn. Seriously, very seriously, he proclaimed on one occasion, "I have been seated in the Tour D'Argent with, oh God, pieces of one of their numbered ducks on the plate in front of me with a crescent of intricate frou frou around the edge and more fine wine than I could drink when all I wanted, I swear, was to be sitting in Bartley's with a double cheddar burger medium rare, fries and a Diet fucking Coke."

So any kind of grind was out, which left them with some kind of scam. Not just any scam. Not for this pair of Harvard's finest. They needed something edifying, something to allude to in their Reunion Class Report, something they could be proud of. So nothing conspicuously tawdry. And something big, something far larger than was already in place inasmuch as Ari Krasnick was not averse to small contributions from certain suppliers of expensive gift items which was one reason his dad, Murray the Terrible, periodically threatened to fire him from the family firm, Cadeaux Noveaux—or Cads, as Ari called it.

Ari said he wanted out because it was his soul-destroying job to craft short, from-the-heart endearments, including snippets of up-market doggerel parading as verse. And nothing, he was wont to declare, absolutely nothing, was too blatant, too corny, too saccharine, too awful. He nearly got fired when his snarky brother, favored son Saul, (as described by Ari) noticed after the fact that a fourteen-line ditty Ari had concocted to go with a Miami real estate mogul's diamond bracelet to his wife on their twenty-fifth wedding anniversary spelled out, acrostically, FUCK YOU DARLING.

Ari maintained a small but lucrative sideline with select clients providing them a quality substance worthy of Fortnum & Mason he labeled Andes Ice. Hence characters like Fritz, his apparent source, who scarcely had a last name much less a fixed address.

For his part, Leopoldo, as one smitten Italian lady called him, though not in a position to extract lucre directly, was not above letting it be known, on location, so to speak, that he was indeed the L. B. O'Boyle, the travel writer, so that a word with the maître 'd, with the manager or assistant manager, with the director, the concierge, or the owner would get him, in return for mere intimations of a favorable notice, all manner of things gratis, a kind of complimentary reciprocity.

A touch of corruption around the edges. Which he could live with comfortably enough. But this *Caper* thing … A lot of sound and no fury signifying less than nothing. A fantasy world. Nothing wrong with that except … He remembered how at the last get-together he had retreated inwardly, like letting his face relax after a spell of obligatory smiling.

So quit, for Christ sake. Call in healthy. Or go and face it.

Part.

Leopold Bloom O'Boyle descended the wide steps of Widener Library and turned left to walk in the direction of University Hall. Erected in 1815 or thereabouts. The handsomest building at Harvard. Bulfinch. Its gray stones were granite quarried in North Chelmsford at Fletchers. Mom's great grand-dad, Paddy Cassidy from Connemara by way of Liverpool, had worked in the pit along with imported Italians who knew the trade. Possible that his great great grandfather had handled these very stones. Cassidy. Hopalong. Neal. Different spelling. Her maiden name, she told him, was from the Gaelic *Caiside*. It meant clever or curly-haired. Some curly hair had come through, but that thanks to Dad.

Out in front of the building, arrayed around the statue of John Harvard, modeled on an archetypal tall WASP, a type specimen, though he may have been a short, skinny wimp, was a collection of East Asians having their pictures taken. No eye contact. In a world of their own.

He continued across what was called The Old Yard, which it was, Massachusetts Hall having been opened in 1718, later used by Washington to quarter troops, and then a freshman dorm—upstairs— where Brooks-Denny misspent his freshman year.

How had Heaney put it? *A spirit moved. John Harvard walked the yard.* The villanelle for the celebration of Harvard's three hundred and fifty years of existence. The march of *ar, ar, al, ar,* even the silent *l* more of an *r.* Scan that, English majors. Iambs? Hexameter? Should learn that stuff. A regular gait. Lower case *y* for Yard. Deliberate? Great difference between yard and Yard. Junk yard. Barn yard. Harvard Yard.

Then stopping and remembering. Seamus or someone had given a short exegesis. There had been cow pens near Harvard at the time. John Harvard's father had been a farmer, cattleman, butcher in Stratford. Heaney's dad had been a cattle dealer in County Derry. Meaning?

Meaning it is Seamus Heaney not Stephen Dedalus who is the real bullock-befriending bard! Not bad, Leo, not bad. But how to work that into any *Redux*? Just mention it. Let the allusion do the alluding. *Oxen of the Sun* and all that. If nothing else, a tidbit to take to Brooks-Denny. Who would pass it on to the befriender of bullocks with due attribution. And to … ah, Dad, where are you?

Through the gate next to the Johnston Gate. Named gates. Who Johnston? Wade the traffic of the avenue, statue of the seated Charles Sumner to his right, all but marooned in the flow. Radical, anti-slavery Republican, caned in the Senate by a stalwart of the Old South. Who remembered Sumner? Who remembered anybody?

Then the gray wooden bulk of the First Church, Unitarian, Old Burying Grounds to the right.

He walked up along the railing of the graveyard and stopped to muse. A grave place is a graveyard. The final yard. Times stops here, at least for those patiently moldering underground. Locale for the Hades scene? Could have his Blooming character wander among the eroding markers recalling the Dublin Leopold's speculation at Glasnevin: *More room if they buried them standing.* Yes, but you couldn't say that so-and-so was laid to rest. Why else line the coffin with comfortable quilting? No big sleep standing up. On your feet for eternity. Wondering what it looks like a few feet down. All honeycombed the ground must be: oblong cells. Plain old dust after long enough. Humus. Remains. What's left behind. *Remains.* Potent word. Implies a soul, an essence that is gone elsewhere.

Humus. The night before in the kitchen with Annabel. A subtle agitation in the air in the wake of the positive reading. Yom Kippur looming in early October and Annabel crafting a sermon about the holiest day in the Jewish calendar that went beyond the usual ecumenical noises about tolerance for and appreciation of other traditions. Annabel running a few passages of her working draft by him, something she did on occasion. Sitting in their late-fifties kitchen, the counters some kind of greenish linoleum edged with metallic trim, ditto the matching table with metal legs that came with plastic-covered chairs starting to split down the seats. Leo, hand around his first whiskey of the night, a smallish Early Times and soda, no ice, listened with interest as the aroma of a chicken-thighs-and-dried-limes concoction baking in the new second-hand stove wafted around them.

Annabel had to hand, lying on the table before her, several printed-out pages already marked up. She read,

> "Is it not significant that Jews regard their day of atonement as the holiest day of the year? So holy that in Leviticus, marital relations are proscribed, meaning sex of any kind."

She glanced up. "The next part comes as an aside."
"Okay."

> "Let us remember that the ancient Hebrews proscribed any sexual activity outside of marriage."

"Good luck."
A grimace. She read,

> "Yom Kippur is also marked by fasting, temple attendance, and prayer. Above all, this holiest of days requires that the observant dwell on their transgressions against others and against their God. Atonement, at-one-ment, points to reconciliation. Why, among the many aspects of Judaism, is it regarded as so important?"

She asked, "What do you think so far?"
"The chicken smells great."
"Mom sent me the recipe. It's Persian."
"A nice way of saying Iranian."
"Yes."
"Your homilectical effort sounds very good as a matter of fact. Perhaps a bit too rhetorical. Why start with a question? Say it out flat. It is significant that the Jews etc. ..."
Nodding and making the change. "Better."
She continued to read.

> "Likewise in the Catholic Church. Confession involves the confessing to a priest one's sins followed by contrition, penance and absolution as long as the penitent promises to

go forth and sin no more. Confession is a sacrament on a par with Baptism, Confirmation, Matrimony, and Extreme Unction, which are the last rites. Should you die after making a good confession, that is, are truly contrite, you will ascend directly to Heaven though your life before had been a long catalogue of mortal sins."

Another glance up.

"A touch of caricature there. A whiff of anti-popishness. You make absolution sound easy. But that's a quibble. Where are you going with all this?"

"Patience." She smiled and took off the wire-rimmed glasses she used for reading and writing. She wore jeans and a leotard top of pale blue that went with her blue eyes and her honey blond hair pinned up leaving wisps around her translucent ears and exposing the cords of her neck. An adjustable exhaust fan whirred in a window. She rose to check the oven.

"We're having rice. Do you want to make a salad?"

"The limes are green. Or once were."

"Why are you looking at me like that?"

"I think I'm in love with you."

"You just want me for my brain."

"No doubt. It's what makes you sexy. Anyway, keep going. I'll follow." She sat down. "Okay. Here goes."

"So what are we missing? Alone in the Judeo-Christian tradition, mainstream Protestantism, aside from a tepid general confession and absolution, does not recognize and mark with significance the avowal, atonement, and forgiveness of sins. Nor does the poetry of the *Lord's Prayer*, old form, 'Forgive us our trespasses as we forgive those who trespass against us,' really cover it."

"Meaning?"

"Meaning that the Congregational Church should set an example, something between the severity of Yom Kippur and the too-frequent laundering of sins that Confession facilitates. I would and will suggest a liturgical body be formed to look into this discrepancy."

"Okay."

"I need a better word than *discrepancy*."

"*Lapse*?"

"Ummm. A lapse implies something lapsed from."

"True. How about *lack. Dearth. Failing. Lacuna. Absence.*" He got up to refresh his drink.

"How many is that?"

"Just my second. And I'm keeping it small. A small whiskey. Whiskey, from the Irish, *uisce beatha*, water of life."

"Your life."

"I think we've said this before."

"We have."

Then, mostly as a diversion, "The 'laundering of sins' sounds a bit prejudicial. But that's okay."

"I know." She continued.

> "What confession and atonement signify in their symbolism and substance is the recognition of faults, transgression, and injuries done to others and to God, however that entity is configured. Perhaps more important are the subsequent acts of repentance, reparation, and forgiveness. Because we are all sinners, are we not?"

A glance up.

"I qualify. Keep going."

> "Most beneficial is that atonement and confession, far from an attempt to keep us in our places, is a path to humility. Humility gets a bad rap in this age of overly esteemed self-esteem. It gets confused with humiliation. And I would argue that there are times when even humiliation is a fitting response to certain trespasses. But the question arises, what exactly is humility? It is both a corrective to our behavior and a perspective on who we are in terms of our loved ones, our neighbors, and the rest of the world. Not to mention the God about whom we all have our questions."

She paused, distracted, listening to herself. "I need to check the chicken."

"Hey, that's not bad. I like the overly-esteemed self-esteem. Where do you take it from there?"

"I'm playing around with the words. Humility. Human. Humus. And that we are all mortal."

"Don't forget hummus."

Sigh of exasperation. "Leopoldy ..."

She brought out the chicken in the wedding present casserole dish, rice on the side, a pitcher of cucumber water. She served him and he poured the water.

"I am only playing with your word play." Glancing at her. "Please go on." He inhaled the aroma of the chicken. "This really smells good." He could sense a fragility in her mood. She usually liked him to spar with her over her sermons. It was a kind of editing.

He said, "I suppose the question in this enlightened age is ... does sin still exist?"

"People still lie, cheat, steal, kill, and commit adultery."

"Is adultery still a sin?"

"Yes. Why do you ask?" Serious.

"I don't know. I find it reassuring."

"In what way?" Skeptical.

"Hmmm ... this chicken is amazing. Put it this way, adultery sounds more interesting as a sin. I mean more interesting than going to a therapist who will be empathetic and supportive in helping you to understand why you're banging the hot little receptionist who gives such good blow jobs." He sniffed the whiskey fumes rising in his nearly empty glass, their beguiling false promise.

Watching him. A touch suspicious. Well, there are lots of new sins."

"Such as?"

"Misogyny. Racism ..."

"Why is racism a sin?"

"Because ..." Thinking. "It's a form of cruelty. And a whole lot more."

"Yeah, okay, but what if someone is a sincere racist? Or a sincere sexist? Or a sincere ..."

"Liar?"

"Yeah. Maybe it's natural to sin. Might there not be a category in your theology called natural sin? Gluttony, maybe? Eating a lot when food is plentiful once had survival value. Fattening up for lean times. It contributed to fitness, to reproductive success. It was a virtue, not a sin. At least in Darwinian terms. By the way, this chicken is really something."

"You sound like Alf."

"Yeah, but it makes sense. Maybe killing is a natural sin. When you think about it. Human history is one long saga of killing, one war after another. It was the cauldron of our evolution …"

"More Alf …"

"Yeah, maybe." This wasn't helping.

"The Hebrew states 'Thou shall not murder.' The word is *retzach*. There's a difference between killing and murder."

Murder.

"Ah …"

At which point they lapsed into silence. *Murder.* The word hung there. Nothing said, the blue eyes blurring. Annabel standing. "I'm not hungry."

"But you should eat something. In your condition."

Condition. Later, pouring himself an infinitesimally small third whiskey and soda, he wondered if voicing that word had been in the nature of a commitment.

Later still, it unnerved him not a little to realize that Annabel had not yet decided. She sat at her desk in their sad living room, her back to him. He said, "Do you want to talk about it?"

She didn't turn around. She just shook her head.

• • •

Condition. The word still resonated as he glanced at the haphazard ranks of weathered stones and what they signified. He turned from the yard of graves. He felt a lift remembering his father's essay on the *Scylla and Charybdis* episode. His words still lived. Or would, if they published it. Frank's words, his thoughts, would become the thoughts in the minds of people still alive or yet to live. That was the magic of writing. Writing that got read.

Standing there, the living coming and going by him on the sidewalk, he found himself on the Hubbard Glacier again. He leaned against the railing, took out the small notebook and began to write, heading it, DETAILS OF AVALANCHE TRAGEDY. He wrote in script, trying to keep it legible:

> The snow covering Daphne is not twenty feet deep, more like ten. But enough to kill her. Cam has a good idea of where she is as he frantically claws at the snow like a large fleece-coated gopher digging for its life. Mike and Myra pull up and realize instantly what has happened. Mike smartly tears the webbing from one of his poles and probes gently through the snow just off to the sides while Myra helps Cam scoop away the cold deadly stuff.
>
> When they have an opening about four feet down, Mike pokes around carefully with the pole, his frown discouraging. Then he brightens. "Off to the left. Here, let me open a breathing hole."
>
> They resume digging, trying not to clog her oxygen life line, as they uncover her by degrees, first an ungloved hand reaching up as though in supplication, then her head and face. She is no longer breathing. In a swoon of hope and dread, Cam attempts mouth-to-mouth resuscitation, his kiss of life bringing back all those other kisses. Again and again and again. She does not respond. She is gone.

In all caps he added:

> HAVE TO SHOW NOT TELL. MORE VISUAL DETAIL. THE TOUCH OF HER COLD LIPS. TIME HERE IS ABSOLUTELY OF THE ESSENCE. NEED CAM TO KEEP CHECKING HIS WATCH AS THEY DIG FOR DAPHNE. SUSPENSE. ALSO TENSE. SIMPLE PAST?

Walking on, wondering why he was going where he was going, Leo O'Boyle scratched again the scab Ari Krasnick had become in his mind. The man so wanted to be a hustler and was something of a natural con man but, like L. B., could never quite get a handle on his own genius, could not break out of a cocoon not so much of failure as of non-success. His own sourness had pickled and shriveled him. Ari not only hated his father, he hated himself, weaving a net of loathing for his own tribe—or most of it. His friend Fritz did not discourage this. One night after a particularly nasty tirade about the low-life Jews he had grown up with on the north shore—they were all getting into their cups—Fritz said to him, "If you feel that way, Ari, maybe you should get your nose fixed."

"Nose fixed, hell, I'm thinking of a foreskin restoration."

Perhaps it was the rough circumstances of coming of age in Revere that had him practicing a kind of pre-emptive anti-Semitism, beating others to the punch, all too ready to believe that he would be maligned for being a Jew.

The immediate and drearily repeated object of Ari's Semitic anti-Semitism was his father Murray on whom he was wholly dependent. "My father, my fucking father," he declared on another occasion when not enough drink had been taken, "is the kind of a-hole Jew that makes the world hate Jews ..." Moving L. B. O'Boyle, a Joycean and part-time Nabokovian, that is, if not philo-Semitic like his dad had been, then at least anti-anti-Semitic, to defend a man he scarcely knew, saying, "If your father is an a-hole, it's because he's an a-hole, not because he's a Jew."

"You know from Jews?"

"I know from a-holes."

Ari could bitch with the best of them, especially about his family, which amounted to little more than variations on a repeated theme. Typically: "I was the one who got into Harvard. I was the one with all As and National Honor Society. Lot of good it did me. You know why? Because Saul is the one that sucks up. Saul the one that went to night school so he could help out in the office. I mean sucking up to big Murray with all the subtlety of a vacuum cleaner, you know, one of those big industrial jobs. And Saul goes to Temple. And he's married to *zaftig* Miriam, who practically fondles Murray's cock and throws around Yiddish she doesn't know how to pronounce and keeps Kosher even for the dog, and of course they named their first born Murray."

The few times Leo had met the family—at the graduation from Harvard, at the wedding of Ari to his second wife, and at a lawn party celebrating mother Judy's seventieth birthday party—he found they bore no resemblance to Ari's caricature of them. They were engaging, knowledgeable, more than cordial, asking intelligent questions about his travel writing as though finding in Leo and what he did a larger world, in which, like a lot of people, they were interested. He could even sense Murray the Terrible wanting to take him aside and chat about Ari, the problem child.

Tall, consciously elegant, the problem child dressed like he was modeling clothes for *GQ*. He didn't smile very often and had a habit of pulling his fingers over his chin as though he had a beard. He wore his black-haired short ponytail with authority. Head lowered, working his lips in a certain way, he could look like a lowlife. Or, lips prim, Mediterranean eyes sighting along the barrel of his formidable nose, prominent forehead wrinkling under uplifted brows, he could disdain with the best.

His air of preoccupation was not feigned as he had much to be preoccupied about. Well launched into his third problematic marriage and with several progeny from the two previous unions, his branch of the family tree had become something of a thicket, a genealogist's nightmare. He indulged in serial polygamy mostly, Leo suspected, to spite his dad, who more than once told his son he didn't have to marry every woman he fucked. Ari liked to say he was taking a swim in the gene pool. Ari needed the job he had penning mushy prose and worse verse for the family's gift-giving service because he had expensive tastes in clothes, food, and cars, not to mention the stuff he took up his nose, not to mention ex-wives. Notes in prose added only five percent to the total cost of the gift, according to the glossy brochure. A note in original verse by their in-house poet cost only an additional seven percent. Ari not only had to write this stuff, he had to vet it with the customer. "Do you realize how many functional illiterates end up being my editor?" was his habitual *cri de coeur*.

What made him visibly cringe was the full page in the Cadeaux Noveaux brochure devoted to Ariel Charles Krasnick as the "in-house" poet complete with an authorial photograph (head and shoulders, fist thoughtfully under chin), and with mention of his Harvard degree and his published book of verse and a sample from it that didn't make a whole lot of sense but which didn't contain the words *shit, fuck,* or *cunt.*

Ari, like Leo, was not so much a failed writer as a writer who had yet to succeed or, for that matter, really try. As a poet, he liked to say he was infected by Philip Larkin, Charles Bukowski, and Allen

Ginsburg, influences that showed in his work but didn't quite add up to a voice. Thus had verbal collages consisting of Ginsburg's excrementalism, Bukowski's quotidian alcoholism, and Larkin's arch pessimism been gathered into a thin volume titled *Down* and published by a now-defunct small press nearly a decade before to less than scant notice.

The odd and yet not-so-surprising thing, Leo thought and rethought, though not in the SOT mode, was Ari's potential as a poet. One of his efforts, a portrait of his grandfather, a coin dealer who had fled Amsterdam when the smell of Nazism could no longer be ignored, began:

> Rembrandt should have painted Jakob.
> I mean the eyes
> That saw the darkness rising.
> I mean the lips
> That spoke the ages.

Then it slackened off into narration as his efforts tended to do. Either narration or a reach for significance that ended in bathos.

He showed them to Leo, but was as leery of any affirmation as of any criticism meant to help. Interestingly enough, he took praise and suggestions from Alf, who had his number, who suggested that he get in touch with some local poets he knew. "You need feedback," he told him more than once. It was Alf who assured Ari, "Low self-esteem is often a sign of intelligence," getting a rueful laugh amounting to acknowledgement. Because Ari did not want to join any club that would have him. Which might have explained his failed marriages.

Not that Ari didn't claim a license, as he saw it, to expatiate grandly on other poets living and dead. "Come on, Leo, Heaney is little more than a very large frog in a very small pond croaking convincingly about the verities of a rural life that no longer exists."

Which brought them closer to a rift at the time than Ari may have realized. If L. B. let it slide it was because Ari tended to denigrate indiscriminately. "Frost is a wannabe hick." Or, "Why does anyone bother to read Elizabeth Bishop?" It occurred to Leo more than once that his friend considered himself too good to have role models in the field he had chosen but seldom bothered to visit.

The real sore spot between them was Annabel. She kept politely cordial around Ari, which made him bluster more than usual. Ari sensed and resented her coolness. "She's an anti-Semite, isn't she?" he challenged Leo one night.

"Like you?"

"You know what I mean."

"I doubt it. Maybe she dislikes you for yourself." Amending. "Okay, dislikes is a bit strong."

"No, she doesn't dislike me, she tolerates me. That's worse. It's ..."

"Intolerable."

Privately, Annabel opined that Ari, to escape the realities of his job and his marital messes, lived the life of a fantasist. When Leo in mild agreement ventured that Ari was his dark side, she snorted that Ari was, on the contrary, his weak side. Then, with a little shove. "I'm your dark side."

"You have very nice sides."

What made Ari's anti-Semitism more theoretical than real was its lack of content. He said nothing about Jews in general, nothing about their influence in the financial system, the media, the government, the bagel industry. Nothing about their influence on culture high and low. Nor did he find Jews lurking everywhere except, oddly enough, in Hitler's entourage.

"Oh, come on, who was their best general other than Rommel? Von Manstein. Yeah, born Lewinsky. And Emil Maurice. Jewish and bi-sexual. Hitler's chauffeur and probable lover. They shared Hitler's niece Geli Raubal until Hitler had her murdered. Maurice helped found the SS. And Reinhard Heydrich. The guy's got *bar mitzvah* written all over him. Himmler. Look at him closely. And Eichman, especially Eichman."

Fritz egging him on with silence.

Leo had snorted his disagreement. "I doubt if any of them were Jews other than Maurice and maybe Heydrich." Then, echoing Hannah Arendt, "The rest of them were ordinary monsters, ordinary as dirt. But why does it matter? A Hindu Nazi is still a Nazi. I mean, really, you're saying that the Holocaust was planned and carried out with the help of Jews."

Ari, pursing his lips, eyes boring into nothingness, then relenting. "I know it sounds crazy, but sometimes it's the only sense I can make of the thing."

"That's insane."

"Yeah, but no more insane than what happened. Nothing is more insane."

Leo wondered if Ari was testing him. Would he bite? Would he bait? As far as Leo would go was to admit that he sometimes got "Jewed out" after too much of the subject. But he also got "Irished out" or "blacked out" or "gayed out." "I seek repose," he said on one occasion, "in being a member of that endangered species—just another human being."

For Ari the state of Israel was a whole different matter. "Those are my kind of Jews," he would say when the subject came up. He day-dreamed, at times out loud, of how he planned to move to Israel and do something with his hands. Exactly what he would do with his hands he never said except to mention once how he would help harvest pomegranates on a kibbutz surrounded by lithe young Israeli women and packing an Uzi.

He got nearly a year's worth of nourishing reveries from a contact in the family business who knew a guy with a shaven skull named Lev or Zev who had been a tank commander in the IDF and who had a friend with a contact in the Mossad who was reportedly looking to recruit an American who had business ties to South Korea. Ari would allude to these possibilities and then turn unnecessarily evasive, saying, in a tone indicating that he wasn't at liberty to divulge more, "Things are developing." Or letting slip, as though accidentally, that the new encryption program on his computer was NSA grade.

Ari as the Citizen in his Bloomsday *Redux*? Nice twist. And parallels didn't have to be parallel. Maybe be better as Buck Mulligan the way, more than once, he had mocked Leo in the Buck's words: "Your absurd name, a canvassing Dublin Jew."

So enthusiasm did not mark Leo's step on this decidedly warming, betimes sunny September day when he paused in the courtyard of the Charles Hotel and peered up at the redbrick walls of windows rising around him. There were abandoned mills in Lowell that had more class. This could have been a shoe factory in Lawrence. Libido for the ugly. But people paid for it.

A mental note to himself: Time is situational, that is, not absolute in a day-to-day situation. Normal people only worry about time in context. Need to think about this.

• • •

L. B. O'Boyle the novelist entered the restaurant with its long bar to the left and tables off to the other side. When it was the Ocean Club it was said you could buy more than drinks in the place.

"You're late," Ari greeted him as he joined The Committee seated around a table, Fritz rubbing his face and Graham looking dignified. They already had drinks and things to nibble on.

"So what?" Leo spoke testily and sat down as though on something nasty. He glanced at the menu and found a new leaf had turned over inside of himself. He wasn't hungry. Or, more to the point, he didn't feel like eating for the sake of eating. Nor, *mirabile dictu*, did he feel like drinking. "A glass of water," he said to the hovering waiter and returned the quiet stares of his co-conspirators. He even resisted explanations such as: I'm not hungry. I have writing to do. Annabel is pregnant.

He was shuffling through his opened satchel to retrieve the folder with *The Caper* materials, fingering the three-ring binder of *Ice Object*, aching to dig into that again, when there she was, the apparition from The Tasty, wafting back into his existence with two others hanging back, whom he figured for graduate students.

Which might not have mattered except that, no sooner seated, she stood up and came over, exclaiming, "Gray Ham, that is you, yes?" She was standing so close to Leo that, bending just a bit, he could have, with a small stretch, nuzzled her splendid haunches.

They exchanged how-have-you-been's and good-to-see-you's. Then Gray Ham Crocker, a man of manners, asked if she would like to sit down with them for a moment, already moving a chair between himself and Fritz so that she could do just that. Then introductions, "Silvia, this is Fritz, Ari, and Leo. Leo's a writer."

"A writer!" Big eyes bigger. Perching on the edge of the chair just across. "Yes, I see you this morning in the little bistro ..."

"The Tasty ..."

"Yes ..." Big smile. "Yes, The Tasty. What does that mean?"

"In Italian ...? *Delicioso*, maybe?"

"That is Spanish, I think." Marvelous laugh. Throaty voice. Her jacket unbelted. "*Gustoso*, better, I think."

"Yes," as though he knew. "*Il Gustoso* ..."

"You were talking about ... *salsiccia* and how to make it from ... *capacolla* ..."

"Hot dogs ... ?"

"Yes, hot dogs. I love the words." Then, "I am thinking someone reminds me of you."

Those eyes. Those marvelous pools of ...

"Where are you from in Italy?"

"Napoli."

Naah pol lee. The music of a name.

"Ah, yes, Napoli."

"You know Napoli?"

"I was there once. To do an article on *Beat the Devil.*"

"*Beat the Devil*?"

"A movie."

"You wrote the movie?"

"No, I was writing about the movie. Mostly about where it was made. Ravello."

"Yes, Ravello. So ... *bella.* You like the view?"

An inner groan. "The Amalfi Coast. Superb. I mean what's not ... ?"

At which point the well-married husband, on the verge of an erotoleptic seizure, groans inwardly again and the ex, lapsed, closet Catholic recalls that putting yourself knowingly in the occasion of sin is a sin in and of itself. But what about what might be called the pre-occasion of sin? Or what if you tripped over sin in the darkness or were, for all intents and purposes, trapped in close proximity to sin? (Ari murmuring in his ear, "Man, are you ever scoring.")

And is not beauty truth and truth beauty? Meaning there is virtue in beauty. How can beauty be a sin if we applaud loudly those who possess it or create it? If we praise beauty wherever we find it. If we travel, travail, the world in search of beauty. Ironically, in this secular age, we wander as though lost in the world's great houses of worship in our worship of beauty. We pilgrimage through museums fighting the fatigue of sensory overload and the feeling of inadequacy to the aesthetic consequence all around us. Or we sit through some teeth-grinding modernist sound effects to get to the delights of Brahms or Ravel. Or, enduring heat, mosquitoes, and other birders, we crane upwards into the forest canopy of the Pantanal happy to catch a glimpse, a fleeting glimpse, of a Hyacinth Macaw.

Her breasts were perfect, the exact right balance of slope and lift. And, no doubt to match her large dark eyes, she would have pertly nippled, large, dark aureoles between which he would nose like a setter on the trail down to where her sublime symmetry converged in her moist flower.

Where the bee sucks ...

He breathed deeply.

"Yes, there used to be a restaurant called The Amalfi near Symphony Hall in Boston. It may still be there."

"You like *sinfonie?*"

"Symphonies ... ?"

"Yes, symphonies. I adore symphonies. My favorite is Beethoven. *La Pastorale,* no? Like summer, no?"

"All of the above."

"Above? Now, now I know. Yes. *Galata Morente.* Gray Ham, *comment dit en anglais ... Le Gaulois Mourant?*"

"*The Dying Gaul.*"

Too close, too close. Inwardly, barely, he resisted a gallantry bordering on the operatic. Instead, with a rue that got a titter he wasn't looking for, he said, "I am only wounded."

A sudden roil of impossibilities. The two tickets to Amman, first class, hotel rooms, meals. Which bloomed into a fantasy of gracious, moonlit dinners. Of conversations about art, love, and destiny. Of endless, lubricious sex in Italian. Of life as a saga out of the F. Scott Fitzgerald playbook from which they would never return. And so real it had the travel writer paling under his blush. Or was that just the gloss he had to give what at best would be an afternoon fling, or several after-noons of furtive love-making until the poetry seeped out of it? Or blossomed into something that would destroy what he had?

In a mental note in the margins, he wondered if she could be the Calypso of his *Bloomiad.* Was he to become her sex slave in the Cambridge equivalent of some remote Aegean island, leashed to a rack of joy and forced to perform for her in her role as an insatiable, whip-wielding dominatrix in high boots with stiletto heels and very little else? Or would she be Circe, changing him into a grunting pig, bringing out his inner swine?

A decision loomed. Hang with the guys. Drink a bit too much. Get her number. Call on the sly. Set something up. Slide back into those pre-Annabel days. Touch and go. Catch and release. Caught and released. He had never been good at it.

To give himself time to think with what was left of his scattered wits, the craven, the craving Gaul Leopold Bloom O'Boyle resorted to the question and answer format. "So tell me, Silvia," a touch of specious, self-protective avuncularity gilding his *Silvia*, "what brings you to Cambridge?"

"I am studying."

"At Harvard?"

"Yes, at the School of Design."

Which, for a micro-second, he misheard as "School of Desire." Recovering, "At the building by Corbusier … ?"

"Yes, Le Corbusier." A slight correction. "The Carpenter Center. You know so much."

Looks like two grand pianos copulating, one faculty wag had remarked at its completion. But Leo didn't want to go into the merits of overlapping planes and cantilevered perspectives and put a damper on a situation he should not be encouraging.

Coup de foudre. Coup de folie more like it as he was still rationalizing, his stream of consciousness turbulent in the shallows. Rationalizing and theorizing. Some internal Q & A:

> Would James Joyce, *pace* Aquinas, say she fulfilled the three requirements of beauty, that is, unity, coherence, and radiance?
>
> Yes.
>
> Was she therefore a work of art and worthy of adulation?
>
> Yes.
>
> Did she not embody the essence and ideal of perfection, a *Venus Aphrodite* come to life?
>
> She did.
>
> Did she conform to O'Boyle's Law, which states that the volume of aesthetic pleasure from whatever source— music, movies, art, literature, another human being, etc.— must exceed the pressure of faculative effort on the part of the recipient by a ratio of at least two to one unless the faculative effort itself adds to or constitutes the quantum of pleasure?

She did.

In what instances might the pleasure of the faculative effort be all?

In the merging with the object of beauty through an act of physical love.

Why?

Because in such an instance the simultaneity of giving and taking pleasure through a distinctive form of faculative effort culminates in a transient and transcendent obliteration of both subject and object.

Is this theoretically sound?

It is.

Why?

Because the young Stephen Dedalus in *Portrait* states that a work of art ought to induce an "aesthetic stasis," an "ideal pity" or an "ideal terror." It is a stasis that, called forth and prolonged, is resolved by the "rhythm of beauty."

And does the act of love incarnate this "rhythm of beauty?"

It does.

Not to mention the culmination thereof.

Exactly.

Another deep breath.

Oddly enough, it helped to dim Leo O'Boyle's dazzlement for him to realize that Silvia was so consciously self-designed, was practically a self-wrought *objet d'art*. It both magnified and diminished her. The heels alone. Her ass on a pedestal. She might be labeled, catalogued, exhibited. Look but don't touch. There are genuine copies available in the gift shop.

Thus muttering to himself, he let himself be distracted into something like ordinary consciousness. Thus, the audible questioning and answering didn't reach the pivotal query: Where are you staying? Translating into, where can I come and all but consume you? Didn't as well because, for all the keenness of his lust, for all his exquisite yearning, Leo knew that while he might palpate her youth first hand, he could not claim it for himself. He would still be *when* he was. She could scarcely claim it for herself. Given time, she would age, might put on weight, grow a little moustache, wear black clothes, and spend time in church praying for somebody's soul.

It was then, un-beckoned, the last lines of a Heaney poem came to him, something about a dream of jealousy and how neither his verses nor prudence could heal his love's wounded stare.

And something else. Dimly, distantly, someone beyond himself and Annabel was now involved in what he did.

The place, the surrounding, the quizzical faces came back into focus. This *Caper* stuff, a pathetic fantasy. Perhaps he should have stood and made a little speech: Friends, my beautiful wife may be pregnant. If she is and we decide … Then I need a whole new life. I need …

Of course he didn't. Instead, with a sense of exhilarating if shaky resolve, he put *The Caper* folder back into his satchel and stood up from the chair. "It has been nice meeting you, Silvia. Good luck at the School of Design. And, gentlemen, I must go as I have matters I must attend to."

Ari was saying something like, "Hey, Leo," but Leo was already up and making for the door, striding purposefully but to where he was not certain.

At the restaurant door, Ari caught up to him. "Hey, what the fuck is going on?"

Hesitating, but with grim determination, Leo said, "I've got things at home to take care of."

"You and Annabel?"

"Me and Annabel. Me and my mother. Me and the rest of the world."

"Don't let that babe scare you off."

"That babe doesn't scare me off." The intonation saying more than the words.

"You need to let yourself live a little."

"This isn't living, Ari. This isn't even playing house."

He rootled in his satchel and took out the *Caper* file. "Here. This is yours."

In that moment, the long spell linking Ari Krasnick and L. B. O'Boyle broke.

Ari nodded, said, "I get it." They regarded each other intently for a minute. Then Ari turned and went back to his friends.

Was he running from life? Leo asked himself. More timid than virtuous? Was Ari right the night he said, "You know what you are, O'Boyle. You're a sexual coward." Worse than that thought Leopold B. O'Boyle at the time, soberness still on the distant side of a looming, near terminal hangover. I am an emotional coward. You impale yourself impaling others. Those smiling lips and other tender labia are far more than portals of pleasure.

But, also, there was the momentum of memory holding the memory and momentum of love. Leo called Annabel the day after the evening he met her at The Plough and Stars. He proposed dinner. She countered with coffee. No easy bedding here. Their initial intercourse was to be verbal. Which darkened his understanding, weakened his will, and left him with a strong inclination to fall in love. He was back in high school, but more patient with his hands. Verbal until a good night kiss turned into a good morning kiss after a nocturne of passionate horizontality. Love like a revelation. Love making him a willing prisoner. Love making him respectful such that he wanted to brag, but didn't, that he had gotten seminal with a seminarian, not to mention a real blonde.

There was a visit to Montgomery. Aging, ailing, saturnine Clyde Floyd Chance, a Confederate flag pin in his lapel and a command of Civil War history at the ready. Not shy with the good bourbon as he told his daughter's Yankee boyfriend about the Irish Brigade and the appalling losses they suffered during the Peninsula Campaign and at Gettysburg. "Yes sir, until they rioted in New York when the blacks began to take their jobs." Clyde had visited Memorial Hall and spent time looking at the plaques. His planter voice sounding oddly Brooklynese, he said, "You know there were graduates of Harvard fought and died for the South. But Harvard doesn't honor them."

Clyde voiced puzzlement as to his daughter's conversion to Congregationalism. "If that's what it toyns out to be. Not that I object. Better than Baptist, anyway."

He drove them around the town. The cemetery where Hank Williams lay buried. The Dexter Avenue Baptist Church where Martin Luther King preached. Cloverdale and the house on Felder Avenue where F. Scott came acourtin' Zelda Sayre.

They had an Episcopal wedding at St. John's—high, but not quite as atmospheric as the Church of the Advent in Boston—with a half-frocked Catholic priest co-officiating to keep Mom happy. Which it didn't. New Orleans honeymoon. Curiously drab. Necropolis best part. Crypts above ground. Put a bell in with the corpse in the old days. Just in case.

Now, approaching Eliot Square, on the rebound, Leo O'Boyle was in love with his wife all over again. So why was he tempted? Only human. Not that Leo O'Boyle had ever taken sex casually. In that he was akin to the Protestants who, like Updike's characters, took seriously their sins of the flesh. They didn't just get laid; their extra-curricular exertions had to have meaning, *gravitas*, consequence. They were Puritanical even in their dissipations. In a like manner, there was for Leo no such thing as safe sex, especially not with Annabel Chance. He still suffered from and indulged spells of infatuation that had him buying champagne and roses as he thought about her shoulders and the way her neck, when she lifted her chin, made him want to press his mouth against her exposed throat and start in about the beauty of her clavicles and end up repeating himself about "jumping her bones."

But in truth, her face, her eyes provocative in their demure cast, was the most beautiful part of her nakedness, as noted by Amis *père*, not only because she had an alluring grace of form and movement, but because that smile, that swoon of eyes, those parted lips were what he wanted to possess in the throes of their lovemaking.

It went beyond the delights of the bed. She had done for him what so many women had done for so many men: she had made him a better person. She had effected an upgrade that, leaving him essentially intact, went beyond improved verbal hygiene and the consciousness that sloppy thinking made for sloppy language. With her silences she had silenced him into being sober or more sober than he had been before. Her independence and diligence in scholarly work—her book-cluttered desk in an alcove off the kitchen—made him rise from the semi-coma of watching television to confront the literary responsibilities begun in moments of heady dreams. She gave his life a coherence he didn't know he lacked until he had it. All of which left him in a state of gratitude and at something of a disadvantage in their contest of wills.

Was it Brooks-Denny who said that romantic love is an artifact of evolution, part of the gratuity, like the huge and encumbering antlers of the extinct Irish elk? In other words, love transcended evolution being an involuntary act of the imagination and the heart that can magnify the attraction of an objective reality—another person—to the point of relative madness.

He looked at his watch with something of a twinge. 2:49. It wasn't just his time anymore. It was their time. And right then it was Annabel's time. He pictured her driving their 1981 two-door maroon Volvo on Storrow Drive, up through the Fens, down Brookline Avenue. He could picture her driving, in her own time and space, window open, blond hair untidy in the breeze, her face naked. Her three o'clock appointment.

It haunted. Like Bloom's periodic distress thinking about Molly's four o'clock tryst with Boylan at Eccles Street. Only a test. Yet it would confirm the presence of another, an alien, a trespasser, a usurper. Catching himself. Not alien, you fool. Your own flesh and blood. Then a snag of a thought for his *U. Redux:* Annabel would be a kind of pre-Mrs. Purefoy. Get details of today's visit. The birthing scene looms. Maybe. Maybe not. Does fictionalizing the living render them more real or less real? Annabel in the world so much more convincing than any impersonation he might achieve with words. How even to describe his own awareness of this other consciousness cheek by cheek with his, looking out at the world, conscious of him being conscious of her.

Their time. Juggling her life like anyone else. Serious about all the God stuff but lately in a different way. More about Christ in the world. Annabel reconciling Darwinism and Christianity. Claiming Christ to be a significant event in the evolution of the species in that what he symbolized and articulated was love for others, even your enemies, to the point of self-sacrifice. Human history populated with Christ figures before and after his advent and crucifixion.

His usual SOTing demurrals: What about the world wars? What about the mass murders of Hitler and Stalin?

There, said the Reverend Annabel Chance, is where faith comes in. We must keep striving to follow the example of Christ. To give up is to give in, to despair, and in that way lies nihilism, nothingness.

He kept falling in love with her, this woman who might rescue Christ from the scrap yard of history. Because she was his Annabel Lee in their thralldom by the sea; his Annabel, emphasis on *bel* in moments of contestation; his Annabella Baby in moments of entreaty; and what now, he mused about telling her—his Annabelly?

Back in the explanatory phase of their courtship, she told him, "I was named for an aunt who was named by her mother who was much taken with the poetry of Edgar Allen Poe."

"But not Annabel Lee Chance?"

Smile. "No chance. We're distant kin of Big Jim Folsom. He was the governor back in the bad old days, and my daddy thought the middle handle would come in handy if I ever went into politics."

"Lee sounds southern enough."

"But Robert E. wasn't kin."

"You chose divinity school instead."

"I did."

"Why?"

"I like to delve into ultimate things."

"I'm not very ultimate."

"More than you may think."

Then a sigh. Larkin's "Breadfruit." The widowed mum. Now nippers. Or at least a nipper.

It struck Leo O'Boyle anew, because he didn't always know what he was thinking about, that he had to decide. Even if it was Annabel's decision. Ultimately. *Hoc est enim …* she might say in smiling mockery of his remnant Catholicism. And she was the one with a job, with a career, with a profession, with, dare he say it, a calling. She fussed over her sermons, which she called homilies—interpreting and commenting on nothing less than the word of God with a capital *G*. Administering, her House of God being a real house, after all, with walls, roof, windows, wiring, plumbing, and leaky basement. What color to repaint the vestibule? The dark blue faction. The light green faction. The shaky pipes on the aging Odell organ. Making the thin ends meet. She had to love people even when she didn't like them. Mrs. Hazel Splinder, the other side of ninety, kept alive with modern medicines and her own healthy venom, suspicious of "new people," a few of them slightly more or less than white. "Why, Mrs. Splinder," the Reverend Chance would gush, dripping enough syrup to turn the old girl diabetic, "they are the children of God." The Reverend Chance visited the sick and comforted the dying and the consequently bereaved.

For this she donned a black or dark gray shirt with an intimation of a clerical collar; a pleated, knee-length skirt of black or dark gray sometimes matching or contrasting with her upper garment; dark nylons and sensible and buckled shoes of a dark hue; all topped with a charcoal jacket only slightly mannish in style. A small cross of old silver hung around her neck on a silver chain. To go with it, not entirely as a jest, her Ellbee had bought her a lacy black bra and matching thong, items she accepted with a smile and put aside for other occasions. Truth be told, he found her sexy beyond words, beyond any minimal bikini, in her ministerial garb. "My Protestant priestess," he would coo; "My Reformation moll."

Unlike her husband, Annabel could not call it in. She had to be there. Which made a major detour, called life, something to think about, to pray about, to talk about. Was it to be or was it not to be? No suitable euphemism had arisen for the word *abortion*, however much it cried out for one. Perhaps *disengender* might suffice for the verb. Ugly enough. *Disengenderation* for the noun. Uglier still. Or *disconception*. It didn't matter. The word and the flesh and blood reality it referred to was on the table, an option, a possibility. She, whose body it was, went back and forth with a calm anguish he could not assuage with words.

Leopold Bloom O'Boyle half the time feared that Annabel Folsom Chance would say yes and half the time that she would say no.

No meant yes to a procedure—awful word, that—in which any new bud of life would be nipped ... in the bud. Meaning that their life would not change appreciably except, perhaps, for the acquiring of a compensatory pet, more than likely a dog, on which to lavish the care and love that would have been bestowed on the child they didn't have. The status quo, in other words. But the status quo—his mind now musing over a familiar track, another SOT—is an illusion. If nothing else they would grow older. They would cobble together a down payment on a modest house in Arlington or move into 68 Strand Street when ... Annabel might hoist herself onto the lower rungs at the Divinity School. Perhaps she would have an affair with a post-doctoral fellow writing a book using post-modern analytics to discourse about culture-based translations of the New Testament. Then they would get divorced and join the growing ranks of the maritally challenged, drifting around trying to connect, trying to find what they thought they had. L. B. O'Boyle would be free to write the novels he was almost writing. Free.

Yes meant yes. The bud of life would sprout around its umbilicus, head, limbs, pre-natal thumb-sucking, and delicate, such delicate eye pods. And a name. Leopold Bloom O'Boyle, Jr. wouldn't make the cut. Perhaps Eleanor Chance O'Boyle, after a favorite aunt if a girl. Another human being. Another universe of becoming.

He stood on Eliot Street on Brattle Square. Eliot Square. Eliot House. Eliot translates as Jehovah is God. Greek form of Elijah. The crumpled throwaway in *Ulysses*. Elijah is coming. Work that in somehow.

Musing over names a lot lately. Annabel just last week surfacing from her books to inform him that *El* means God in Hebrew. Find it in a lot of names. "Your friend Ari, for instance. From Ari*el*, lion of God. *El*izabeth is from *El*isheva, My God is an oath. Immanu*el*. God is with us. Micha*el*, who is like God. Dani*el*, God is my judge. Gabri*el*, man of God. Isra*el*, God prevails."

A display of sorts, for him. He didn't damp things at all by asking, "What about *El*vis?'

She laughed one of her short happy laughs. "You silly! *El*vis is one of our pagan gods."

• • •

A flow of one-way traffic came along Brattle Street. *Ice Object 13* pulsed within him again. He needed a place to create. Back to Lamont? Too far. Sleepy. Algiers Cafe right here. Front of the Brattle Theatre in the old days. He went up the stairs. Copper espresso machine for show. Lattice. Decorative hookahs. Caffeinated air. Lunch crowd clearing out. Turkish coffee and a side of pita bread and hummus. Small table. Enough.

From his satchel, he extracted the binder and the chaos that was *Ice Object 13*. He knew what he had to do. Leave the world. Inhabit the alternative world you are creating. Live in it. Breathe it. Touch it. But you also had to stand outside of it and deliberate deliberately. Back story. Their life together. Ranch. Starting a family. Relatives. Keep that vague. In the future. And an ending.

Thinking: So Cam McInally succeeds, after several hitches, in having the Object nuked. He flies home to their ranch in Idaho. He comes up the drive. And there she is, as beautiful, as real as before. About as real as Tinker Bell.

And why, right now, was TSE's "Little Gidding" nagging at him, quoting itself to him?

> And the end of all our exploring
> Will be to arrive where we started
> And know the place for the first time.

Not all that chaotic. Opening chapter and several others in decent shape. He flipped ahead to the part where members of the team have to approach the Object on foot from their base camp because the electronics on any motorized vehicle get frazzled within two kilometers.

Noted in margin:

HOW REALISTIC TO HAVE YOUR CONSCIOUS-NESS REPROGRAMMED?

Hell, nearly happened a short while ago with the Silvia creature. Ready to immolate himself and Annabel and company.

He picked up where he had left off in Widener with the interior dialogue and the Object's question to Cam: *Tell us what you think you are.*

Cam answering: Good question. Nobody's quite sure. We are also a life form. How long have you been here?

Ten Thousand and more of your revolutions. What you call years.

What about your own years?

We don't live in a temporal sphere. We are atemporal. Sometimes, but sometimes is the wrong word, we revert to multi-temporality.

How do you do that?

We exist in a continuous present.

Continuous present?

Sorry, but your communications are not adequate for correct conceptualization.

How can I help you?

We need a pulse of very high energy.

I don't think we have that technology.

Of course you do.

I don't …

The best way would be a nuclear weapon.

Just drop it on you?

Yes. A medium sized-tactical weapon would do. The one-kiloton W33 would be ideal.

That will take some doing.

Understood.

Cam's mind raced aware that this other side of his mind knew what he was thinking.

I have a favor to ask in return.

Yes.

I have a friend. My wife.

Yes, *Homo sapiens* still practice sexual reproduction.

She died in a skiing accident. Can you bring her back?

Pause. What remains?

Ashes.

Need DNA for hydrocarbon entities such as human life.

You can't manipulate time?

Unusual pause. That is not entirely possible even when freed from this temporal matrix. DNA simpler. Do you have any?

I have a swatch of her hair. Perhaps blood samples.

That will do.

What about her memories, memory?

I'm not sure what you mean?

Did she have a computer?

Yes.

And you have it?

Yes.

Things that she wrote?

Yes.

Her music? Her movies? Her writing? Her books? Photographs?

Yes.

Her voice?

Yes.

It will be a reconstructed consciousness. You'll have to help her build on it.

She'll just appear?

Yes.

The author paused to pen a block-lettered note in the margin:

TOO DIRECT. DAPHNE CAN'T JUST REAPPEAR. NEED OBJECT TO EXPLAIN THAT IT WILL PROVIDE THE INFORMATION ABOUT THE PROCESSES NECESSARY FOR THE CLONING TO BE DONE. CLONING AND RAPID GROWTH TO HAVE DAPHNE BROUGHT BACK AS AN ADULT.

How will we explain … ?

Your problem. We can't perform miracles.

By our standards … But when?

As soon as we are back in a continuous plasma state.

A waiter brought his order to the small table at which he sat. Leo thanked him. He tore off a piece of the pliable bread and used it to scoop up a portion of hummus. He put it decorously in his mouth and chewed. Ummm. Hummus. Ground-up chick peas, lemon, sesame oil, salt and pepper. High in protein. That pita bread on the road to Amman. Cooked on heated stone surface. Could have lived on that.

On the next page more scaffolding.

So how best to convince the military to use a small nuke on the thing? And where are the points of suspense? Though the Ice Object exists in an atemporal sphere on the time-bound Earth, they are running low on energy which means they are running out of time. How much time? Another ten thousand years? No, make urgent. Clock ticking.

Reverse here. Usually how to keep the military from blowing the thing up, the usual Hollywood stereotype about gung-ho stupid military brass. Tension: How to get the Colonel to call in an FB-111 with, say, a one-kiloton device. Appeal to his humanity? But these, this thing, is not human. Better to let it expire. The colonel telling him what the brass want: This thing has high-tech military significance.

How to convince the colonel, the generals, that Ice Object 13 poses a threat to the whole world? Can't you enter his brain? he asks the alternative thought center. Not large enough. Could cause irreparable damage. REDONE. CHECK.

Rooting around, L. B. O'Boyle found that he had already written the solution. Reminding himself again that you have to remember what you've done. It was on a sheet of notepad and taped to the page.

Cam suggests in his thoughts to the thing: Why don't you appear to Colonel Farley in a dream?

A note to the note:

COL. FARLEY IS CAM'S IMMEDIATE COMMANDING OFFICER ON THIS MISSION. INTRODUCE EARLIER. ESTABLISH TENSION BETWEEN THEM.

Pausing for another sip of coffee and dip of hummus. Might ask for the recipe.

Then, continuing mental dialogue with Object:

And do what?
Tell him that you are here to establish a space colony for your home planet.
We don't have a home planet.
Make one up.
Why would we do that?
As an excuse for resources. Your home planet has a shortage of, say, carbon.
But we don't need carbon.
I know, I know.
What will we call our planet?

I don't know. Ur … Urpenis. Christ, man …

We are not a man.

Right. If you want to get nuked, you have to convince the military that you are a dire threat to the planet. If you were to deplete all the carbon on our planet, life as we know it would cease.

I see. Exercise deception.

Exactly.

The writer paused to appraise his writing. Not bad. *Fiction 101*: If you don't like what you're writing, no one else will. If you like it too much you are probably deluding yourself. Like any author or would-be author, L. B. O'Boyle took pleasure in imagining the pleasure, perhaps even a touch of admiration tinged with awe and a tad of envy, that his friends and family would take in what he was creating. Annabel, of course, who didn't quite take his travel writing seriously. Alf, a good editor and critic. Liam Walsh and a few others in the travel business. Ari, who might make his compliments sound like a sneer. Stratis, perhaps? Not Mom, who thought books a waste of time. And now someone else, someone more prospective than actual, someone hovering. Dad? Possibly. The man did persist.

Then thoughts about Annabel at Brigham and Women's. Waiting room. Ten more minutes. Larkin's "The Building" in his head of a sudden: *And more rooms yet, each one further off/And harder to return from …*

But, Philip, people leave hospital with mended bodies, with new life …

Just as bad …

Musing resumed. Okay, can't be that simple. Colonel has a vivid dream. Calls up Pentagon. Area cleared. FB-111 roars in. Detonation. Too simple. Then what?

No, colonel dies that day of an apparent cerebral thrombosis. Medevac chopper comes in to get body. Top secret autopsy. Forensic medical people stymied. Never seen anything like it. General shows up. Press getting nosy. Need to expand. Sketching:

In near-blinding sun coming off the surrounding ice and snow, the colonel stalks right up to the thing. (FIRST

THE SCENE IN WHICH COL. IMPLIES THAT CAM &
CO. ARE A BUNCH OF PUSSIES.) They watch amazed as
he gets within twenty-five feet of the alarmingly pulsating
Object. The colonel stops. He clutches at his head, bends
over as if to vomit, and then starts to stagger back. He is
still in the danger zone when he falls face down in the
snow. Cam, risking his own life and feeling an intense
whirring in his head, reaches the colonel and drags him
back to the group. The man has no pulse, no breath, no eye
flutter. He is dead.

NOTE: NEED TO FLESH OUT SCENE JUST
PREVIOUS. CAM TRIES TO PERSUADE COL. FROM
APPROACHING TOO CLOSE. THE COL., HIS
COURAGE QUESTIONED, WAVES CAM ASIDE AS
THOUGH TO SAY, I'LL SHOW YOU.

A coffee buzz going, his muse hovering and then sitting lightly on
his lap and whispering in his ear. L. B. O'Boyle went into a veritable
furor scribendi. He wrote:

Cam contacts his extraterrestrial contact. What
happened?

Came too close. Overload maybe. We were going to fix
it, but not worth it.

While Cam is dialoguing with the Object, a chopper
lands near the base camp. Two-star Air Force General Matt
Burle climbs down and walks directly to where Cam and
his crew are gathered around the body of the colonel. A
large man with fierce eyes and a face going just a bit jowly,
the general motions the others away and turns on Cam.

"Tell me what's going on here, McInally."

"I'll tell you as much as I can."

"You'll tell me what you know."

Cam has to restrain himself. "General, let me remind
you that I am no longer a member of the armed forces."

"Meaning?"

"Meaning I can tell you to go …" He breaks off. "It will
help, General, if you keep your tone civilian with me."

"Okay, okay. But I know we've got a situation here. Tell me what happened to Colonel Farley?"

"He approached too closely. Against my express advice." (BACK FILL ON THIS ... DESCRIBE HIS ATTEMPT TO TALK THE COL. OUT OF APPROACHING TOO CLOSELY.)

The general nods. "Let's move back. Let's get to the tent. I could use a cup of coffee."

While a couple of crew from the chopper secure the colonel's body to a stretcher, Cam and the general make the trek back to the operations tent and settle themselves in chairs. Piko brings them mugs of coffee from the makeshift canteen.

Cam takes a second measure of the man in front of him. He plays out his cards slowly and deliberately.

"The Object is an extraterrestrial."

"How do you know?"

"It's been in contact with me."

"How?"

"Mental telepathy."

"You're shitting me."

Cam sighs. "Look at the initial report, General. [REFER TO EARLIER] None of our units have been able to get within a hundred meters without becoming violently ill. Even in space-worthy hazmat gear. It's done without radiation or any other measurable emanation."

"But they have gotten in touch with you?"

"Unless I'm hallucinating."

"Could be. What do they, it, say?"

Cam McInally pauses. This is the tricky part. His hunch tells him to tell the general everything. His common sense tells him to edit. He starts slowly: "It tells me it's been here ten thousand years. Since the last ice age."

"And you believe them ... it?"

"Yes. And, for your information, it is probably monitoring this conversation."

"So how come it picked you? Why not the colonel or some other member of your team?"

"I apparently have the right brain chemistry."

"How do I know you're not just making all of this up?"

"You don't. I could contact it and ask it to get in touch with you."

"Is that what you did for the colonel?"

"No. He just walked up to it on his own authority."

"So it's dangerous."

"I'd say it is very dangerous. But not deliberately so."

"What do you recommend?"

"I think we should nuke the thing, vaporize it."

"You're suggesting that we destroy the first verifiable extraterrestrial object in the history of the world?"

"Yes."

"Why? If it's been here ten thousand years and harmed no one except, maybe, an Air Force colonel, why suddenly get rid of it? You're not making sense, McInally. Think of what it could teach us. I'm not just talking about some new military gadgets."

"Yes, sir. But that's what it wants us to do."

"Destroy it?"

"It won't destroy it. It wants to get back to interstellar space. It apparently does that in some kind of plasma form. It doesn't have the energy … because of a malfunction having to do with the glacier. Anyway, a small nuke would give it just what it needs in terms of energy."

The general is dubious. He paces about. Then he says, "You say it can read our thoughts?"

"Mine, anyway."

"What about mine?"

"What are you suggesting?"

"A test."

"Really?"

Leo inserted an all-caps note:

(DOES CAM HAVE TO BE RELATIVELY CLOSE TO COMMUNICATE WITH THE OBJECT? IF SO THEY WALK BACK WITHIN RANGE. ATMOSPHERICS

HERE. THEY STAND ABOUT THE LENGTH OF A
FOOTBALL FIELD FROM THE THING. THEY HAVE
TO TALK LOUDLY BECAUSE OF THE WIND.)

"Easy enough. You get in contact. I'm right here. I have a specific thought. They read it and tell you. You tell me."

"We can try."

Cam closes his eyes. He summons the thoughts. Nothing. Then, there it is, like another consciousness in his mind.

"I know what you want. If we do this, will it make any difference?"

"Maybe a lot of difference. I need someone like the general to believe me."

To the general, Cam says, "You ready?"

"Ready."

NOTE: SHOULD TYPOGRAPHY CHANGE FOR
THIS EXCHANGE?

The general's thought comes as words to himself. This is so much bullshit.

"This is so much bullshit."

"Jesus!" The general is aghast.

I don't believe this.

"I don't believe this."

The general's mouth hangs open.

Four thousand three hundred and twenty.

"Four thousand three hundred and twenty."

Orange. Black. Burgundy.

"Orange. Black. Burgundy."

It must be some kind of trick. Hypnosis maybe. I don't feel that well.

"It must be some kind of trick. Hypnosis maybe. I don't feel that well."

We should cease for now, Cam thinks to the other thought center in his head.

Switching off. Good luck.

"You okay, General?"

"Jesus Christ, man, what … It's real."

"I think so."

"No … tricks. No hypnosis."

"Even if I could hypnotize you, I couldn't read your thoughts. Or have you believe I had read them."

The novelist paused to wipe the hummus bowl with a last piece of pita bread. Could put Algiers Cafe in *Redux*. His Bloom sips coffee instead of Burgundy. His Bloom muses about Ireland instead of Israel. What had Dr. Kiersey told Alf in that Dublin medical's voice? "Ireland. It's a disease. There's nothing there."

He scribbled a long note:

> Possible development: In exchange for technical information about some of the world's problems and perhaps just a bit of technology of military value, the general, as a member of a special committee, agrees to nuke the Object. Cam is the go-between. The question becomes, what are the priorities in solving the world's problems? Overpopulation is on the list. Easy, use a pathogen on as much of the population as you want to eliminate. Or, more slowly and "humanely," pay mothers after two or three kids to get their tubes tied. All kinds of stuff like this. Removing carbon from the atmosphere? Use solar-powered extractors in desert areas. Bury the collected carbon on-site. Future of life. Etc. Drags out. Committee breaks promises. Cam agonizes. And does what? Arranges a visit by the committee. Object makes several of them deathly ill. Recovered, they decide finally to nuke the thing.

Thinking, not good enough. Thinking, the solution to any significant problem in a novel cannot be too simple or too easy.

The watch that had been his dad's read 3:26. His phobia lurked again, shadowy now, a mocking imp reminding him how foolish he had been and would be again if he forgot.

Forgot what?

His thoughts turned To Annabel. Did she have to get into a johnny and ride the stirrups? Amazing how personal doctors get. They see parts of you that you will never see. Especially surgeons. You have lovely kidneys, Mrs. Smith.

Or is it just a urine sample and wait in the waiting room? Should have gone with her. Offered to. She shook her head. "Why don't you write instead?"

Which surprised him, made him love her. She seldom said anything regarding his attempts at imaginative literature. She might say, "Either write the thing or don't write the thing. Do it or forget it." Another time, referring to *Ice Object 13*: "In what way, Poldy dear, is it more than an adventure yarn starring some character modeled on implausible action heroes out of movies based on comic book characters created to appeal to infantile minds? Or as a projection of what you would like to be?"

To which he had replied with as much dignity as he could muster under the circumstances (early evening, well passed his whisky limit, aching for a long-forsaken cigarette, too fuzzed to read never mind write, the near death of watching television looming), "The Object in fact is a device for another perspective or perspectives on the human race or, to be grand about it, the human condition."

"Such as?"

"Well, for instance, the Object regards us the way we might regard what we find when we turn over a rotted log or what we might find in a petri dish kept warm and moist too long."

"That's not a bad start." Thinking, her lips pursing. "Unless the Object is like a researcher, one from outer space. Or a travel writer."

Ah! Was that it?

"In a way. But I haven't established why it's there."

He couldn't tell whether she was trying to discourage him or egg him on. Either way, he rose from their bed in the early hours of the next day and sat at the ThinkPad thinking, typing in a few bits and pieces. What would a highly advanced extraterrestrial think of the Earth and its alpha species? Why would it care?

Now, pondering more caffeination, he rooted around for the notes he had about the purposes of the thing. Because everything had to have a purpose. Somewhere in folders within the binder. Why was the Object come to earth? Or was it Earth as a geographical entity? What had it been doing? More than travel reporting, surely. Interstellar exploration? Space tourists from an advanced system somewhere?

A different note came to light. It took him time to unravel his scrawl.

> How much background on Daphne? Her parents. Karen
> and Karl? What about Cam's antecedents? Is Cam trying
> to prove something to an absent father? Or does he stay
> a pure hero? How to make the novel more than a verbal
> cartoon?

How to make the novel Cam/Deke is not going to write more than a verbal cartoon? *The Mystery of Hacienda don Carlos. Mystery? Curse* better.

Then a memory floating up. A cup of coffee with Alf in The Tasty, up against the wall. Alf remembering. "I found out something that your dad would have loved to know."

"I'm listening."

"It's entirely possible if not likely that Eamon de Valera had *Converso* antecedents."

"*Converso?*"

"A secret Jew."

"Right! In Spain, the Inquisition. Before and after the expulsion. That's amazing! One of modern Ireland's founding fathers was a Jew! I love it. But I don't know about Dad. He'd be conflicted. He was a Michael Collins man. He said more than once that it was a black day in Irish history when de Valera went to the German legation to sign the book of condolences after Hitler shot himself. But I wonder if Joyce knew it? Maybe he guessed. Molly was partly Spanish, Jewish ..."

"Molly mentions the novelist Valera in her soliloquy."

"I wonder ..."

Might work that into the plot. *The Curse of Hacienda don Carlos de Valera.* Bo O'Malley uncovers a blood libel against Don Carlos who was and wasn't a *Converso.* There were betrayals. Deadly feuds. Bo slowly and painfully unravels it all. He gets the deed to the ranch. He wins the beautiful Esmeralda. With a mate and territory, he sets the stage for his progenitive future.

A verbal cartoon. And why would Cam need to write novels? He has a life.

Getting back to the cold reality of his own novel, Leo found, under the heading ICE OBJECT PLOTTING/DIALOGUE, a decipherable scrawl reading:

How does Cam and the thing on the side of the glacier and inside his head get the military to use a nuke to free it? A public relations campaign? Does Cam spill his truth to General Burle? The thing has promised to resurrect my wife if I help it get free. No bearing. Military caught between threat and opportunity. More mental dialogue between Cam and Object:

We want something in exchange.

What is that?

We need a weapon or the basis of research leading to a weapon that will make us secure no matter what.

That is impossible.

Why?

Because your systems are made to be hacked as you call it. The Chinese and the Russians will steal any secret we give you almost before you get it.

Then tell us how to protect the secrets you give us.

This is not easy. It would be like you trying to teach some primitive tribe that is just learning to knap stones how to program a computer.

If you do not help us, why should we help you?

Because we are working with other elements of our KIND to induce a solar flare that would provide the energy we need to transform and go.

Meaning the destruction of the Earth?

More than likely. That is of no consequence.

How can you say that?

Your life form is too basic to make a difference. You would not hesitate to dispose of something infested with maggots.

The differences are that radical?

Beyond your imagining.

He noted in the margin:

SUN FLARE THREAT NOT PLAUSIBLE. IF OBJECT CAN ORGANIZE SUCH A MASSIVE DISRUPTION ON THE SUN, IT CAN SURELY GET ITSELF OFF THE GLACIER.

Another typed note labeled PHILOSOPHIZING (INTERIOR DIALOGUE WITH OBJECT)

Are there many other life forms in the universe?
Yes. There are organized forces in the universe far greater than you can imagine.
Are you among the highest?
We are surviving.
So Darwinism still pertains?
Evolution planned, inadvertent, or both still pertains.

The author musing as to where to fit these fragments into the flow of the story. Or cut them. Especially:

Do you believe in God?
By God you mean an all-encompassing power of creation that created the universe as it is known?
Yes.
Some do. Some don't. It is not knowable.
Some? Are you individuals or are you one big …?
Collective?
Yes.
Both. There is no sharp distinction. We divide and cohere, depending.
On circumstances?
On many things.
Do you reproduce?
Only in the sense that we evolve.

A pause, jotting down an idea:

Cam is tempted by an offer to be ionized and join the Object. You would be something of a pet, it tells him. The equivalent of a pet grasshopper, though the disparity is really too large for you to grasp. Would it mean I would

never die, Cam asks. Yes. But you would have to evolve.
Also, Object tells Cam they are like tourists only they also
conduct research and collect data.

Of a sudden, Leo O'Boyle, letting his mind wander, found himself
un-mused. Gone. She was probably up in Maine dallying with Stephen
King or on the North Shore sitting on Updike's lap and stroking his
imagination with Barthian insights. A moment of doubt. So why not
quit this novel stuff? Keep to travel writing. Those kind of books sell. *My
Year in Dublin*. Lots of notes. Probably get a contract. Or a memoir of
survival. *Chronicles of a Chronic Chronophobe*. His muse would return.
He could feel it.

A spasm of remorse about walking away from Ari and Ari's dreams.
More like Ari's nightmares. He'd call him later. Father and son thing
again. Frank X. and Joyce did not have enough father. Ari had too much
father. Never made the break. My own just about right. Dad working
through his dreams. Visiting them on his son. The Harvard thing easy
enough. Not so easy the heavy stuff about life and literature. Came a bit
too early. My name. Then the stark question as though voiced by his
father: What kind of a father will you make, Leopold?

The author looked at his watch. The seconds hand ticked along
sweeping upwards. No sneering imp this time but a distinct and odd
pang of unease, a chronological anxiety, but one at a remove, one not
of this sphere. It was—he realized with an inner smile—the imaginary
time of his novel that needed shaping. And in that realm he was the God
of time. He was God, period. If only, in his omnipotence, he could come
up with an ending, an ending with the promise of another beginning.

• • •

Godlike L. B. O'Boyle collected his things preparatory to paying
his check and walking in the direction of the Museum of Comparative
Zoology, his wits scattering into random thought. The MCZ was
founded in 1859, the same year as the publication of *The Origin of
Species* and one year before the outbreak of the Civil War. Curious term,
Civil War, wars by definition being as uncivil as you can get. But orga-
nized, relentless killing is how our intelligence evolved, according to
Alf. The light has dark origins.

Thus musing, he pointed his steps across the business end of Brattle Street to the front of Billings & Stover Apothecary. Then a curving, one-story flow of shops—Baak Gallery, Cahaly's, Calliope, Brattle Square Florist. Should he get flowers for Annabel for tonight? Whatever they decide? To let be or not let be. Flowers for weddings and funerals so why not pregnancies and abortions? But they hadn't decided. He hadn't decided. And flowers are a message. Brine's Sporting Goods. Warburton's Bakery & Cafe. Shades of Henry James. Should have called it Lord Warburton's Tea Shop. Bertucci's Pizzeria. Across the street Dickson Hardware. Just upstairs the Harvard Square Business Association. Domain of Sassie Brooks-Denny. MayFair. OktoberFest. Umpapa band. Putting up wreaths and Christmas lights over the major thoroughfares. Palmer Street. Back end of the Coop. Harvard insignia on everything. Going like hotcakes. Cardullo's again. Nini's Corner. Should have just gone up Church Street. Navigationally challenged.

Across the kiosk and through the dazed and the clueless he strode to a rack of payphones. Fishing out the Elms of Cambridge number and a quarter. Didn't really need to call. Making the commitment helped somehow. Yes, this is Leo O'Boyle, Mrs. O'Boyle's son. I would like to stop by for a visit this afternoon … say five. Of course, Mr. O'Boyle. We'll tell Mrs. O'Boyle. We're sure she'll be glad to see you.

Well, maybe. Mom. Fading. Every life does end.

Leo paused and contemplated again Dmitri's *Omphalos*.

Omphalos the stud farm for ladies in need of impregnation that Buck Mulligan was going to start on that island … Lamprey, no, Lambay, just north of Dublin. Lord Talbot de Malahide its holder. Alf had a riff going on it for a short novel. Ladies escorted over in a special ferry. Discretion assured. Serviced left, right, and center by the indefatigable Buck. Spillover handled by select friends of certifiable pedigree. Satisfaction guaranteed and the fee modest, considering the blood lines involved. Great sport with various characters, with angry, impotent husbands and with denunciations from pulpits of all persuasions. All going swimmingly until disaster strikes: Buck Mulligan falls in love. Did Oliver St. John—pronounced SinGin—Gogarty ever marry? Dad would have known.

Cross with the light. Into the Old Yard between Lehman Hall and Wadsworth House. Who Lehman? Who Wadsworth? The latter wooden, ancient. Behind Weld and Grays Hall. Who Weld? Who Grays? Angling across the New Yard. Did anything else matter if he was writing? Because this small world radiated now with a benign glow. Yes, you are welcome, arriving students. Don't waste your Harvard years. Or if you do, waste them memorably. Memories, in the end, will be all you'll have.

He stopped on the path and moved aside in the sway of a startling idea: Was it possible that instead of identifying with his larger-than-life hero Cam McInally, he yearned, like the Object in his novel, to escape his predicament, to escape into the light, to be blasted into timelessness? He walked on musing.

He stopped again and took out his Moleskine notebook. He jotted down his recent thought about escaping into timelessness. Then another thought:

> PIKO GOES MISSING DURING A FOGGY, SWIRLING
> STORM AT NIGHT WHILE OUT GETTING SNOW
> FOR COOKING AND CLEANING. HE FORGOT TO
> TAKE HIS LOCATOR ALONG. HAD HE GOTTEN
> TOO CLOSE TO THE OBJECT? HAD HE FALLEN
> DOWN A CREVASSE?

More tourists taking their pictures in front of the fictionally represented John Harvard. But then, did anyone know what Christ looked like? Millions of pictures, statues, unlikenesses. Did he ever smile? Is there one smiling Christ anywhere? How to describe him if he borrowed Alf's *Second Coming and Going* for a novel: Of medium height, dark-haired, noble-browed with aquiline nose, and eyes, what, beyond wise, beyond gentle, mostly sad, so sad. *Jesus wept, and no wonder, by Christ.*

Memorial Church. Bailiwick of the Reverend Peter Gomes. Would Peter hear his confession? Bless me, Peter, for I have sinned. Haven't we all, Leopold. That accent. Would have made more than a cameo appearance in any redux of *Ulysses* set in Harvard Square. *The Reverend Peter Gomes, Minister in the Church and Plummer Professor of Christian Morals, stepped out of the front door of brightly yellow painted Sparks House across from Memorial Hall ...* The unfeigned haughtiness. Making affectation respectable. More Brahmin than the Saltonstalls. That accent. More Harvard than John Harvard. Not just of Africa, but with a Portuguee name and still one of Harvard's Afro-Saxons. Annabel

a fan. Attends. The Yeatsian roll of his sermons. And gay. Causing bene-
factor and Harvard elder Tom Cabot to object when the Minister in
the Church came out of his commodious closet. But who in the *Redux*?
A kind of Father Conmee? Could check out his sermons. Quote from
them. With permission of course. But whom did Conmee represent in
the original saga of Odysseus if anyone? The problem with doing an
interpretation of an interpretation.

Not to mention the sheer work. What does the Reverend Gomes
do all day? Where does he walk to and from? Same for Ed Doctoroff,
Alf Brooks-Denny, Sassie Brooks-Denny, Stratis Haviaras, Annabel
Chance, Dean Epps, Ari Krasnick, Silvia, his mom, Charlie in The Tasty,
his father's shade, himself as the man in the brown McIntosh. Their
paths crossing and re-crossing with themselves and other characters he
would invent for the sake of synchronicity.

In fact … In fact he couldn't do it. It couldn't be done. *Le sublime
Dubinois* crafted a cathedral of living words, its light blinding, its dark-
nesses forbidding, any attempt at imitation pathetic. It was beyond
parody in its self-parody. Each seemingly throwaway phrase a bit that
fit precisely into the over-arching mosaic of meaning and madness.
The endless allusiveness. The smithy of the man's soul had operated at
intense heat and pressure, its materials from the vast storehouse of his
mind anvilled into shape by the arts of mimicry and imagination.

Still …

Sever Hall. H. H. Richardson in brick. Frieze from the Parthenon
reproduced in one of the halls. Impressive. Teach a class in there. *Nestor*
episode?

Memorial Hall loomed. Harvard's monument to its Civil War dead.
In going around it toward Oxford Street, Leo paused. Dad brought him
here as an eleven-year-old. Francis X. wanted his son to know about the
larger world they inhabited. He wanted him to understand that these
names stood for the young men who gave their lives for something
beyond themselves. It stuck. As an undergraduate and later, Leo had
been drawn to the place, especially the transept with its white marble
plaques. It beckoned now. He glanced at his watch. He had time.

Be mindful of these people, Frank O'Boyle had told his son. They
created a civilization out of a wilderness. A contrarian view for a loyal

son of Eire. But in candid moments, Dad would dismiss his own tribe as a narrow, in-looking, priest-ridden enclave who carefully nursed their grievances over the decades while willfully oblivious to the greater, expansive WASP world all around them. By that he meant the museums, the symphony orchestra, the literary tradition, the universities, the industry, the evolving technology, the very landscape of New England. Except for JFK, of course. But Kennedy was more Harvard than Holy Cross, more Beacon Hill than Southie, more the lofty rhetoric written for him by Ted Sorenson than the witty jibes of Massachusetts Senate President Billy Bulger, brother of Whitey.

Leo mounted the south steps to the shrine stopping to think that had he a hat on he would remove it. And puzzling over the realization that his visits to this place were more to escape from himself than from time. Yet this hall of memory stood beyond time in its own way, the massive stained-glass windows high above the heavy doors on either side signifying a holy site however secular in its churchy sort of way. No easy scoffing in this place where sacrifice was honored with little more than the names of the dead engraved in white marble tablets along with their class year and when and where they died. Here by the dozens. A fair proportion. Because in those days Harvard was small, at least compared to the corporate sprawl it had become.

The names haunted. *Gerald Fitz-Gerald, Divinity School 1859, 3 May 1863, Chancellorsville.* A chaplain? A soldier killed, killing, in Christ's name? To free the slaves? Could be why Leo O'Boyle felt a sense of moral inferiority to these men. They were Harvards, Brahmin names all over the place, privileged. That is, most could have bought their way out. They didn't. Some enlisted before they graduated. *Sumner Paine, 1865, Gettysburg, 3 July 1863.*

So that, for a few moments Leopold Bloom O'Boyle stopped thinking about Leopold Bloom O'Boyle except in terms of others. Others. The looming Other. At which point, the nebulous, avoided anxiety that had teased him since waking again crystallized into the stark, unanswerable question: Would he make a good dad given the depth of his ambivalence, his hesitation, his fear?

A tussle with Larkin: Listen, Philip, if you don't give your kid (your kids?) the faults you have, they'll get their faults somewhere else. More than likely worse faults. Strange faults. Idiotic faults. Self-destructive faults. In fact, Philip, I rather like the faults I got from my mom and dad, especially from Dad. He told me that getting drunk every once in a while was a good way to stay sober. He told me you should strive for the moral high ground but never presume you held it. He told me that the cruelty of a witticism has to be justified by its wit. He told me not to be too careful because you can only learn from your mistakes if you make a few. It's not his fault I made some of his virtues into faults. Perhaps I drink too much in the name of sobriety. Perhaps I am overly modest and lacking ambition in my claims to morality. Perhaps I make too many mistakes and don't learn from them. Perhaps I indulge in cruelties, if only verbal, at the expense of wit. I tend to dither a bit like he did. Big plans and little follow through. Impatience with people who repeat themselves even as I repeat myself. Indulging in hankering for what cannot be. Sentimentality. The list goes on. But what about all the good stuff? He taught me how to think, how to question everything, everything, including the little pieties that bad conservatives and nice liberals repeat like mantras to themselves and each other. He taught me that you take one person at a time, even if they have a Nobel Prize on the shelf or are carrying a spear, metaphorically or otherwise. He taught me it was okay to be obsessed as long as you didn't try to foist your obsessions on others. Except, maybe, your kids.

So fuck you, Philip Larkin.

Besides, I have a few faults of my own, that is, completely *sui generis*—such as a tendency to throw around phrases in Latin and French that a lot of people don't understand.

Cleared those decks. Sort of. The question remained:—Darwin hovering now—did he, L. B. O'Boyle, have the fathering gene? Did he esteem himself sufficiently to esteem his offspring? Did he esteem himself too much to bother? Did you not have to love yourself, but not too much, before you loved others?

Might not a child free him from himself? Free him from the curse of his fear of time? Or was he afraid of losing his fears? If nothing else, they were reliable. They could be managed. Managed. Another buzz word. Nothing worse than new fears. A fear of fears. Could you be phobiaphobic?

Then a brightening, fleeting thought, catching his heart off guard: He would bring his child here and try to explain to him or to her the significance of these names and why this attempt at permanence. An inner bridling. How could he explain the mystery of sacrifice to the young stranger standing beside him? As a toddler? As a teenager? Alf rattled on about altruism and how sociobiology explained it. Kin selection. Group selection. Too cut and dried. But what it took to do a deed of bravery. The self-forgetting. It transcended social science. It transcended art. Because what these mostly young men gave with their lives was their times, the times of those lives and all the possibilities those times meant for them, times never to be.

Such that, however affecting, these gestures of memorializing all around him appeared piteously inadequate next to what they symbolized. The where and when of each name. For that you had to imagine the face of the young soldier, bayonet fixed, scared, brave, walking steadfast into the hail of Confederate lead. *Johnny we hardly knew you.* How do you tell a kid that?

Or that these were the names that counted. These the names to be read and remembered, these, incised on their modest marble tablets, who gave the last full measure in dying for … for their country. Or to free the slaves. They died for our sins. In your mother's book, young strange person, these were among the innumerable Christs of history. Their names are here and on village greens, on battlefields, in memorial parks, in churches, all over the old Union.

What about the Confederate dead he had asked Annabel, who had more than a few Rebels in her family that did not survive the bloodletting. Your own kin. Tate doesn't do much for them. A lot of leaves blowing around the graves. The wear of time. Are they the damned of history? Where are their memorials?

A stupid question. She had looked at him in incredulous amazement. "Ellbee, the South is one big memorial to our Civil War dead. We have our statues and places. They, too, were defending their country."

"Are they, too, counted among the Christs of history?"

Constituting the thorny question for the attractive theologian's essay into the theology of Christology writ large. Not just the Confederate dead. What about the brave Nazi soldier who fought and died for a cause he thought sacred? What about the brave, dedicated Communist functionary who risked his life—if only by being purged—in helping starve to death millions of Ukrainians in the name of historical inevitability? Are these people also among the lesser Christs of history?

Heavily pondering but with a lighter tread, Leo O'Boyle issued through heavy doors on the south side and back into the light of day as present in the juncture of Kirkland and Oxford Streets. On the latter, where he paused, rose stately Lowell Lecture Hall to the right and the concretely Sertish Science Center on his left. A. Lawrence Lowell. Former president of Harvard. The honor earned, not bought. Appropriate, he thought. These buildings should be named after university worthies and, more appropriately, after the real giants, not the money men. Where was Edward O. Wilson's name? Dudley Herschbach's? Ernst Mayr's? James Watson's? Robert Burns Woodward's? Bit of a SOT.

Leo O'Boyle dimly regretted making the hook-up with his friend Alf. Going for advice he'd already gotten. Mostly, he itched to get back to his manuscript. Which it was literarily, at least in part, that is, scripted by hand.

Because he had heard Alf's rant on the subject of child-bearing before. "Yeah, you meet these people, thirty-somethings, and you can tell they're just too precious to be doing something as base as reproducing. Or those young good-looking educated women with a degree and some piss-ass little job with a title trying to prove they're as good as men when they could have a couple of kids and prove they're a whole lot better than most men could hope to be. Or they're trying to convince themselves they're making a difference in the lives of others." Then muttering something about how Jack the Ripper and Charles Manson had made a difference in the lives of others.

Then he would relent and unwind his argument. "Hey, look, there are couples who can't have kids or shouldn't have them if they don't want them. But that's different from thinking you're too important or too busy or simply wanting to prolong your adolescence." On occasion he would rewind himself all the way. "You no longer have to reproduce to participate in human evolution. Alexander Graham Bell impacted the species far more with his inventions than with any genetic contribution he left behind. Alan Turing, gay and childless by the way, conceived and built a thinking machine—the computer—and thereby transformed humankind, especially with the Internet wiring us all together into something more than what we are."

Or he would say, "If having kids is a mistake, my kids are the best mistake I ever made."

But then Brooks-Denny held that life was a matter of making the best of your inevitable mistakes. He also said that a lot of people, including himself, spend their adulthoods trying to repair their childhoods. Which wasn't the same as over-thinking your personal life. The over-examined life, he called it. In part the legacy of the Viennese Quack. "People like us don't get married and have kids anymore. People like us have relationships. And when you say 'relationship,' you speciously objectify something that should be half feral and maybe half institutional and not quite definable, meaning alive. Because when one of these relationships, these pampered, over-thought, over-wrought, over-precious things, turns pale or runs a fever, they put it in one of those padded refrigerator bags used to transport donated organs and take it to a therapist. And there, to the predictable psycho-babble and pseudo-clinical stuff about expectations, boundaries, self-esteem, mutual respect, and fuck knows what else, they pick the poor thing apart until the vivisection becomes an autopsy as what this couple might have had finally shrivels and dies. Nothing, mind you, gets mentioned about love, passion, poetry, good old-fashioned loathing, vows, fidelity. But the poor dead thing gets resurrected at the next session around some succeeding, faltering relationship. It's nothing more than a cover for self-absorption. Which the Quack legitimized. With considerable help from Oscar Wilde and others. The great Karl Kraus had it right: Psychoanalysis is the disease of which it purports to be the cure."

It was in one of his novels, something about people in love going to Paris and people in a relationship going to therapists. Yeah, but how do you go to Paris when you've got a squealer on board? The vistas of the Hemingway life—bouts of hard writing followed by bouts of hard drinking—may be unreal, but at least they were vistas. His own vistas had become memories. That long afternoon sitting in the sidewalk cafe on the Piazza Navona, a Pernod and cappuccino to hand, Camel fuming in the ashtray, writing away like a regular ex-pat. Or that morning in the garden at Greisemont House in Kildare, home of the Ashes, Carolyn and Robert, overlooking the cattle-studded field next to the stream and ruin of an old Quaker mill, notebook out, ideas flowing. Or Paris to Istanbul on the Orient Express, reduced to a migrant worker shuttle ("*Merde* on the Orient Express," quipped Sassie about the toilet facilities) with a compartment miraculously to himself penning his way across

Communist Bulgaria with uniformed thugs coming through periodically to check passports and shake down passengers. The remembered life now the dreamed life.

Like Alf's caricatures, Leo and Annabel had discussed more than once, quite dispassionately, the prospect of children or at least a child. They had established having a child as an option, options being very important to them as they belonged to that class of people who valued their capacity for deliberate decision-making based on available options. Was it an option they could afford? In terms of money? In terms of time? In terms of interest?

What they did not discuss openly was the presumption that their careers were simply too important and too engrossing to include the possibility of a child much less children. Given their professions, would they have the time and energy, not to mention the love, to devote to parenting? L. B. O'Boyle had his travel writing and, yes, novels to write. Not for him membership in that emerging species known as the house-husband. Because? Well, hard to admit this, but would that designation provide him a sufficiently virile self-image with which to rouse his sleepy muse and get to work? Or how much time would house husbanding leave for him to forge in the smithy of his soul the uncreated conscience of what he didn't quite know despite the unfinished novels, the notebooks with ideas, summaries, treatments, character sketches. All of which called to him like some far-off, exquisitely picturesque mountain village glimpsed from the window of a speeding train called Time.

As for the Reverend Chance? Again left unsaid but in reality front and center was that Annabel had an actual career, or the beginning of one that already involved an office to which she went most days. She had meetings, budgets, buildings, and responsibilities. That is, she had her ministry or sub-ministry and, in the offing, academic prospects in the cosmos of theological thought.

So their conversation might run, starting with mundanities, "Can we afford it?" Unvoiced—L. B. not speaking—"Can we afford it on your modest salary and the hit-and-miss checks I get?" They quibbled over pronouns. *It* meaning for the prospective father both the abstract and all-too-real reality of having a child. Annabel reminding him they were talking about a *her* or a *him*. Then the details. Maternity leave for junior ministers being a fuzzy area to say the least. A job for Leo. Even a part-time job. With good benefits. Benefits? More like necessities with an infant in tow. Repetitions: Look at all the people with a lot less who have children, sometimes lots of them. Yeah, look at them. Which struck home as they shared a horror of poverty, being already borderline in that state as it was.

Then he, in the comprehending, sympathetic mode, "But Annabella Baby, what about your book?" There being professional editors preparing her thesis for publication. (Which at times galled the would-be novelist L. B. O'Boyle though he tried to be big about it.) *Updike's Version: A Barthian God in a Godless World* would sooner or later appear as an actual book. And now pregnant with real life as well. Because on that warm afternoon in Maine in the lower house they had mated like healthy mammals bent on reproduction whether they acknowledged it or not.

• • •

Mallinckrodt to the right, Gordon McKay to the left. Who Mallinckrodt? Who McKay? Hard science. Bill Doering in Mallinckrodt. Something to do with synthesizing chlorophyll and a lot of other things with Woodward. One of those. Met him at an MCZ party. Pal of Liz Shannon and Deane Lord. Worldly, smart, witty. ("The critical element in an up martini is the amount of ice melt.") What you think about when you think about a Harvard professor.

Then thinking: When it came to being biological, and what could be more biological than child-bearing, Alf provided an evolutionary context for those who needed one. Not necessarily an encouragement. That is, he put your selfish genes in perspective. The you that is you—Larkin's million-petaled flower of being here—doesn't last very long. "You not only die but you lose the unique combination that is you very quickly in evolutionary time. Your grandchildren share only one-fourth of your DNA, your great-grandchildren one-eighth, your great-great-grandchildren one sixteenth until, for all practical purposes, what was you has been mixed back into the great heaving gene pool. More like an ocean. Unless you live on a small island or in some situation where there's inbreeding. Enough of that and all the recessive gene problems start popping up."

Then explaining how we are all accidents if you go back the other way even if your existence came about consequent to an arranged marriage and planned parenthood. "Think of it," Alf boring in, "upwards of a billion spermatozoa with each ejaculation. And, before that necessary juncture, how did your parents meet? How did theirs and theirs, back and back, exponentially. With one little break in that tenuous, ever-branching thread reaching back and back, there would be no *you*, someone very like perhaps, but no *you*."

"It sounds like what we need," said Annabel, puncturing Alf's balloon of words with just a pinch, "is a theology of the accidental."

Hoffman Geological Laboratories, wing on the right wing of the main pile, Agassiz's monument, redbrick, set back on a generous lawn with a curving drive to the front door. Five stories of the University Museums of Natural History. Zoology. Botany. Mineralogy.

L. B. O'Boyle the novelist paused again and leaned on one of the squared granite bollards that bordered the lawn where it met the sidewalk. Alf wouldn't mind if he didn't show up. Alf was one of those slyly busy guys, not so much with a secret agenda as an agenda he didn't seem to have.

It was Alf who convinced Annabel that any system that didn't take into account the reality of evolution was for all intents and purposes irrelevant. Summer evening, the side garden in Belmont, Alf holding forth: "If we are made in the image and likeness of God, then God, like us, must be a product of evolution and is still evolving." Alf talking, converting Annabel to the Church of Charles Darwin. Alf, ever an absolutist on evolution, saying, "People think it's out there somewhere or that it's already happened or that it doesn't concern them. But it's going on right now, especially in technology. Cybernetics is nothing less than an evolving extension of the human brain. It will not only match human intelligence, it will surpass it; it will make Einstein seem just a bit slow. It may replace us." A pause to sip his gin and tonic, no ice. "What I'm saying is that everything is in a state of evolving. It occurs minute by minute, second by second and at every level. It is the universe fine-tuning itself."

"You really think God is evolving?" asked the Reverend Chance, who, her husband could tell, was taking mental notes.

"Why not? You could say he's evolving as an idea whether she exists or not. Or God is evolving through us: We are the avatar—a Teilhardian idea and a bit on the homo-centric side." Then, "Darwin didn't disprove God's existence, he merely made it unnecessary."

On into the night.

Sassie, taking her husband's arm, "Let others say something."

Sassie a marvelous, quiet presence. Alf made the splash but Sassie grew on you. A quiet wit and mercifully free of partisan cant. And still eminently … yes, at fifty. Why do we hanker after our friends' wives? Because they're there, we know them, Updike wrote somewhere. Something else, too.

It was Alf who encouraged Leo O'Boyle to write even while saying "We are all the main character in the novel of the life we are leading be it tragedy or comedy or a dull soap."

Leo saying, "But all of our life novels end in death."

Brooks-Denny had smiled. "But there is new life along the way. Death is not the same as extinction." Later adding, "The novels of our lives are more like over-lapping stories, our life and the lives of others."

Diverting them into Mallarmé on *Hamlet* … *lisant au livre de lui-meme.* "We all read the book of ourselves," said Alf. "I got that from your dad who got it from Stuart Gilbert who was describing the source of the soliloquizing in *Ulysses.*"

Leo O'Boyle approached the central entrance of the museum remembering how his mom had brought him here as a nine-year-old to see the glass flowers, she being the only one in the family interested in anything like nature. The beautifully wrought all-too-life-like creations by the Bohemian father and son had palled on him, but not the enormous Siberian tigers, the Harvard *Mastodon americanus*, the head of the *Triceratops*, the *Kronosaurus* and the slow and decisive realization that time had been around a long time.

Like most people, he grasped evolution in a general way. It was Alf's at times rambling expatiations on Darwin's *Origin* that made him aware of it as more than some grand theory of everything living and dead. How Darwin started with artificial selection. Knew pigeon fanciers, dog breeders, farmers. Selective breeding for desired traits. Phenotypes, our actual forms, are malleable over time indicating the same for our genotypes, the underlying coding. Natural selection is what happens in nature. How Malthus gave him the forcing mechanism—only a small percent of offspring survive in nature for most species. He intuited randomness. Did not know that a Silesian monk named Gregor Mendel, the founder of genetics, was publishing around the same time as the *Origin* his research on pea plants. But what resonated with the chronophobic Leo was how the Scots geologist Charles Lyell provided Darwin with the time for the slow grind of natural selection, gave him millions and millions of years instead of the few millennia allowed by Holy Scripture.

Alf describing how Andy Knoll patiently attends a water-cooled cutting saw slicing razor-thin slices from granite billions of years old. Then putting the sections under the microscope, teasing out the evidence of those first tracks of life. Time so vast that the human mind, in its crack of light, can scarcely comprehend it.

As such, Leo O'Boyle, resuming his way along the curving drive to the front entrance, considered this museum not so much a refuge from time as a temple of time, a place filled with the trophies of time, filled with the astounding, nearly absurd, creativity of time. Such that he had been, in yet another manifestation of his phobia, intimidated by time.

Before opening the big door, he paused, a snatch of dialogue coming to him. He rifled through his satchel for his notebook which he found in his shirt pocket. The Object wouldn't dismiss time as merely another measure of energy and motion.

He scribbled:

> The Object pronounced in words in a thought in his bifurcated mind, "Time is the medium of evolution. Time is created by energy and motion. Evolution results from all three."
>
> Cam asks, "Is evolution still random?"
>
> "Yes. But it is self-generated in the intermediate stages by advanced intelligences."

Under it he noted,

> CONNECT TO INTERVIEW WITH OBJECT RE PLANNING

• • •

Big double doors. Down a short flight. Door to the left. Knock.
"Open."

Alf behind his desk in the inner office in profile working the keyboard of a computer eye level with the lawn outside. He turned. "Leopold Bloom O'Boyle again. Jesus Christ, you can't make that up. Your father had balls." Rising, smiling, extending hand, handshake. "Good to see you again. Have a seat."

"I will. How goes your day?"

"Laying waste my powers ..."

"Getting and spending ...?"

"Don't I wish."

"I've often wondered, did Wordsworth mean 'spending' in the ejaculatory sense?"

The open face suddenly alert. "You know, I hadn't thought of that, but it makes sense. Hemingway thought sex laid waste his powers."

"That didn't stop him."

"From writing or sex?"

"We know about the writing. We have to infer the sex. He did have children."

"Lots of people have sex without having children. It's the new norm."

"So where are you off to next?" Said Leo, not yet ready for the subject and glancing at the world map on the wall. Pins all over it. Been everywhere.

"Repositioning trip in November. They're taking the *World Discover* down the west coast of South America."

"For the fjords?"

"Fjords and then Antarctica for the season."

"You're not doing the whole thing?"

"Too long. We're on from Arica to Puerto Montt. Fantastic country. Iquique. No recorded rainfall. Atacama Desert. Some of those volcanic islands are really ..."

"Sassie going?"

"Better believe it. If I was going to hell she'd insist on coming. Afraid she'll miss something."

A laugh. "Yeah, Annabel's like that. She'd take notes. Weren't you just north."

"Wager Bay."

"Wager Bay?"

"Northwest corner of Hudson. Small boat. Polar bears in the water right next to you. Caribou. Gyre falcons. Lousy food. Good local guide. He told me that seal blubber is a guaranteed aphrodisiac."

"For those nymphets of the north?"

"No for the guys."

"Savenor's might have some."

Then, "Got something to show you." Leo reached into his satchel and produced the article his father had written for *Erato*. He handed it across the desk. "Stratis wants to publish it."

Alf put the article on his desk, bent over it, and read. He came up as though for air. "Good stuff. I can hear your dad's voice."

As well he might. Alf and Francis X. had gone in and out of *Ulysses* more than once over a pint in the Potato and other venues. They agreed in a rephrasing of the ponderous Saxon Haines about Shakespeare to the effect that Joyce is the happy hunting ground of those who have lost their balance. And most gladly. Not that Alf could keep up with Frank in navigating the universe created by James Augustine Aloysius Joyce except where he might bring natural history to bear. The *Proteus* episode where Stephen is walking on Sandymount Strand musing on the reality of reality came up more than once or twice. Alf: "Our perceptions of reality were shaped in an evolutionary process directly related to whether or not they contributed to our fitness, that is, our ability to survive long enough to reproduce. The rest is ingenious fluff. Evolution permeates all life."

"Yes," allowed his Dad. "But you also say there is a gratuity to human life created by evolution that takes us beyond the exigencies of evolution." Dad had tended to use the King's English around Alf.

"Right. What French silk chocolate pie and a Mozart symphony contribute to fitness is not readily apparent and part of what I would call that gratuity. As is the prose of James Joyce. What I'm saying in a larger context is that these notions of perception, of ineluctable modalities and all the rest of that can't be viewed without reference to evolution."

"Are you saying they are part of the gratuity? That they are gratuitous."

Alf listening, thinking. Alf saying, "The gratuity is a realm of freedom. It is a product of evolution and it is both evolving and affecting what might be called base line evolution. Mostly, as part of that gratuity, it is ... well, gratuitous."

Leo thinking that, in partaking of that gratuity, the poignancy of perceiving any reality was how quickly it changed or vanished.

"Evolution is alive and well in *Ulysses*," Frank told a doubting Alf on one occasion. "You take the *Oxen of the Sun* episode, that's the one in the hospital where Mrs. Purefoy is having a difficult birth. Anyway, he refers to, and I quote, 'the late ingenious Mr. Darwin.' Not only that, Alf, a hand going out to touch the skeptic's forearm, "there's much in it devoted to the evolution of language as it is deployed over the centuries by writers of English."

Alf nodding. "Right. The evolution of language is supposed to mirror the stages of the child's growth in the womb."

"Exactly. The text is interlaced with references—webbed hands, fish without heads, oxtail, jaws ..."

"But a child's development in the womb is teleological, not evolutionary. Unless he's alluding to the idea that ontogeny recapitulates phylogeny. Fancy words, I know. The phrase refers to the notion that in its embryonic development any organism goes through the stages of its evolutionary history. It's largely discredited now." Alf sounding like he might consign Joyce to those, among them Marx, Freud, B.F. Skinner, and others, whose works had failed because they had not read or, having read, had not heeded Darwin.

"Yes. But for Joyce it's more than teleological because the evolution continues. He considered the language of *Finnigans Wake* to be the language of the future."

Alf smiling, conceding. "Something to chew on."

Another time, visiting the museum and calling on Alf's natural history bent, Frank asked, "What in hell is a sandblind upupa?"

"Spell that."

"U. P. U. P. A. Here's the quote: 'Agendath is a waste land, a home of screech owls and the sandblind upupa.'"

Alf brightening and reaching for his *Birds of Europe*. "*Upupa epops*, the only species in the genus, the Hoopoe." The illustration showed a large, tawny, crested bird with a long beak and black, white-striped wings and tail.

Asked Leo, "How did you remember that?"

"How can you forget a name like *Upupa epops*? The Hoopoe's in Aristophanes' play about birds. The range is Eurasian. It's the national bird of Israel."

"Modern Israel didn't exist until … 1948? But Bloom had that flyer about citrus groves in Agendath Netaim." Dad thinking. "I think it's a repeat of up, UP, U.P., that occurs earlier … but about which no one seems to have a good theory."

Alf with a knowing smirk. "You poopa. Maybe the sound appealed to his coprophilic bent."

Frank saying, "Yes, but another image of himself as a bird. Sandblind. Joyce had trouble with his eyes. And with his moral vision. The way he treated his mother on her deathbed." More thought. "Or, he's confusing it or matching it with the lapwing. Migratory. Himself going back and forth to Trieste before he quit Ireland altogether."

Then, nose up, summoning, quoting from memory: "Fabulous artificer, the hawklike man. You flew. Whereto? Newhaven-Dieppe, steerage passenger. Paris and back. Lapwing. Icarus. Pater, ait. Seabedraggled, fallen, weltering. Lapwing you are. Lapwing he."

Alf impressed, thumbing to the page of plovers. "*Vanellus vanellus*." Smiles all around. Alf saying, "About twelve inches, the same size as the hoopoe. Also a pronounced crest. Joyce the birder?"

"Joyce the birdman. Joyce the everything."

Leo butting in, "You might say, paraphrasing what Nabokov said of Shakespeare—'Nature produced an Irishman whose head was a hive of words.'"

Frank nodding. "And ideas. Perhaps too many ideas."

Thus it had gone. On and on. What they agreed on was the great art of Joyce, especially the more accessible parts of *Ulysses*: You remember it not as literature but as life.

Alf stood. "Let's do a walkabout."

Together they climbed past the admissions desk. Up another two flights. Birds and mammals to the left, geology to the right, glass flowers straight ahead. They walked left, looking, pausing, until in front of the exhibit of equine evolution, Leo O'Boyle said to his friend Alf Brooks-Denny, "Annabel's pregnant."

Surprise, the pleasure a touch condescending. Or was it pitying? "You sure?"

"About ninety-nine percent."

"Congratulations." Warm, strong handshake.

"You sure?"

"Hell yeah, keep the party going."

"I don't know …"

Bones of the great ground sloth loomed over them.

"Ah, the great ambivalence. What does Annabel think?"

"I think it's what she wants. I kind of know it is. But she insists it's up to both of us."

"So what's your hesitation? Aside from incurring a living responsibility and a source of private terror for the rest of your conscious life."

Deep breath. Smile. Confess. "It would be life-changing."

"It damn well better be."

"I'll have to get a real job."

"A curse worse than death. There's always Expository Writing."

"Compare and contrast … Jesus, anything but that."

"I could talk to Shaun O'Connell or Lloyd Schwartz at U. Mass."

"Good guys, but I don't know."

"Or Mike Schnagel at Extension."

"I thought about that."

"No more travel writing?"

"I'd have to travel more. Scrounge around for better gigs. I mean Annabel's the one with the real job, sketchy as it is."

They entered the Romer Room. A chamber of time. Giant fossilized tortoise shell. *Coelacanth* in alcohol, living fossil fish. Long-clawed *Deinonychus*, a raptor right out of *Jurassic Park*. *Edophosaurus*. Sail Lizard. They sat on a bench facing the glassed-in fossilized skeleton of the forty-foot-long *Kronosaurus queenslandicus*. Giant gaping mouth, four huge paddles, long tail. Chronosaurus? More likely from Kronos, overthrown father of the gods. Aphrodite emerging from the foam of his castrated testicles. Weird stuff. Sixty-three million years ago. Curiously soothing all that time, gone, but the effects still here behind glass.

Leo began, "The real issue … aside from self-image and fantasies of the grand literary life …"

"My God, what else is there?"

"Time."

"Ah, the god of everything …"

"I won't have any. A job, a kid, helping Annabel …"

"It doesn't work that way. Not for me."

"I don't follow you."

"When time gets precious, you find you have more of it. You spend it better. You don't take it for granted. You want to write?"

"Of course."

"Then write. Get up at five in the morning and write. By eight o'clock you'll have three hours of work done. You go to work free. Except for a notebook. For ideas."

Easy for Brooks-Denny to say. His kids, two beautiful girls now young women. His nice big house and the gorgeous Sassie in the holy townland of Belmont. Still dry.

"And that's just the beginning."

"The matitudinal hours?"

"Right. Most jobs, especially at Harvard, have lots of holes in the day. So you grab an hour here, a couple of hours there, a sick day, whatever ..."

"But to write?"

"Maybe not the pure creative stuff, but all the note-keeping, the bits and pieces. It adds up."

From the Romer Room they went into the Great Mammal Hall. High above them from the ceiling hung the skeletons of whales. *An astounding crate full of air*. Reaching towards them a towering giraffe and giraffe skeleton. An exhibit of stuffed *primata* sans *Homo*. Why not a stuffed human? *Mounted* the nicer word. Say a retired professor. Or a graduate student prematurely deceased. People donate their bodies to medical research so why not museum exhibits? Would get political. Why a man and not a woman? Why a white person? Because if you put a stuffed black person in an exhibit with a bunch of greater and lesser apes ... Get Lenin on loan from his Stalinist tomb. *Homo homocidens*. Hats off, the frowning guard gestured. A Bolshevik holy site. Neat little goatee, shirt and tie. Leave the clothes on.

Lenin would be a jarring note, a touch of the obscene dressed or not amidst not so much the beauty as the extravagance of nature. Evolution creative in the default mode. More and more. A case batty with bats. The Indian gaur looking like the mother of all bovids. Wombat. Kangaroo. Tasmanian devil. Wildebeest. All of which Leo O'Boyle had seen before but regarded now as though through eyes not quite his own.

On his first visit to the place, Frank O'Boyle had resorted to *Ulysses*, intoning:

> Elk and Yak, the bulls of Bushan and Babylon, mammoth and mastodon, they come trooping to the sunken sea, Lacus Mortis. Ominous, revengeful zodiacal host! They moan, passing upon the clouds, horned and capricorned, the trumpeted with the tusked, the lion-maned, the giant-antlered, snouter and crawler, rodent, ruminant and pachyderm, all their moving moaning multitude, murderers of the sun.

Alf walking and talking, saying something about how Darwin figured out sexual selection. Competition within a species. Who gets to breed. Who gets to pass on their genes. We're not that much different from the rest of nature. Competition for mates. Like any organism. Our genitals are the flower, our navels the stem. We are birthed, we blossom, we pollinate, we reproduce, and we die. Eventually.

Leo thinking: Annabel had selected him. Now she was pollinated. Inwardly distracted by some emerging, unshaped epiphany, he said, "Larkin was having none of that."

"'Get out as soon as you can and don't have any kids yourself.'"

"Right. But you have kids."

"When we were young and I was a font of genetic material. Mostly blind instinct back then."

They were inspecting the case of bats.

"Nothing really planned?"

"Yeah. Better that way. There ought to be something haphazard about life. Let it happen."

"You weren't scared? I mean …"

"Bloody terrified."

Alf Brooks-Denny stopped and held up a hand, index finger extended. "You want to know something? You can have this job. I'm about finished." The expression was set, almost pleading.

"You're kidding?"

"I'm dead serious."

"I'm not strong on natural history."

"It's mostly administration and hand holding. We call it eco-travel, but it's more like ego-travel."

A laugh at his own pleasantry. Typical Alf.

"You're absolutely serious?"

"I've been thinking about nothing else lately. God's truth." Alf nodding to himself, pleased at the idea.

"But why? Burned out?"

"Not really. I'm eligible for early retirement. I want time to write."

"Ain't that the truth."

"I'll train you, not that you'll need much. You've been around. You can come in part time on the casual payroll. It won't take long. Hey, look, this isn't exactly Larkin's 'Toads.'"

"Tell me about it."

"One condition."

"Okay."

"I get to lead at least one trip a year."

"Deal. But … getting the appointment?"

"We'll get you on board. Start coming in. Get you to meet some folks. Especially the director. I'll mention possibilities. Once he gets used to the idea, there'll be no problem."

"Man, I've got to think this over. Good salary?"

"Around forty to start."

To the coping mind of Leo O'Boyle the possibility seemed as improbable as the towering, not quite credible giraffe before which he stood with craning neck. Then, lost in the reticulations of the animal's hide, it seemed entirely possible. And, along with that inner nod, as from nowhere, something nudging him blossomed into a sharp, pleasant pang of expectation: He would bring his child here and show him or her this absurd creature. He could all but feel the small hand in his. It provoked a smile he kept to himself, this Rockwellian image of himself and a toddler viewing the wonders of nature as presented in these exhibits. Then a head-lightening sensation of expanding time, of release from the chronophobic constrictions he suffered, as though, however vicariously, he would be inhabiting another sphere of time. That of his child. And a realization beyond intimation: By having a child, he and Annabel would be continuing time, their own time.

He savored the thought. These forms were creatures of time as was he and as was the tiny pod of cells dividing and multiplying in Annabel's womb. Womb. And his and Annabel's time would overlap with … Until he experienced something like a revelation, one so obvious and so liberating, he couldn't believe he hadn't thought of it before or read it somewhere. He spoke it out in his mind: *Everyone lives in his own time with a beginning, a middle, and an end. And all of these times overlap and interweave with the times of others in a continuum, in a crumpled flow that goes on and on and on.*

To relieve the overload on his mind and his heart as he stood there with his friend Alf, he asked, "Wasn't there another room beyond here?"

"The Coral Reef Room. It's been closed."

"Too bad." Leo remembered large models of Pacific atolls, one with a giant octopus mounted above it, its tentacles spreading. Alf explaining on that first visit how Darwin was no mean geologist himself. Figured out how atolls formed from coral built up atop slowly sinking volcanoes. Then talked how Darwin published *Origin of Species* in 1859, same year MCZ was founded. Agassiz, the pioneering glaciologist did not subscribe to Darwinism. Hence the name Museum of Comparative Zoology rather than Museum of Evolutionary Zoology. Missed that boat.

All of which played like a kind of background music to the chords of realization sounding in the mind of Leopold Bloom O'Boyle. Right now. Back then. Next week. Right then. And all those other times, all those times of others, flowing, overlapping, intertwining, ceasing, starting, each precious to each, each alive, so that his time was but one strand in this living, weaving web that would continue when his own strand ended.

None other than Edward O. Wilson came through a door on the balustraded balcony and started down the stairway.

Amazing to see the change in friend Alf's demeanor. He might have been one of the apostles meeting Christ coming ashore on the Sea of Galilee, walking on water.

Lanky, courtly, the great man paused to greet them, shaking hands with both. "Working on a novel?" he asked Alf, having read and admired his first effort.

"As always. And you?"

A smile and dip of his head. "The novel of my life. A memoir." Then a wave good-bye.

Leo O'Boyle took in the whale skeletons suspended above them. "Christ, that is like meeting Darwin at Down House."

Alf nodding. "You do not exaggerate."

"Myrmecology, right?"

"Ants and a whole lot more. Island biogeography. And one of the architects of sociobiology."

"And still controversial ...?"

"Not as much as it used to be." Alf paused, thinking. "Leftists still don't want to accept that important aspects of human behavior are evolved, meaning hard-wired."

"Meaning not the *tabula rasa* for the behaviorists and others who would create a new humanity."

"Exactly. Or a new inhumanity. Back in the seventies the commissars of correct scientific inquiry Gould and Lewontin tried to have Wilson dragged off to the Lubyanka. Figuratively speaking."

"I never understood that." Said knowing that it might provoke Brooks-Denny's rant about Stephen J. Gould.

This time, they avoided it.

Back in Alf's office, Alf sat down behind his desk. Leo stood dawdling, shouldering his bag, wondering what it would be like to work in this place.

He glanced at the wall map of the world and all the push-pinned places. He said, realization and words erupting at the same instant, "My biggest worry, frankly, is whether I'd make a good dad or not. I mean someone like my own dad. Not that he wasn't almost too much of a good thing."

Alf nodded thoughtfully. "Sit down for a minute. Then I've got to get to work."

Leo, bag shouldered, sat down.

No easy answer this time, no jesting aphorism to put the imponderable in perspective. Then, "I think it's probably a good sign that you worry about it." Another few ticks of silence. "You know, no one ever talks any more about the deep, visceral enchantment of being a mother or a father. These are your flowers growing up and growing out. They are your living link to the future. And, let's face it, for most people it will be the most creative thing they'll ever do. And in the end, family is all that's left, family and a few friends. Most everything else in life ends up for sale or in storage or at the dump."

Which didn't help Leo a whole lot.

Then Alf said, "You might ask yourself, what kind of son have I been? What kind of son am I?"

Leo smiled dimly and nodded, dissembling the impact of his friend's words. Finally, "You're right. I should give that some thought. It does go both ways."

At some unspoken sign, they both stood up. They shook hands across the desk in an oddly formal way. Alf said, "What are you waiting for, Leo? You're not going to get any younger and neither is Annabel."

These words registered as well. That's what he had been doing. Waiting. Waiting for his mother to die. Waiting to finish and publish a novel. Waiting to have time to, for ... his ship to come in? In a silence he repeated a few lines of Larkin to himself:

> Only one ship is seeking us, a black-
> Sailed unfamiliar, towing at her back
> A huge and birdless silence. In her wake
> No waters breed or break.

He said, "I need time."

"Unless you act, your past will never live up to the promise of your future."

They went out into the entrance of the building and stood near the massive doors leading outside and the glassed-in fossil of *Smiladon californicus*, its gaping jaw showing its great saber fangs. Alf said, "I'm serious about your working here."

A nod. "I want to think about it."

Alf said, "Aren't you at least curious?"

"About what?"

"About what your little man or your little woman would be like?"

"The thought scares the piss out of me. It would be the end of my life."

"Or it would be the beginning of your life."

"I have to go. I haven't seen my mother in an age."

"Yes, mothers." Alf gave his shoulder a squeeze. "Where would we be without them?"

• • •

Exiting from the Museum of Comparative Zoology, Leo the son crossed Oxford Street and entered another yard of paths and lawn enclosed largely by the Law School. Another universe. Any connection between torts and torture? Must look up.

He exited the grounds of the Law School between the Richardsonian United Methodist Church and Pound Hall. Who Pound? Oscar Pound? Legal scholar. He crossed the four busy lanes of Massachusetts Avenue and went along Waterhouse Street, past Waterhouse House to Garden Street. Sheraton Commander on the left and bearing left onto Concord Avenue across from the Longy School of Music. All the while thinking, sorting out the effects of the visit with Alf. Alf's job. Regular hours. Or regular irregular hours. Hand holding the clients. Bone up on natural history. Meet the tour operators. Go look at places to go. Do all that and write? Once time becomes precious you take better care of it. Said Alf.

Then the words that pierced: What kind of son have you been?

Then his own Damascene moment peering up at the giraffe: Thinking again, time is shared. We share it and in sharing add to it. Or something like that. More felt that thought.

Then thoughts of Annabel. Driving home? Home already? She in her own time. Their times. Together. Could, should call her. Later. Sort it all out first.

Then Alf again, repeating himself, saying write. Don't talk about it. Don't even think about it. Write. And then write some more. Then think about it. Live your life and make it your material. Or don't. You can have your cake and eat it. Make it your drug of choice. Make it so you have to have a fix. Every day. Leo had heard it before in several iterations. Now it stuck. He would become, as Alf Brooks-Denny called it, the father of words.

But where would he put Alfred Brooks-Denny in his born-again *Ulysses*? No one on that June day in Dublin quite matches. Go back to the *Odyssey*. One of the hospitable Greeks.

The 74 Bus went by. He kept walking, climbing. In a wooded area behind a chain-link fence, the Harvard Smithsonian Observatory. Must go there some day and look through the telescope. Talk about travel to the Moon. To Mars. Not so far-fetched. What would one of the home-steaders trekking in a covered wagon from St. Louis all the way to the west coast think of getting on a Boeing and doing it in three or four hours? With a book and a couple of whiskeys to help pass the slow time.

For a few musing moments, he pondered again Alf's offer of his job. On the one hand, he had grown weary of traveling and writing about where he traveled. There was the tedium of being in an airplane for hours on end, sitting in a minimal space, tired yet sleepless, re-breathing everyone's air, time stretching and stretching, inverting his chronophobic tendencies such that he felt threatened by the seeming endlessness of time.

Actually, he did want to travel. But he didn't want to write about it unless moved to. He didn't want to be on duty, to have his paper notebook or his mental notebook open, pen in hand, being observant so that his readers might be assured in their quest for the real to be told of some small, achingly bucolic, local eatery where other tourists almost never go and where the gnocchi or the pirogues or the ravioli (filled with local mushrooms and cheese made from the milk of local goats that feed on local heather that give it a distinctive pungency found nowhere else) are made fresh daily by the aproned, stout wife of the smiling couple and their surly son who brings you glasses of the local wine, a surprisingly sophisticated yet sturdy red with the same heatherish echoes that inform the cheese, all topped with tiny cups of bitter coffee, teeth-breaking biscuits, and complimentary shots of the fiery local grappa. Followed by a session on the bear pads.

Such that the quaint little bistro is shortly to be overrun with hordes of knowledgeable travelers in search of authenticity, trying to find a seat at the moveable feast which was nowhere anymore because it was everywhere where credit cards left their imprint.

Would Alf's job be any better? Keeping people happy is not always easy. Especially the ones who are not happy unless they're unhappy. But Alf had said that keeping those kinds happily unhappy is easier than it sounds given how resourceful they are.

Okay, but if not travel writing or Alf's gig, what? The gnaw of uncertainty. Larkin's nippers nipping. Breadfruit the most boring food on the planet. The hungry slaves of the Caribbean wouldn't eat it. Meaning … ?

He didn't know. His mind SOTing. Yeah, but how many people are full-time novelists? Another familiar rut, the coulda, shoulda, woulda. Instead of hanging around with Ari when Ari got back from New York and a failed career copywriting at an ad agency, he should have packed up for L.A. Pick Nobles, another Winthrop House pal, had an in at Fox. Reading scripts, but so what? You read scripts, then you wrote scripts, and before you knew it, you were in the dazzlement of the Oscars, surrounded by A-listers, on your way, already there. Or he could have found himself an academic tit or a government job. Not much to do and time to write. He should have ... written.

But written what? SELF DOUBT with all caps. Did he have anything to say that wasn't already being said? Or had been said? Or could be said better by others? Or was worth saying? Not so much a violin in a void as a violin no one wanted to listen to. Why did it appeal to him, this monastic, onanistic, self-flagellating grind of lining up words one after another, to the last syllable of recorded what ...? Actually, it clearly didn't as he would spend more time at it if it did. Then why be solicitous of a future in which to do precisely that when, to be honest, he wasn't doing it when he had saved, borrowed, taken, and stolen vast wastes of time in which to write the great American whatever. Instead he had done everything but write. He had dithered, read the works of friends (often with silent disparagement—I could do better than that), called same friends, listened to music, day-dreamed, called friends, done lunch, been done by lunch and, finally, all too close to an after-thought or after-thoughts, wrote. Or at least jotted. Always jotting. But jotting wasn't the same as writing. He had seen Brooks-Denny's drafts. Bloody endless.

But then there were those moments when the muse opened herself to him. Those sentences like gifts. The description of the melting glacier in *Ice Object 13*. "The shamble of strewn rocks alive with runoff from the deliquescing ice was shrouded in drifting tendrils of white mist." If only ... If only what?

He had scant interest in the fringe benefits of being a writer, that is, an artist. As sanctioned by tradition if not best practices, he, as a writer, had a license to drink more than those who did not claim to be a writer. A license to drink to keep body and soul apart and to make others more interesting as he wrote his way to an Oscar. He had a license to be aloof, obsessive, slightly mad, self-indulgent, proud, vain, and interestingly offensive. A license to dress or not dress in any manner he chose. On the other hand, it was a myth that writers were obliged to have untidy love lives as fodder for their fiction or as something for biographers to pick over. Vladimir was faithful in his way to his Vera. Joyce might have turned his fantasies about Nora Barnacle's non-existent infidelities into literature, but he didn't stray himself. Seamus is true to his Marie. He to his Annabel Lee.

His muse. She had returned, was tapping him on the shoulder, whispering in his ear. Marvelous. Where to sit and write? There should be enclosed stations with desk and chair for writers spaced around places like Harvard Square, like those things in Churchill to shelter from wandering polar bears.

He paused beside St. Peter's School. Sister Bernadette. Bride of Christ. Doing Christ's work. Thousands like her across the globe. In schools and hospitals. Back of the beyond. No appreciation. You needed to be Christ-like for that.

Alf's words again: What kind of son have you been?

His mind cast back to a Sunday morning when he was sixteen and had decided he was no longer going to go to Mass or lie about going to Mass when he hadn't.

"Because I don't believe in it, Mom." Who had withdrawn into herself to hide her hurt and disappointment. "I'm sorry. I can't make myself believe something I don't believe. I can't do it just to please you. Dad, you've said it again and again, 'self-hypocrisy is the worst kind.'"

Dad nodding and calmly saying, "It's something we all go through."

"I never doubted for a second," said his mother, eyes accusing now.

"Okay, Dad, tell me, what do you believe? Do you think you're going to go to Heaven or Hell or Purgatory when you die?"

"I neither believe nor disbelieve except for the teaching of Christ." He paused then and smiled. "I also believe in grace. And, let's face it, we all yearn for something sacred in our lives."

Which led to a walk and a talk, Francis X. knowing but having to turn into words what he knew. And what he felt. "Grace is everywhere, of course. In nature. In other people. In poetry and art. But, mostly, I find it in church when I pray … Meditate might be the more hip word for it. I can't even tell you what it is. A sense of blessing, benediction, a moment of seeing, of knowing that it all makes sense. It comes and goes. But afterwards, I find myself refocused, my life and the world in some kind of perspective."

Which didn't send teenage Leo back to Mass on a regular basis. But he kept his father's words to the extent that he, too, had begun to search for and leave himself open to what was called grace.

His mother never quite forgave him his apostasy. When he got into Harvard, she said, "That's nice, dear, your dad's very proud of you."

"And you're not?" Only a touch facetious.

"Of course I am."

Of course.

She had begged off flying to Montgomery for their wedding. He had made sure she had seen the invitation on which he had underlined "the Reverend R. Edward Leonards, S.J., officiating with …" Without telling her that The Rev. Father Leonards was on probation over an argument with the Holy See as to whether or not unrepentant homosexuals could get into the Kingdom of Heaven. Never quite forgave him for marrying a Protestant minister. Asking, later on, in one of her fogs, married to a Protestant minister, Leo? You're not queer, are you, Leo? Annabel is a woman, Mom. Oh, one of those.

The usual self-cross-examination under oath. Had he not gone out of his way to get her into The Elms of Cambridge, "A Retirement Home of Distinction?" What else could he have done? Move back in with and live like an Irish bachelor of old? Talk about queer. Did he not, on occasion, take her out for tea, usually to the English place in Belmont Center. (In that way avoiding their old neighborhood lest she make a break for home and the nightmare of …) Did he not attempt not to think that her demise would solve any number of problems, financial mostly. Would he miss her? Not until one morning he woke up and realized that another large piece of his own life had slid away with hers. That she, Mom, was gone. Missing her. Their shared past catching up with him.

Till he SOTed himself into a funk.

Huron Avenue. Paddy's Lunch. Down a block and a few blocks over on the right across from Massey's. Where the Lord of Talk was wont to hold early court. An impulse to bolt. Not this time a discarded fantasy of strange love with the sylvan creature of chance meeting. More a quick shot and a slow chaser. Help him think. Help him not think. Then another quick shot and slow chaser, lapsing into the past, resisting the future, alcohol as good a way as any to burn the time. Mom could wait. It's what she was doing anyway. Her final wait.

He had started down Concord Avenue in the direction of Paddy's when he paused, remembering the cameloid head of the giraffe with its two silly horns atop the towering neck. And himself craning up with a toddler by his side, holding a hand, a little person calling him Daddy. His dad again. Joyce again. *Life.*

• • •

He stepped back on the curb. Across Huron Avenue to the left of Amando's Pizza was the Hickey & Son Funeral Home. *Et in academia ego.* Though Harvard had yet to over-run this part of Cambridge. From where his mother would be waked and buried. His mother. What kind of son are you? And wasn't Sheila Cassidy O'Boyle also part of his time, part of the warping and woofing of that very real imaginary fabric he had begun to spin in his mind, in his heart? Yes, but that would mean …

His muse tugged at his sleeve. Armando's. Small salad and a coke. Buying a chair and a space to write. He glanced at his watch as any normal mortal would. 4:32. Mom would have to wait, just a while.

Twinge about Ari. He would call him later. Later.

He took out the three-ring binder. More reading than writing. Odd note here and there. More filler about the Object's perspective: What is our future? More mind-in-mind dialogue. He read:

> The human race has clearly begun to transition to a cybernetic form of life.
> How will that happen?
> At some point the processing power of your computers will exceed that of your brains. At that point you will be able to upload, as you call it, your consciousness.
> And make backups?
> If you choose.
> Meaning …?
> Meaning everything.
> Is that what you used to be?
> Many moons and suns ago.
> So evolution continues?
> Evolution never stops.

What will happen to the world?

You mean to *Homo sapiens sapiens* as you call yourselves?

Yes.

Most likely there will be a race between end-stage cybernetic evolution and catastrophic habitat failure leading to extinction.

Can you manipulate time?

We don't have to.

I don't follow you.

Mortals are obsessed with time because when the individual dies time stops. Once ceasing ends, time becomes another dimension of energy and motion.

So you don't have to fill time?

What do you mean?

How do you amuse yourselves?

We make up stories.

Some things …

We explore and catalogue.

Human life?

Yes, and other primitive forms.

Is there much life in the universe?

The universe pulses with life.

Why haven't we been able to contact or be contacted by other extraterrestrials?

You would call it snobbery. Hydrocarbon manifestations are at such a low level of development no one is really interested.

But a lot has happened in the ten thousand years you have been here.

That is true. Back then you were barely out of a feral state, a feral state by your standards. In another hundred of your years what you call consciousness will be etherized. If you survive.

Okay, not bad. But more filler than necessary movement. Was it Hemingway said there was a difference between motion and movement? How does the Object get freed from its gravitational snare?

Good bread. He made a kind of salad sandwich. Touch of feta. Bloom's gorgonzola sandwich. Could get a wedge of the pepperoni No. He wrote:

> How does the Object get free?
> One, the Object, speaking through Cam, tells the authorities that if it is not given a dose of energy in the form of a small nuclear explosion, it will use its solar magnifiers to burn cities and towns in the area starting with Anchorage. And, as its power increases, it will extend its range. The Object could prove its threat by picking out an abandoned mining town and making it burst into flames as though through spontaneous combustion. That's the stick.
> Two, the carrot would be a transfer of ultra-high-technology such that the largest mainframe in the U.S. is barely able to handle it. That occurs when a powerful transmitter is flown in and situated near the base camp. It takes the feed from the Object and sends it to the computer. At Langely? IBM. (LOOK UP)
> Development here: Both aspects touch and go. Media gets the story. Great outcry. Talking heads talk about trying to preserve extraterrestrial. Glitches with technology transfer. NSA gets involved. Presidential briefings. A journalist slips past the security net around the Object and gets his brains fried.

But still no ending. So it gets nuked and Cam ends up with a resurrected wife? Stop. Think. No, more than think, less than think, imagine. Let it come. He began to write on a five-by-eight pad:

> 1) The Object escapes one way or another. Cam on board in an ionized state after retrieving Daphne's DNA, samples of her voice, etc. She comes back to life. Darling, where are we?
> 2) On Earth the process of re-incarnation using DNA starts. Skip ahead five months. They are together at the ranch, on horseback overlooking a magnificent view of

mountains, streams, etc. Daphne turns to Cam. "Yes, I do remember this, I do! Darling, how did you do it?"

3) After tense negotiations with the military, etc., Cam succeeds in getting Daphne's DNA, etc., transferred to the Object, with the understanding that it will, somehow, effect the cloning. After a transfer of technology, etc., the thing is duly nuked (Cam watching, not believing he will ever see Daphne again). Skip to a month ahead. Cam is riding home alone, lonesome cowboy style. (HE SHOULD HAVE A FAVORITE HORSE, A BIG BAY GELDING NAMED GALLOP OR SOMETHING LIKE THAT) When he sees a figure in the distance riding towards him, he stops in disbelief. He can tell by the way the rider sits her horse that it's Daphne. He lowers his head, spurs his mount, and charges to meet her.

Still no ending. Not really.

He gathered his things and his thoughts and continued down Concord Avenue. Now all but oblivious to the few shops and houses along the way. Little League field. Tried out. Couldn't judge fly balls. National Guard Armory. Charlie Company.

Rotary at Fresh Pond. Worth your life to get across. The pond. Used to cut ice and send it all over the world. Sharp Yankees. Ice houses. Ice lasted all summer encased in sawdust. *Ou sont la glace ...?* He was SOTing on and crossing more or less with the light, cars whizzing by when it came to him: how time can be both linear and circular. It was a bit like traffic in a rotary, the traffic coming down Route 2, circling, peeling off for Belmont or on to Boston.

He stood to one side out of the way of joggers and cyclists, shoulders hunched, Moleskine in left hand, pen in right. He wrote as best he could:

TIME IS A SPIRAL. TIME CIRCLES FRACTORIALLY
IN SUB SUB NANO-SECOND SPIRALS THAT
SPIRAL INTO WHOLE SECONDS, THEN MINUTES,
ETC. KEEPING IT CIRCULAR AND THREE-
DIMENSIONAL, MOVING THROUGH SPACE.
COULD IT BE THAT TIME CREATES SPACE AS IT

CORKSCREWS THROUGH THE VOID? PERHAPS
TIME CREATES EVERYTHING. PERHAPS TIME IS
GOD MANIFESTING.

He walked on musing on his musing. How to fit his own braid of time into that cosmology? Human time. Perhaps it has its own evolutionary spiral. Whatever. Perhaps the idea of the spiral is what the Object tells Cam when he asks, what is time?

• • •

The Elms might have been college dorms what with their redbrick attempts at residential gentility. Nice grounds and trees, but no elms, they having all died out. Which did not assuage Leo O'Boyle's low-grade dread of what awaited him. Mom would in her room. Fading, less and less of her there. Even as he took in the graying, frayed form, he would be aware of his filial regard turning dutiful. Edged with an incipient opportunism he no longer resisted as convincingly as he once did. Because when she passed—he didn't use the word "died" as it offended his bogus sensibility—he would inherit the family duplex on Strand Street just off Huron Avenue in Cambridge. Getting valuable. Scarcely any mortgage. Upstairs rented out to the Hassan family. Her place downstairs empty, waiting. Renting both apartments would bring in a nice bit of change, enough to live on. Particularly if Annabel was called to a congregation that provided a modest habitation for its minister.

The Elms, with its disguised minimalism, its sense of begrudged adequacy, and the wafting of covered odors, seemed as one with his dutifulness, his scarcely smothered hope that he would find her all but dead. A touch of Dedalus here. *Agenbite of inwit.* How low could a mortal get? Going through the slow motions. Worse that she had gone from her home of nearly five decades protesting. She hated the genteel warehouse he had found for her. In her lucid moments: When am I ever going home, Leo?

Why aren't they screaming?

They are, Philip, they are, we just can't hear them. Because we block our ears. For six, nearly seven months now, since March, he had listened to his mother's muffled screams. Muffled by him. On good authority. It's what the doctor ordered. Or what the doctor strongly recommended. Along with the social worker, a brisk young woman of unimpeachable competence and formidable certitude. It's for your own good, Mom. It's to keep you safe. All of it backstage to what could have been a one-act play with two actors—aging mother and her son, verging on early middle age.

Sheila: I'm not living here, Leo, I'm dying here. I want to go home.

Leo: But, Mom, if you fall again …

Sheila: Someone can pick me up.

Leo: What about your meals …?

Sheila: Mrs. Curran down the hall says there's a lot of in-house care these days. Wheels on meals or something like that.

Leo: But you said you didn't want anyone to coming into the house.

Sheila: I said I didn't want someone all the time.

Leo: But, Mom …

A one-act play or a scene for his updated *Ulysses*?

At the reception desk. "Yes, Mr. O'Boyle. We told Mrs. O'Boyle about your visit. Your mother is not having one of her good days. She's been sleeping a lot lately. Be sure and knock first."

He went down the corridor. Some doors open, ghost-like eyes peering out. The not-unpleasant reek of institutional food in the air. A trolley of trays would shortly come around for those unable or unwilling to go to the dining room.

Sleeping a lot. Rehearsing? Not said. Could get pre-hearsing out of it. Not really. Words do fail.

He knocked gently. He pushed open the door.

Sheila O'Boyle, born Cassidy, slept quietly on the single bed, hands folded over her chest. She was dressed in a gray dress with a white collar, not unlike the habit of a secular nun. Her room more like a cell, but a comfortable cell. On the bureau ranged framed family photos including several of him at various stages of his growing up. A wedding picture in a silver frame and one of Francis X., head and shoulders, as a dashing young soldier.

I married a Sheila, Frank would say of the dark-haired, azure-eyed, freshly-complected variant, Iberian Celt, not from the sinking Armada, that being a myth, but from Spanish Galicia, back in mythic time. An acquiescent type, very pretty in her bloom, Sheila had gone along with her husband's modest Bohemianism—a little weed, Joan Baez on the turntable, some civil rights activity, vehemently anti-Vietnam. Dad talked and Mom listened. Dad talked and Mom acted. She arranged the purchase of their duplex when they were going cheap. She arranged the insurance policies and modest investments. She didn't just turn off the idiot box but read to her growing son: *The Wind in the Willows, Charlotte's Web, Narnia,* and later, *Treasure Island,* her voice a caress of narrative, closing the book, saying, "to be continued," meaning the story, meaning her love.

He sat in the comfortable armchair next to the bureau and felt keenly again the futility of regret. Unthinking, resorting to the disconnected ruts of what he had thought before, to SOTs about SOTs he tried to avoid. His mother was old and dying. Isn't it good to survive to old age before dying? Only she was alone, grieving the loss of the life as she had lived it on Strand Street for all those years.

And grief, too, for her mate. For his loss and for the futility of his life. Because Francis, as she sometimes addressed him in life and in death, "could never get a handle on his own smartness." Then a litany. The half-written books. The half-developed schemes. The rejected reviews. The essays worked on and never finished. Leo thinking, Dad was afraid of success, as though the quality of its disappointment would not match that of failure. People with a tenth of his talent and imagination beating the world. And he knew it. Drove him crazy at times. All that useless knowledge. For its own sake, of course. But it needs to be animated in life. Needs application to some end.

"Be careful, Leopold," he had said, contradicting what he had said before, "Literature and the blandishments of the literary life can be as big an escape from the world as alcohol or drugs. And more insidious because it has a moral force beyond the power of any politician or preacher."

Son Leo wondered if his dad wasn't describing his own life. Frank O'Boyle didn't practice what he preached, memorizing whole chapters of *Ulysses* before he began *Finnegans Wake,* before he grew depressed,

before he shriveled, maddened ever so slightly, and died from an over-
dose of literature. Which thought Leo kept to himself.

It wasn't that Frank and Sheila didn't have a life. Albums full of
snapshots proved they had lived well. Friends in Cambridge. A shot of
Frank shaking hands with Robert Frost. That happy instant. Their black-
and-white wedding pictures. All kinds of snaps. The Catholic church
in North Chelmsford. Home of the bride. How did he come about?
Some enchanted evening. Accident. Clock ticking last chance. Awkward
thinking about your parents' love life. But they had to have had one.
Without it he would not exist. Perhaps even passionate. Amounting
to what? But why does anything, especially love, have to amount to
anything but itself? *Time the fire in which ...* And *Sweet transience.*

Still, there were the facts of death. SOTing again. Should his mother
die, then all his problems, his monetary problems would be solved. He
and Annabel could, with good conscience, move into the vacated but
still furnished first-floor apartment of the duplex on Strand Street. Or,
maybe even better, if Annabel were called to that church in Woburn
that included a parish house, they could rent both units for a tidy sum.

So there perched vulturine Leo, waiting to feed on the carcass of his
mother's life. Or gliding over on ragged wings, a blot on the sun. But
who was he to question unquestionable medical expertise? At home
she could easily fall down and die of helplessness. And in all fairness to
himself, about which he was scrupulous to a fault, that was what nearly
happened in March. She had fallen down and fractured her hip and lain
there for hours. She had healed slowly with complications because of
a heart condition. But she could go home and have help come in. And
they had these things that you can use to call in an emergency. She had
a son who might drop by more than he had or come by for a cup of tea
or even to take her to Ken's Steak House where she and Frank would
revert every once in a while to their roots of red meat and creamy sauce
on the salad. He could. He could care for her.

Was it moral turpitude? Or just a case of Hamletian dithering?
About what exactly? What could he do? He could do something more
than mask his grubbing speculations about inheritances with his fake
trappings of woe.

In those moments of full disclosure with himself, rare but real, he
would admit that, however insidiously, bad news about her condition

would register as good news before he could censure his reaction. Any day now. Sincerely enough, he would ask if she were suffering, meaning physically, when he knew damn well she was in an agony to go home, to go back to life, however attenuated that life would be, however much a prelude to death.

And, of course, she was a mere cipher of the person she had been a few years ago. Back then, she had walked up to St. Peter's to go to Mass. Back then, she had a couple of friends that called and even dropped in for tea. Back then, she kept up with her brother Jack who lived in New Hampshire and her sister Eileen, who had retired with her husband to Arizona. Back then, she subscribed to *Time* and even read it occasionally. Back then.

But now son Leo felt a sudden sharp pang in the light of his Damascene moment regarding the interwoven texture of his time with the times of those he said he loved. Because, would he not for ignoble ends let unravel and be snipped his mother's strand of time?

Followed by another jolt. Should he tell his mom that Annabel was pregnant? Would it not make her happy? Would it not commit him? Because they hadn't decided yet. It was entirely possible if not that probable that Annabel would opt for no. Or that together they would shy away in favor of a childless future.

Then Alf's question: What kind of son have you been?

His mother stirred and woke, her eyes fluttering open. "Leo, is that you?"

"Hi, Mom."

"I must have been sleeping."

"Just a snooze."

She sat up and leaned back against the pillows like a patient. Lucid, he could tell, from her voice and her eyes.

"I was in church today, Mom."

"Were you?"

"St. Paul."

"Frank's church."

"I know."

"Did you see anyone?"

"Not really." He couldn't tell her about Dad. She'd get confused. "Father Hehir might have been there."

"Yes, a nice family. I wonder what became of them. They don't tell you about this when you're growing up."

"Tell you what?"

"That it all disappears. Disappears like it never existed."

"Too true," he murmured. Then, brightly, "I was at the Poetry Room earlier, you know, at Harvard, and the curator there showed me an essay by Dad about a scene in *Ulysses* ..."

"Yes, that book. I had forty years of that book."

"They're thinking of publishing the article in the *Harvard Review*."

She smiled dimly. "Sometimes I think he cared more about the people in that book than he did about us. I think they were more real to him. He certainly listened to them more than he listened to me. I think he used to talk to them."

Leo cocked his ears. This was a rare glimpse into what he presumed had been a faultless marriage. Perhaps more like a no-fault marriage. Had she, all those years, resented her husband's Joyce mania? Resentment being next of kin to tolerance. Not so much excluded from it as simply not interested in his endless fascination with the characters, speech, and times that still lived on those pages. Not to mention the learned obscurities.

She smiled. She almost gave a titter of a laugh. "He was a good man, Leo, a very good man. I was a very lucky girl. You were a very lucky boy. Except for your name."

Too heartily, relieved that she was on her uppers, he said, "I love my name. Now I do. In high school it was rough at times. I wanted to be Bob or Jim or Jack. Then, I don't know, I began to strut it a bit. It helped with girls. I'd tell them it was a character in a novel that stupid people had no hope of ever reading. Even stupid people don't want to be thought of as stupid."

Now she tittered. And it took them back to when he was young and they had a kind of conspiracy against the Seriousness of Dad. Even as the Seriousness of Dad stuck. "Leo lad, literature isn't just literature, you know, pretty words and great thoughts on the page, a joy to read. I mean, sure, it does that. It diverts us. But it also focuses us. It helps us find the way. And not by slamming us over the head. Remember Polonius in *Hamlet*, 'By indirections find directions ...'"

But also a drug.

Which he was recalling and musing on how Joyce's fiction animated his father in a way that made him take all of his life—his students, his friends, his colleagues and, especially his family, more seriously than did most people. He wanted to remind his mother of this without making it sound like a rebuke.

Because the silence began to hang between them, growing, thickening, threatening the rapport they were indulging. She got this way just before she began their one-act tragedy.

He said, "Annabel's pregnant."

Nothing. A flicker of resentment, eyes frozen blue.

"Doesn't that make you happy?"

No response. Then, "Why should I be happy? It will have nothing to do with me." Unsaid: I'll be here dying and you'll be there having your life.

So he bit the bullet. "You still want to go home, don't you, Mom?"

"You know I do." Like he was an idiot, or worse, a fraud.

The usual phrases lined up. He said, "The problem is …"

"The problem is, Leo, I don't want to be here." The sharp eyes boring in. "I don't know these people. I want to go home."

More phrases at the ready: It's not that simple … What we're concerned about … The doctor says … The director says … Followed by elaboration. No one at home to take care of you. Steps. Falls. Meals.

This time the words failed to reach the teleprompter of his mind. He surprised himself then, another mind in his mind voicing thoughts before thinking about them.

"Why not, Mom?"

"Why not what?" Puzzled.

"Why not go home?"

The confusion of incredulity. "What are you saying, Leo?"

"I'm saying let's get you home." He smiled to encourage himself as much as her. What was he saying?

"You mean it, Leo?" She sat up now, her body stiffening.

Christ Almighty, he did.

"We could get help in when you need it. And when the upstairs comes free, we could move in. I'll ask Annabel."

He watched his aged, shrunken mother take a deep breath, smile, come back to life. "You really mean it, Leo?"

"Of course, I do." Even if it meant an old recurrent dread coming true: nursing his ailing mom down cemetery road.

He stood. "I'll be back."

"You're not leaving?"

"I'll be right back."

Another thought as he went back down the haunted corridor: Was he Telemachus come to take Penelope back to Ithaca?

A hall off the reception area led to the office of the director, one Estelle Kiley. Her secretary, a young man of gayish aspect getting ready to leave, looked at his watch. "She may not be ..." But he buzzed her. After a moment, Leo was admitted.

She was an impeccably groomed, no-nonsense woman of indeterminate middle years with such evident austerity of presence and voice that L. B. O'Boyle, author and self-licensed voyeur, had, at earlier encounters, wondered about her personal life. More than that, this woman intimidated him. He presumed she intuited his unseemly ambivalences about his mother's fate if only because she had an appraising eye and dealt with waiting next-of-kin on a daily basis.

From behind her desk, rising, extending hand to shake. "Mr. O'Boyle, what can I do for you?"

"I'm going to take my mother home."

"I see. To live with you?"

"To her own place."

"Will she be safe there?"

"She'll be happy there."

A glint of respect in the crystalline eyes behind crystalline glasses. Thin nose rising, mouth thoughtful. "That is a consideration. It assumes she is not happy here."

"She wants to go home."

"A lot of our residents want to go home. Even those who no longer have a home to go to." A shuffle of papers. "It's a serious decision, Mr. O'Boyle. She will need in-home help."

"I understand. I would hope you would help us arrange that." His own declarative tone surprised him.

"Her insurance may not cover it all. May not cover ... Round-the-clock coverage can be prohibitive."

"I don't think she'll need that."

"Perhaps, but I want you to understand that."

"You don't have any out-patient arrangements? Not that she's a patient." Unless old age and decrepitude are illnesses.

"It's something we're developing. But it may be more expensive than …"

"That is a consideration, but not the most important one."

The formidable woman adjusted her glasses. She said, "When would you like this to happen?"

"Tomorrow afternoon."

"Can we say the day after tomorrow? That would give us time to make the necessary arrangements."

"Good. I'll let her know. We'll get her place ready. As ready as we can."

She paused and tapped a ballpoint pen in the palm of her hand. "You may find, Mr. O'Boyle, that your mother, despite her protestations to the contrary, may be reluctant to leave when the time comes."

"I suppose …"

"Or she may find that being home alone isn't quite the reality she now thinks it is." A cryptic smile. "May I speak to you frankly, Mr. O'Boyle?"

"Please do." He found her formality refreshing.

"You are not of course the first family member to retrieve from The Elms an elderly family member. But you should know that it often doesn't work out, not when the resident has been here a few months. Don't be surprised if, after a few days, she wants to return."

He did not have to feign a frown to go with his "I see."

"They can be querulous with each other, but it doesn't mean they don't care about each other. Few of them are who they used to be. And even if they don't have any close friends, there are people around. They know they're safe. After a few days at home, especially if they live alone, they ask to come back. What they can't change is the fact that they are old and in decline. Going home, wherever home is, doesn't change that."

"In that case could she come back?"

"It might be easier for all if instead of a formal discharge, we arrange for a furlough. Say a week or two weeks."

He considered. It was wise to listen to those who know. "Okay."

She said, "Perhaps you could come by tomorrow and sign some papers."

They both stood.

"Despite my cautions, Mr. O'Boyle, I think you are making the right decision. But just for the record, The Elms will be on record as opposing Mrs. O'Boyle's return home even on a temporary basis."

"I understand."

He also understood that his mother did have friends at the dying Elms. She flaunted him at times to Mrs. Simonian from Watertown, "whose son is a doctor, which she never lets us forget." Or Mrs. Kelly from East Cambridge, which was somehow significant. And several others. Leo sensed these friendships had a contingency about them—like those of bomber crews in World War II, the attrition rates being high.

Still he stood five-foot-eleven as he walked back to his mother's room to tell her what was going to happen. He wanted to see her smile again. He wanted to hear her start to plan to get out of this house of the slowly deceasing if only for a week or two. He wanted to feel like a good son.

She was dozing, almost corpse-like, her head back on the pillow, mouth open, breathing slow and shallow. Let sleeping moms lie. He sat down in the easy chair and extracted his novel from his satchel. From the three-ring binder he took out the five-by-eight-inch lined pad he had bought at Slates. He uncovered his Pilot V Razor Point, Extra Fine, dark purple. He stopped.

He remained stymied by the ending of *Ice Object 13*. However you play it, resurrection is a tricky business. He reviewed his notes from Armando's. Not really. Cam can't just find Daphne at home on the range reading a magazine. Hi, darling, how was your trip? Explaining to friends and neighbors how it had all been a ghastly mistake. Fending off nosy reporters.

Thinking. So she's back, but she's not at all the same person. How could she be? Perhaps she's nothing more than a figment of his mind implanted there by the Object after it was blasted free into a photonic state and warped off into space. Because others don't seem to be aware of her existence. The hero and his beloved hallucination live happily ever after like The Ghost and Mrs. Muir. Doesn't work. He wrote in long hand:

So Daphne has to be real in whatever iteration. They have reconstituted her using her DNA. But other than her body, what actually would remain—to stay barely in the realm of possibility? Would she have any memories at all? Do memories become part of a person's DNA? Sounds Lamarckian. What about language? Voice? Smile? Her weakness for C&W music? Her liking for Jack Daniels? Her love for him? Her love-making idiosyncrasies? How could you rebuild what can only be described as her soul—her life experience, that which animated her physical presence? Without that what he would have on his hands would be her remains, her living remains, a kind of zombie.

Side note here:

NEED TO DEVELOP DAPHNE AS A CHARACTER, A PERSON, NOT JUST A BARBIE TYPE WITH A NICE ASS. DO THAT WITH FLASHBACKS ON THE EXPEDITION SHIP AS THEY COME UP THE SOUTH COAST OF ALASKA. ALSO BACK STORY ON THE RANCH.

More thought: No easy fix. Too interesting to fake. How, working together, Cam and Daphne reconstruct her mind and memories. It would take over the novel. Perhaps start with the aftermath and then fill in the adventure part. But in that case, it would have to be more, far more than a dressed-up amnesia plot? It wouldn't be just a few missing files. Her hard drive would be empty.

Alf had said it: Dead-ends are easy. You back out and keep going. It's the open road taking you where you don't want to go that's the problem. It's easy to get lost. Worse than that, you get invested in your lostness after a lot of time and words before you realize it isn't working. Happens in novels. Happens in lives.

What if you did start with the ending? It's a big mystery to her but not to him. The front story becomes the back story. The sensation when he goes public with what happened. Full report. Too complicated. Too many possibilities. Murky depths of identity. Just what are we finally as individuals? What makes us what we are? More than the sum of all these parts.

Sheila O'Boyle coughed, opened her eyes, and smiled. "I think I've been sleeping."

"No, Mom, I'm the one who's been sleeping."

"I was just dreaming about you."

"A good dream, I hope."

"You were telling me that you were going to take me home."

He put his novel aside. "That wasn't a dream, Mrs. O'Boyle," as he sometimes addressed her. "I am taking you home."

Realization dawned perceptibly in her eyes, young again with shrewdness, her slow smile rejuvenating her face. "Yes, it wasn't just a dream. Leo, really …"

He got up and sat on the bed. He took her hand in his. "Here's the deal. I talked to the director. She advised against it and will put it in writing, but that's for the lawyers. What we'll start with is a furlough of a week, ten days at most. If at any time for any reason you want to come back."

"Why would I want to come back?"

"Sometimes people … Okay, here's how I think we should handle this …" He broke off.

The azure eyes his dad had loved regarded him with what might have been faint amusement. She liked this different Leo. She nodded. Speak.

"You go home for a week, ten days and see how it goes. Then you come back here for a while."

"Here?" A touch of puzzlement.

"Right. I have to go on assignment for at least a week. I'll be away. I want to know you're safe."

"Why wouldn't I be safe?" The light in her eyes flickering, dimming. "They lock the doors. And they have guards."

"I mean safe at home."

"I've always been safe at home."

Reality like a stone wall. A toppled stonewall. Never simple. He soldiered on, talking to himself aloud. "We'll set up a system. Layla Hassan can drop in on you. We'll arrange meals on wheels. The Elms can have someone visit, maybe once a day. You'll have to wear one of those emergency things around your neck."

Then, as happens, she was back with him. "When can we go?"

"The day after tomorrow. Mrs. Kiley told me she needs a day to get the paperwork done. And to arrange some in-home help. And, remember you're going to have to wear one of those emergency call buttons around your neck. All the time."

She held her hands up to her face. The tears came through her fingers.

"Mom ... Jesus, don't cry ..."

Through her hands, "I know. I'm just happy."

"Just one question."

His mother uncovered her face. Smiling through tears.

"We need to make sure you really want to do this. It could be something of a shock. You've been here a long time."

Another touch of puzzlement. Then his mom of old again. "Of course I want to go home. Lord, Leo, I've thought of nothing else."

"Okay. Annabel and I will go over tomorrow and get the place ready, you know, a little dusting, some groceries, phone hook-up, that sort of thing."

"You'll come and pick me up?"

"I will, of course. Day after tomorrow. I'll arrange it with the director. Damn, I should have done this months ago. Been asleep at the switch."

Sheila O'Boyle rose off the bed and stood, straightening her dress. She took her son's face in both her hands and looked up into his eyes. "You are a blessing, Leo. And I am so happy about Annabel. It's like ..." She hesitated, wiped at a tear. "It's like a new day."

• • •

Sitting in the bus shelter waiting for the 78 Bus to Arlington, the author resorted to the Moleskine notebook. Moleskine meaning moleskin. Fake, of course. Was there such a thing as moleskin? Were the wee beasties trapped and skinned, their tiny hides scraped and tanned and then stitched together? Doubt it. Not even the Italians. Back in the day. Have to look it up.

His mother's son, Leo thought but didn't write. Warming up with random thoughts, avoiding the tough nut of an ending for *Ice Object 13*. Reduxing again. He was Telemachus just visiting his mom Penelope.

And now he's Odysseus on his way to reclaim his wife Penelope. He's Bloom and Dedalus rolled into one. Would have to create some suitors. Some guys to vanquish, if only from her heart. Won't work.

Nor will the idea of Cam writing a novel. Pure projection on his part. The novelist writing about a novelist writing a novel. It's out of character. Cam is a man of action, a doer not a thinker, not that he doesn't think. Duly noted.

Projection. Pen poised. He thinks. He writes:

> None of these endings relies on the mastery or manipulation of time. But why does it have to? To help me cope with my own problems with time? Writing should never be therapy even when it's therapeutic. Then to give it depth? But you can't fake profundity.

Again, the lines from "Little Gidding" ran through his casting mind: … *Will be to arrive where we started/And know the place for the first time.*

The bus pulled up. He flashed his pass at the heavy woman in tight uniform trousers wedged behind the wheel. She nodded. He walked by other passengers without seeing them. He found a seat alone. The five-by-eight writing pad came out this time.

A moment later, with a lurch of the bus, his muse whispering inside his head, the ending arrived. Bracing the notebook and his writing hand against the movement of the ride, he wrote:

> Daphne is there, as the Object promised, a bit fuzzy around the edges but definitely there, a reconstitution after all. He fears, as he comes into and goes out of consciousness, wondering why he had been asleep and where, that she might be like the Object, there and not there, hovering, her words like thoughts, then more like sounds as though someone is turning up the volume. They, it, got the voice right. She's saying nonsensical things like, "His color is much better today." Then, "If he comes around will he …?" Then, very clearly, "I think he's back!"
>
> Which happens. Cam McInally opens his eyes fully into visual brightness and his faculties turn on like a room with lost power restored. (REWORK) His hearing tuning in, his sight focusing, feeling in his hands and legs, conscious of

his breathing, of a catheter in his cock (PENIS?) and tubes in his arms, one in his chest.

She hovers over him. She says, "Cam, Cam darling, you're back." Then, hand to her mouth, then dabbing at her eyes, she hovers over him.

He says, "Where have I been?"

"In a coma. Don't talk if …"

"I'm fine now. I'm hungry."

She is kissing him on the lips, then stops. "I shouldn't …"

She's back, he's thinking, but am I? Because there are vast empty areas of his mind once populated with memories, thoughts, anxieties.

"Where are we?"

"Anchorage. In the hospital."

"But how … ?"

The bus, moving slowly in heavy traffic, stopping along the way, had turned right onto Bright Road past Sancta Maria Hospital. Mom worked there for a spell. Now a nursing home. A few businesses. Hillside Garden Supply. A small Pentecostal church. L. B. O'Boyle wrote, trying to keep it legible.

A nurse comes in. She's evidently surprised. "Mr. McInally, how are you feeling?"

"I'm fine. Why am I … ?"

"You have to go easy."

Cam McInally's eyes can focus but not his mind. He lies back and drifts, then resists, rouses himself. "I don't understand." He lapses back, but not into a coma as into a fitful sleep in which he can hear sounds in the room and feel Daphne's hand holding his.

A young doctor comes in later and checks his signs. "Everything looks good. Almost normal."

He block prints a note in the margin:

MORE HERE. NEED TO LOOK UP CASES OF AWAKENING FROM COMA. PROCEDURES, ETC. NOT THAT IT HAS TO BE ALL THAT CLINICAL. CAM IS NOT LIKE EVERYONE ELSE.

Leo O'Boyle stopped and peered out at the neat lawns and prosperous houses of old suburbia. But right then unreal. He had been reduced to an amanuensis of his imagination. He turned a page on the notebook and wrote:

> Later, though still tubed up, Cam is able to take some soup and crackers. In bits and pieces, Daphne takes him back through what had happened.
>
> "I was ahead of you, showing off a little bit when I heard you call. Then I knew. I could hear it and feel it. I tried to wave you back, but it was too late. I don't know how you survived. I went back to where I thought you had been buried and began digging."

Another note in the margins:

> MORE HERE ON FRIENDS HELPING, CALLING IN RESCUE/ALSO, TO ADD TO THE ELEMENT OF MYSTERY.

The 78 Bus might have sprouted wings, pulled up its wheels, and lifted off the ground for all that the author L. B. O'Boyle was aware. Although he did, however peripherally, experience a sense of ascending as the bus drove up the road paralleling Route 2, ascending as it did the slope of an ancient caldera.

Another block-lettered note in the margin:

> NEED TO ADJUST THE SCENE WHERE THE AVALANCHE HITS. SHE HAS HEARD HIM AND ESCAPES. HE, GOING AFTER HER, SKIS DIRECTLY INTO THE DANGER. MAKE IT A NEAR THING. WITH TIME HE VAGUELY REMEMBERS THE RUSH OF AIR, THE SUN-BLANKING COLDNESS, THE SLOW OBLIVION.

Back to the draft, scribbling, trying to keep it legible.

> "I had the weirdest dream," Cam says, chaffing now, wanting to shuck the tubes and get up and walk around. The soup and crackers are working. His mind is opening up, nearly tripping over itself as it unfolds.

Daphne is smiling at him, her eyes moist. "Don't talk if ..."

"I need to talk. The dream. It was realer than real. One of those long ones. And coherent. It just went on and on."

The television on the wall facing the foot of the bed has a news program in dumb show, the mute button on. A reporter is talking to an Air Force general. They are in a windy, snow-blown place.

Daphne is saying something, but Cam interrupts her. "What's that?" He clicks the sound on.

The reporter is saying, "That was General Banks of the Alaska National Guard. As you heard, he won't say more than that they have brought in an emergency reaction team and cordoned off an area of at least two miles around the mysterious object."

Daphne waves a hand at the set. "Oh, that. It's the weirdest thing. You know the avalanche that nearly killed you, well it seems that it uncovered something on the side of the glacier that's been there a long time. Apparently." (HOW CLOSE WAS IT TO WHERE CAM HAD BEEN BURIED?)

"What is it?"

"That's just it. The thing doesn't show up on any flyover photographs or other sensing equipment. But they can see it, at least some of the time. People are starting to talk about it being an extraterrestrial."

Cam McInally feels his pulse go up. "I need to get out of here. I know what it is."

"What are you talking about?"

"I think it's already communicated with me."

"Cam, you've been in a coma."

"How close were we to the thing when the avalanche hit?"

"Real close, actually. They were speculating about cause and effect."

Then what? Another note in the margins:

SWITCH TO FINAL SCENE. TWO HELICOPTERS
HOVER OVER A SITE NOT FAR FROM THE THING.
CAM, RECOVERED, IS DROPPING FROM ONE OF
THE CHOPPERS WITH A HAND-PICKED TEAM.
CIMEMATIC FADE OUT. AN ENDING AND A
BEGINNING.

• • •

The author put down his pen to find the bus stopped and empty
save for himself and the driver. She was looking at him quizzically. "You
headed back?"

"Actually, no." With unhurried deliberation, he smoothed down
the pages of his notebook and placed it in his satchel, which he closed
and buckled. A first draft. Lots of work to do. His *bébé mort* gurgling
happily.

Thanking the bus driver with more than usual civility, the author
emerged into the parkland that was Park Circle. Nearby rose the gray
mass of the Arlington water tower, a replica of the Arsinoe Rotunda at
Samothrace right down to a march of columns circling the upper part.
Gravity feed. Two million gallons. Bloom filling the kettle from the tap.
Did it flow? Yes. From Roundwood reservoir in county Wicklow … Redux
it? Annabel turning the taps in the shower, the water spraying over her
upturned face. His Penelope primping for her Odysseus?

The image stirred him to a dawning then erupting realization: L.B.
O'Boyle had, of a sudden and once again, fallen ridiculously in love
with his wife. He had fallen in love with her many times before. That is,
he had been smitten with something transcending by several orders of
magnitude the steady conjugality of their marriage. On this occasion,
a warm late afternoon in late summer, the light crystallizing as the air
began to cool, the sublime, antic headiness of love came with a sense of
repossession as though, along the way, he had forgotten about, ignored,
neglected, or simply lost his very own Annabel Lee.

Making him wonder what was he doing hankering after other
worlds. Which thoughts he resisted wanting then not to think but
simply to indulge in this elation that had him stepping sprightly along
the sidewalk in the direction of home, fondling in his mind his mate in

all her aspects, not the least her lounging around in a sluttish negligee on hot summer evening in the unconditioned air. Her beauty. Those eyes. That smile. That variable voice, husky in passion, bell clear from the pulpit. Or White Trashy taking out the trash, doing the dirty work of living. Or the fragrance of her warmed skin after a bath. Or her distance, her self-containment as she bent to her studies.

Then a flickering of trepidation, of second, third thoughts clouding his sunny love. What about *it*? Correcting himself. What about a him or a her? A brave new world. Or a not-so-brave old world. Such that he stopped in his tracks. He didn't want to think about it. He didn't want to decide. So catch the bus back. Back to where? There was no going back even if he went back. Unless she had already decided. Or wanted him to decide. He looked at the trees, at the sky, at the world. Again, his dad. Again, Joyce. Again, *life*.

•   •   •

Key into the lock. Up the sun-warmed stairway. Door open. Annabel waiting, radiant. Hugging and kissing.

He said, "So it's definite?"

"Yes, it's definite. But we knew that."

"But definitively definite?"

"Definitely, definitively definite. Yes."

They were close, his hands on her hips, his fingers just touching her backside through the thin cotton dress summer yellow with pale stripes like some blossom. He was lost, sinking into her blue depths. Some voice, his own, talking, sounding those depths, telling.

"Okay … Listen, I did more today on the novel than I've done in months. It was just there, being handed to me. I have a draft. It needs a lot of work, but it's real, it has a beginning, a middle, and finally, finally, an end."

Her smile wavered between uncertain and coy. "Do you think it might be because of what's happening to us?"

It took a moment for the significance of her words to register because he had become distracted by her neck, which was exposed by the way she had pinned up her hair like a proper Boston lady of old. And a certain mutual pressure in the pelvic region. In truth he had not consciously linked their new situation with the way his day had bloomed and transfigured him. The realization made him smile. She had woken him from a waking coma from which he was still coming around.

He said, "Okay, a couple of things …"

"I'm listening."

"Alf says I can have his job. Says he's taking early retirement."

"But …"

"I know. It will be full-time. Especially at first. But he says he's found time to write. And he'll be around to help. Oh, and by the way, I've been nagged all day by this idea for another novel. One I got from Alf. It's a kind of redux of *Ulysses* only set in and around Harvard Square …"

"When will you start at the museum?"

"I don't know. This fall sometime probably. I'll start part-time on the casual payroll. He'll work me in. It could be perfect."

Her smile grew. She looked at him from under her brows the way she did. "What about your travel writing?"

"What about it?"

"You said …"

But he had said so many things. "I know. I can fold it into the travel I'll have to do for the museum. Maybe. It's not important."

"You're sure?" She took him by the lapels of his jacket.

He was bending to her, not yet kissing, but smiling at her smile. "I want you to come to Jordan and Petra with me. I have tickets, hotel rooms, the whole thing. We'll resurrect the Nabataeans! I can arrange a side trip to Israel. Jerusalem. It's the Holy Land. It's your bailiwick. For Christ sake."

"But …"

"No buts. You've already got that sermon in the bank …"

"Homily."

"Right, homily, the one on Yom Kippur. You could get another one ready just in case."

"Just in case what?"

"Just in case. Look, someone else can read them. The gospel according to Annabel."

"I'll need to make a few calls."

"Then it's a deal."

"It's a deal?"

Then, suddenly, lifting his hand, she said, "And your watch! You're wearing your dad's watch."

"I know."

"All day?"

"All day."

"So you're … ?"

"I think so. I hope so." He shook his head with a laugh. "Time will tell."

"You are having some kind of day."

He sensed a nudge, but let it go, going on about himself. "Yeah. I broke it off with Ari. That *Caper* nonsense …"

"Really?"

"Not really with him. I need to call him. I think I can help him with his poetry. Not me directly. Alf knows people, poets, you know, Fred Marchant, Tom Sleigh, Stratis in the Poetry Room …"

He pulled back a little and his voice turned tentative. "Also, I'm getting Mom out of that home. It's not a home. She hates it there."

Smile fading. "Where will she go?"

"Her own place."

Pulling back, standing, arms folded. "I wish you had talked to me first."

Deep sigh. "Yeah, I know, but …"

"Ellbee … she's all but helpless. Who's going to take care of her?"

"She's not as helpless as you think. I'm arranging coverage with the Elms. They've started an out-patient care thing. Not that she's a patient. The director is pretty sure the insurance will cover it. You won't get stuck with her."

"That's what you say now."

"I mean it."

"I know you mean it, but you'll be traveling and something will happen and I'll end up taking care of her. Which I wouldn't mind, but she snipes from cover and then smiles that way she has. She hates me."

"She doesn't hate you. And I told you, I'll be around. I'll be taking over from Alf …"

"He travels all the time."

"Not really. A couple of trips a year."

It was a standing disputation. Leo's two closest women had never warmed to each other. That taking care of Mom could turn into another career for her was a fear Annabel voiced with some regularity.

Relenting just a bit, she said, "Just as long as we don't have to move in upstairs."

"We won't have to but we can if we want to. It's her house. And we're her family."

"You said …"

"Yeah, I know. But Annabella Baby, she's my mother. I'm her son. I'll work it out. She may not like being home. But if she does, we'll make it work. I'll make it work. I'm her son."

A slow dawning. The blueness brightening with her smile. She moved in close and pulled him back to her. They were joined again at the hips. "You're saying 'yes,' aren't you?"

"Yes."

"To our … ?"

"Yes."

"Why didn't you say so before?"

"I wasn't sure."

"But you're sure now?"

"I'm sure now."

"You're not just saying that."

"I'm saying I'm sure if you're sure."

"And I'm saying I'm sure if you're sure."

"Then we're both sure."

"More than sure."

Her arms went around him and she buried her face in his chest. A moment later she came up happy and agonized. "Why didn't you say so before?"

"You never really asked. All we did was talk around it."

"I know."

"Why?"

"I was afraid …"

"That I'd say no?"

"That you would say no or that I would say no."

"Ambivalence squared," he muttered to himself. Now vanquished. "Okay, I'm saying yes, once and for all, yes."

"You have to say it again. By itself."

"Yes, yes, yes, yes, a thousand times, yes."

Arms around her, his eyes lost again in those depths. He said, "Now it's your turn. Will you say yes?"

The blueness began to blur. "Yes. I will. Yes."

•   •   •

About the Author

Born in 1941 to an Irish mother and an English lorry driver, Alfred Alcorn, born Denny, spent his early years exploring the heavily bombed docklands in Wallesey, just across the Mersey from Liverpool. When his parents died a few years after the war, he went to live with his grandfather in County Roscommon, Ireland. A year later he was adopted by an aunt who had immigrated to New England and married a farmer named Alcorn. He grew up on a dairy farm in South Chelmsford, Massachusetts, belonged to the 4H Club, played football in high school, and received a scholarship to Harvard. During a varied career in journalism, he worked for CBS, the *Boston Herald Traveler*, the *Worcester Telegram*, and the *Montgomery Advertiser* in Alabama. For several years he ran the travel program at the Harvard Museum of Natural History, organizing and leading natural history trips before retiring to write full time. His novels include *The Pull of the Earth, Vestments, The Long Run of Myles Mayberry, Natural Selection, Extinction,* and a parodic series starting with *Murder in the Museum of Man. Time Is The Fire* is his ninth novel.